The Magistrate's Tale

Nora Naish was born in India, one of seven children of an Irish father in the Indian Civil Service, and did not come to England until she was eight years old. She was educated at a convent in Wimbledon and London University before qualifying as a doctor at King's College Hospital during the war. She married and brought up four children in Gloucestershire. In middle life she went back to medicine as a GP in Avon. Her elder brother was the late P.R. Reid, the author of *The Colditz Story*. *The Magistrate's Tale* is her third novel.

*Also by Nora Naish
and available in Mandarin*

Sunday Lunch
The Butterfly Box

NORA NAISH

The Magistrate's Tale

Mandarin

A Mandarin Paperback
THE MAGISTRATE'S TALE

First published in Great Britain 1995
by William Heinemann Ltd
This edition published 1996
by Mandarin Paperbacks
an imprint of Reed International Books Ltd
Michelin House, 81 Fulham Road, London SW3 6RB
and Auckland, Melbourne, Singapore and Toronto

Copyright © Nora Naish 1995
The author has asserted her moral rights

A CIP catalogue record for this title
is available from the British Library
ISBN 0 7493 1906 2

Printed and bound in Great Britain
by Cox & Wyman Ltd, Reading, Berkshire

THE MAGISTRATE'S TALE

PART ONE

The Magistrate's Tale

ONE

'Stand up please!' shouted the clerk. As the magistrates rose, picking up their scattered papers, everybody in the courtroom stood up too. The clerk stood up himself. He cast a quick look over his shoulder at his newest Justice of the Peace as she pushed back a stray lock of blonde hair from her face and slipped behind the heavy curtain into the retiring room behind the bench. He was glad to see her disappear. Mary Chicon was the first lady magistrate he had ever dealt with, this was her very first court session and her presence made him feel uneasy. Then, leaning his left elbow on the edge of his high desk he scraped with his right forefinger a flake of breakfast egg yolk congealed on the pot belly of his waistcoat.

Gregory Barton was a clever, uncultivated man. He had come to Frenester nearly fifty years ago, a skinny, threadbare, bespectacled boy (so Higgs the local ironmonger told Mary) to work as a clerk in the offices of Preene, Parsons and Parsons, and through his native wit and persistence had qualified himself as a solicitor. The old-fashioned gentlemen of the law, not recognising their cuckoo in the nest, fostered his talent and encouraged him. In time he completely ousted Messrs Parsons and Parsons. Poor old Preene by then had faded away from senility and weariness. Gregory Barton took control not only of that rather

3

bumbling firm but also indirectly of many lives. Higgs used to say there wasn't a pie in the district into which he hadn't poked a finger. Mary's father described him as Dickensian. As a matter of fact everything about that rural court was Dickensian.

'Even more archaic than Dickens,' Colonel Chicon said.

'The other magistrates are not like you, Colly,' said Mary.

'I don't believe they've altered much since Shakespeare's day. That Mr Justice Shallow of Gloucester in the *Merry Wives of Windsor* still sits on the Frenester Bench.'

'Perhaps it doesn't matter much,' said Mary thoughtfully. 'As magistrates we only take the place of the jury. The average judgement of society is what is needed. Twelve good men and true and all that. . . .'

Mentally he clicked his heels and in soldierly fashion saluted her common sense. 'That's about the ticket. They're judge and jury rolled into one. No great intelligence is asked of magistrates, provided they be good men and true. But it is your job to try to make things a little better,' he exhorted her. 'I believe I improved things a bit, and you must carry on my work. I'm a great believer in the little leaven that leavens the whole.'

Mary had to admit that Gregory Barton was a hard worker. And many people felt affection for him. Some were grateful for his cranky benevolence; and it was even rumoured that he occasionally helped the guilty, *sub rosa* of course, and through them their families, if they kowtowed to him enough. He died rich, 'the uncrowned king of Frenester', to quote old Higgs again; but he lived frugally and remained throughout life, as he liked to tell people, a humble man. At the time of Mary's first meeting with him he was very far from dead.

He had an immense respect for the law; but he didn't like Mary, especially on what he called 'My Bench' as a member of 'My Magistrates'. When he first shook her hand he looked her over rudely and openly, sizing her up pretty shrewdly too. He knew her to be an inexperienced female who had led a more or less protected existence hitherto, running her own Girl Guide platoon to be sure, and dabbling a bit with calf-rearing on her father's farm, but a middle-class spinster who had never had to earn her own living. He cautioned himself that she was her father's daughter, and might not be easily cowed. Many were the times, in the days when old Francis Chicon was chairman of the bench, they had crossed swords, and usually Barton got the worst of those crossings. In his own opinion the proper place for a woman was in the kitchen or in bed, though he realised (and Mary could guess his thoughts as his sour glance slid over her) she would not be desirable in either place. She had an angular figure, she knew, and too big a nose; but by the time she reached her mid-forties she had grown to accept her own appearance, and was able to acknowledge her disadvantages without bitterness.

The law demands that each juvenile court must be constituted of not more than three magistrates and shall include a man and a woman. So Gregory Barton had to put up with her, not only on the juvenile bench but in adult courts where she had to take her turn as well. He treated her with mildly sarcastic gallantry, egging on the other justices to feel amused contempt for her. She suspected that behind her back, at Bisons' Club dinners and the like, when they were all boys together, he was more ribald. She could hear him saying: 'I don't think she'd be profitable in bed.' And Turner would laugh, adding, 'No. She'd be a dead loss there.' Their imaginations she felt sure, would be anchored to the concepts of profit and loss. Perhaps they said even worse things about her; but of course all this could not be tolerated in the courtroom where Barton liked to cover the proceedings with a veil of pomp. This was often very rudely torn by his own bad manners, his bullying of witnesses when irritated, and by his undignified, sometimes ungrammatical speech. In Colonel Chicon's day as chairman he had managed to check the clerk, cutting short some of his rhetoric, and forbidding absolutely his attempts to join the justices' deliberations in their retiring room, 'to prevent any mistakes', as Gregory Barton put it. But the Colonel had dismissed him promptly. 'It's your duty to keep us inside the law,' he said. 'It's not for you to influence our verdict.' So Barton had been a bit afraid of Mary Chicon's father.

Mary once overheard old Higgs describe her father to a customer who wanted to buy some four-inch nails. She hid in the doorway, overcome with embarrassment at being an eavesdropper; but she couldn't help hearing what was said: 'Old Colonel Chicon was a Desert Rat, you know. Blown up in a cloud of sand at El Alamein. Riddled with shrapnel, and left for dead. Terrible thing – in that heat! But he survived, you see. A strong man, the Colonel. And good at laying down the law. Best for folks to keep on the right side of him – and the law!' Higgs laughed, and so did his customer.

Higgs was right about Chicon's being good at laying down the law, which he had done for years in petty sessional driblets to the fear of some and the satisfaction of many, as is required in the magistrates' courts, but he was wrong, Mary knew, about his being a Desert Rat. Strictly speaking that honour belonged only to the Seventh Armoured Division, which alone bore the insignia of the little rodent. He had fought at El Alamein. That battle finished his army career. He was hospitalised, invalided out and then discharged, limping badly, into civilian life when he visited her at school towards the end of the war. He was a brave man, a survivor, and very sure of himself.

Mary was much less confident. She did not take easily to her new office. Sometimes she felt totally bewildered. She slept badly after days in court. She was most anxious to do the right thing, but often feared she'd done the opposite. She had studied all those dull little red handbooks for new justices, attended some lectures and visited a prison, a remand home, and a detention centre in her conscientious efforts to learn how to cope with her new job; but she felt very keenly her inadequacies and the weight of her responsibilities.

On that first morning, which she always looked back on with hot embarrassment, the defendant before them was a poor fellow who had pinched some frilly knickers off his neighbour's washing line. Mary wondered what on earth he could want them for. The chairman, Mr Turner, explained shortly: 'He's a pervert. That's why.' They were sitting in a little room no bigger than an alcove behind the bench, hidden from view and out of earshot of the rest of the court.

'If that's the case,' she said, 'he should see a psychiatrist.'

The other magistrates looked at her pityingly. Mr Dunster, who was a farmer and a mild man, said: 'I don't suppose that would do much good, Miss Chicon, would it?'

'Well, if it hasn't been tried it should be,' she insisted.

Mr Turner laughed. 'OK,' he said. 'This man has done this before, and fines haven't stopped him yet. So let's try it.' He was a very busy man, a builder, able and active in local affairs and a district councillor as well, and was anxious to get through the list of cases as soon as possible.

When Barton heard their decision he was dumbfounded for a moment, but agreed to adjourn the case for reports from probation officer and psychiatrist. He addressed the defendant in a loud sarcastic voice: 'One of my magistrates thinks a psychiatrist would do you good. I don't think much of psychiatry myself; but in the circumstances we'll give it a go.'

Mary was furious. He had no right to express his opinion in defiance of theirs. Battle between them was thus declared after that very first case she heard. He won the first round. Six months later the same man was brought before them again on the same charge. When in the dock he spoke up for himself: 'I seen the psychiatry doctor, and he says as how I can't help myself.' This time he was fined amid laughter in court; and Mary was made to look a fool, which perhaps she was. The other magistrates enjoyed

7

themselves laughing at her later over a pint with Barton in the pub. But later still (it must have been in the second year after her appointment) Turner and Dunster took a liking to her. It happened over a young man with very long hair. He was brought before the court by an irate matron who had heard him using obscene language at a bus stop. Barton explained to the justices that there was still in existence some quaint law or by-law forbidding the use of obscene language in a public place; and the lady thought she was doing a public service by bringing up the case. The young man in question had been standing in the street with a macho friend who accused him of being a sissy. The policewoman read aloud the indictment in a steady expressionless voice without dropping a single h: 'The defendant then said: "I've got more fucking hairs on my fucking balls than you've got on your fucking head!" '

It was Mary who burst out laughing first. Her laughter was checked only when across the courtroom she caught the steely blue gaze of the policewoman, who was understandably offended because she'd tried so hard to state her case in a professional manner. She didn't even smile; but the magistrates were finding it difficult to suppress their hilarity. They retired as quickly as possible to consider their verdict, and in the little room behind the bench they broke down into loud guffaws.

'Why! It's the kind of language farm workers use all the time!' said Mary. 'They don't mean any harm. They just haven't enough vocabulary to find the right adjectives.'

Mr Dunster wiped his eyes. 'It's all a bit silly, isn't it? But if it's the law. . . .'

'That young man has read nothing at school except comics, and only the tabloids since,' she declared, riding one of her hobby-horses, 'and probably has a reading age of nine. We should regard him as a juvenile.'

'We can't do that,' said Turner. 'He's obviously got too much hair.' And they both dissolved into laughter again.

'What a pity we can't make him sit in the police station

until he has copied out a page of the dictionary,' Mary said. 'That might teach him a few more words.'

'No seriously, what can we do? It's obviously a trivial charge. The woman who brought it has been wasting the time of the court. It's she who should be fined.'

'Why not an absolute discharge?' suggested Dunster.

'OK,' agreed Turner. 'We'll find him guilty, but give him an absolute discharge.'

And that was what they did, to the relief of the defendant and the outrage of the irate woman. This incident for some reason softened Mary's colleagues' attitude towards her, though it did not alter Barton's; and from then on, at least while she was in the magistrates' retiring room, she became almost one of the boys.

By the time Hannah Batherswick was brought before them as a juvenile in moral danger and in need of care or protection Mary's whole outlook was more relaxed. Nevertheless it gave her a shock, especially when she learned that the girl was Maeve Delaney's daughter, to see her standing there, and yes, it gave her heart a nasty wrench to note her astonishing beauty. Although she drooped her head Hannah carried an air of wounded, indignant innocence. Mary remembered her mother well. As children they often went riding together when Mary was home for the holidays. After all the evidence had been heard, and the magistrates had retired to consider the case, Mr Turner began to mutter: 'What a shocking business! At her age too!'

'What can we do with her, Miss Chicon?' Dunster turned his troubled eyes to her.

'She's fifteen next month,' Mary said hesitantly. 'Care or protection must continue till the age of eighteen, I believe?'

'Hannah Batherswick is an old-fashioned-sounding name,' mused Dunster, 'but she's not exactly an old-fashioned girl, is she?'

'She's a trollop!' said Turner. 'And a disgrace to our town!

9

Her own father has refused to have her back home. And I'm not surprised. She's quite out of control.'

'Her father is a ruffian,' Mary said.

Turner continued as if she hadn't spoken: 'Running away and living with all sorts of men! Going to pubs, and then trying to do away with herself by drinking a bottle of Lysol . . . She was picked up I see in a public lavatory, where she passed out.'

Mary was reading the probation officer's report, from which images of the child's first seduction, so baldly described, stuck in her mind like thorns: ' "He pushed me down in the back of his lorry," she said. "It was a gravel lorry; but it wasn't ordinary gravel. It was a red earth and dust from the reddle mine down Madstock way; and the driver's clothes, and even his skin was stained red with that dye. He'd given me a lovely meal of egg, bacon, sausage and chips at a transport caff, so I was grateful. I was scared too, because I didn't know what he'd do. You don't, do you? till it happens to you. Gran never told me anything about sex. Whenever I asked her any questions about it she used to say: 'I'll tell you when you're old enough'; but she never did, because she died too soon. Of course I knew lambs were pushed out between the ewe's hind legs, and I'd often seen young steers playing at mounting heifers in a field. Sometimes the girls in my class used to huddle into a heap in some corner to tell a sexy joke, and then burst apart laughing; but I never used to see the point of it. So when I came to lie down in that lorry I didn't know much; and I was scared.

' "He undid my blouse and lifted my breasts as if he was weighing bags of sugar. 'Like apple dumplings they are,' he said. 'Like my mum used to make, with a little pastry knob on top. So nice I could eat them.' For a moment I thought he might; but he didn't use his teeth. I cried out when he pushed his Thing inside me. He stopped then for a moment. He must have realised I was a virgin. 'Take it easy kiddo,' he said, and waited while he stroked my bum. He was quite nice really. Afterwards I was grateful for the quiet. I thought how strange it was. Not a bit nice, not for me anyway. I wondered what my dad's blondes did it for.

' "When morning came and I saw how covered in red sand I was I decided to move off. I bided my time till he parked the lorry near a pub and went inside for a pint. Then I jumped down and ran as fast as I could back along the road we'd travelled to a service station I'd spotted on the way. I reckoned there'd be a toilet there, and perhaps a washbasin too. It was while I was standing naked over the basin to wash my pants and bra that a woman came in and began to eye me suspiciously. No wonder, since all the water in the basin was bright red. She must have thought I was bleeding and needed an ambulance. So I grabbed my clothes and rushed into the toilet to dress." '
The probation officer added her own bleak comment to Hannah's story: 'She seemed more upset by the colour of her underclothes than by the loss of her virginity.'

Mary picked up the psychiatrist's report next. It was not too puzzling because he'd taken the trouble to write it in plain English: 'She described her adventures as if talking about something which had happened to someone else. Apart from the shelter she found in vans and the cabs and backs of lorries she seems to have been homeless. She said all this was OK till it got really cold in December. She couldn't stand the cold, she said. When asked wasn't her father's house better than a lorry in winter she suddenly came to life. "Please don't send me back to him," she begged. "Please! Please! He killed my mum driving drunk with her in his car. It's because of him I've got no mum. He used to hit me too. Black and blue I was sometimes. That's why I ran away."

'Presumably her hatred of her father and her homelessness gave rise to an insoluble dilemma, which was what drove her to attempt suicide. She was picked up in a public lavatory after having swallowed some Lysol she found on the windowsill. "A black woman came into the toilet as I

11

was staggering about," was how she described the incident to me. "You having a haemorrhage or something?" Hannah remembered throwing the empty Lysol bottle in a litter bin, but can't remember anything more till she found herself in hospital. I think if she were sent back to live with her father the whole history would repeat itself. What she needs is a calm, secure and affectionate family background for the remainder of her adolescence. She is a girl of above-average intelligence; with care, and a bit of luck, her cognitive ability might yet steer her out of the emotional traumas of her childhood.'

Dunster sighed as he looked up from the papers. 'No relative has come forward,' he said gloomily. 'Her grandmother is dead, and the aunt can't look after her, since she herself is a chronic invalid in a nursing home.'

'We'll have to send her to an approved school then?' said Turner briskly. He was used to making quick decisions in business, and that's how he wanted justice to be done.

'No! No!' Mary protested vehemently. 'She's not a criminal. In that approved school she'd mix with all sorts of bad girls who'd teach her all sorts of bad habits. Even taking drugs. And then perhaps she'd finish up in a Borstal before she's eighteen.'

'She's a very bad girl herself,' said Turner indignantly. He had no children himself. 'If I had,' he once modestly explained to Mary, 'I wouldn't be able to give so much time to public life.' Her own opinion of his altruism was that the addition of JP to his name weighted the scales slightly to his advantage when he applied for planning permission to extend a Grade II Listed Building, or to spread new houses on a green site. So she argued with him.

'But the child's had no mother since she was four years old. It's obvious the father's no good.' She thought of him sitting there in the courtroom turning his big flabby face this way and that, fiddling with those enormous moustaches grown to emphasise his virility. 'You can see that.

What she needs is care or protection, a mother, in other words – not incarceration in an approved school.'

The two men looked at her in silence. She could read their thoughts: That was the worst of women on the bench! Always letting their feelings run away with their judgement!

'Well, what else can we do, Miss Chicon?' asked Dunster kindly, with a little helpless gesture of one hand.

'There's no alternative then?' said Turner. So they filed back into court.

'Stand up Hannah Batherswick!' shouted the clerk.

When Hannah heard that she was going to be shut up in an institution where it was hoped she would be trained to lead a sober and industrious life she suddenly uttered a piercing scream, and leaning across the table where her father calmly sat – who had publicly disowned her by declaring he was unable to keep her under control, and was it seemed to her the cause of this terrible punishment – she bared her teeth like a carnivore, and cried out: 'You viper! You dirty snake!'

The court was shocked into complete silence. The scorching venom in her strong young voice rushed through Mary's soul, making her shudder. She supposed that after a lifetime of discipline in her father's house she was an exceptionally orderly person. Her days were certainly planned, quiet and composed, her hours pigeon-holed. Hannah's rage swept through the tidy compartments of her mind like a hot wind, leaving them strewn with dust. Her mouth felt dry. She knew she was inexperienced, foolish even, but she felt in her bones the suffering and need of the girl standing, savage but quivering and wounded, only a few feet away from her. In spite of her history there was a sort of innocence in Hannah's face, and her big beautiful eyes blazed with a sense of outrage. She obviously felt an abominable injustice was being done to her. And so did Mary. She remembered the lessons learned from her handbook for new magistrates: 'In dealing with the adult criminal your first duty is to protect society; but in dealing with the juvenile delinquent your first duty is to consider the welfare of the child.'

She must have turned pale because her cheeks felt suddenly cold; but she took a deep breath, and leaning forward she tapped Gregory Barton on the shoulder.

'I will offer myself as a foster mother,' she said. He turned crossly to stare at her. Everybody must have heard what she said. The silence was intense and seemed interminable. At last Barton rose and turned towards his magistrates.

'This is most unusual, if not irregular,' he whispered hoarsely. His eyes behind his spectacles bulged over purple cheeks at the enormity of what had been suggested. The other two magistrates stared at Mary in stunned disbelief. The clerk's clerk, whose job it was to copy into a big book the whole proceedings laboriously in longhand, stopped writing and stared at his pen. The policewoman and Hannah's father eyed each other in consternation, and Hannah's sobbing died away to a whine.

'Are you sure you understand what you're suggesting Miss . . . madam?' hissed Barton with a highly audible hiss.

'I think so,' she replied.

'I've never in all my experience known such a situation,' he grumbled; and then, turning to the chairman, 'Do you agree to this?'

Mary felt the blood rushing to her cheeks, and spoke quickly: 'Is there any reason in law why I may not foster this girl?'

'Well, no,' he admitted. 'But it's most unusual.'

The chairman now intervened. He stood up and spoke firmly: 'We shall retire again to consider these further aspects of the case.' And again they filed into the alcove.

'Do you really have any idea what you're suggesting?' asked Turner irritably.

'She wouldn't be an easy girl to manage,' said Dunster.

This time Mary did let her emotions go in a torrent of words. 'We knew her grandmother quite well, you see. The Delaneys used to supply a lot of our winter cattle feed in the old days. And I knew Hannah's mother. Maeve was younger than me, but we did ride together a few times. I can remember the day my father sold her one of our ponies. The Delaneys were keen for her to learn to ride; and I taught her a few things about horses myself. And then she married this ruffian. God knows why! He was good-looking, of course. Women are so foolish in love . . .'

She could see Turner gesturing in an attempt to stem the flow of her story, but she refused to be stemmed. 'Then she was killed in that terrible car crash. New Year's Eve it was. The man was probably drunk. Everybody knew about it. Everybody was shocked. And now here's this child. She hasn't had much luck really, has she? All the dice loaded against her . . . her life in tatters already . . .' She choked, and for a few appalled seconds the men must have thought she was going to weep. They didn't know her. It wasn't grief, it was rage that choked her. There was a short silence.

'Well, of course I can see that in the circumstances . . .' said Dunster. 'There are special circumstances in this case, are there not?'

'No relative has come forward,' said Turner slowly. 'And perhaps in a way you are as near as possible to a relative we are likely to find.' He spoke grudgingly. 'How do you think your father will take it?'

She was beginning to wonder about that herself.

'The Colonel might supply the order and discipline the girl needs,' was Dunster's comment.

Gregory Barton, who had believed the other magistrates would persuade Mary to drop her silly idea, was very put out when he heard their decision. He shook his head and muttered loud enough for everybody in the court to hear: 'I'm sure this won't be the end of the matter!' Then sitting down again in his high desk he shouted: 'Hannah Batherswick stand up please!'

The chairman then announced the magistrates' decision that an interim care order committing Hannah to the care of the local authority for twenty-eight days would be made to enable full reports to be put before the court for proper assessment of the foster home offered.

As Hannah was led out, Mary could hear her protesting: 'I don't want to be fostered by that mangy old cat!' Barton grinned openly, and the clerk's clerk bent his head to hide his smile as he scribbled. Turner pursed his lips in an expression of 'I told you so!' but Dunster nodded at Mary across the bench, now littered with loose papers, and murmured,

'We shall see . . .'

TWO

Miss Harris, the social worker to whose casebook Hannah had been allotted, interviewed Miss Chicon and her father at home. She was impressed by Gatt's Rise Farm. Who would not be? The lovely old house with its long façade displaying four windows on each of two storeys, and from the attics under the roof four dormer windows, hooded like the eyes of old women blinking in the sun, its stone-flagged entrance and great central chimneypiece stacked on either side with logs to feed the slow-burning but voracious stove, would welcome the least sensitive of souls. Like so many Gloucestershire farmhouses it was built in the seventeenth century, but probably had older foundations. It stood on a small hill, Gatt's Rise, whose south-facing slope, fenced in to form a paddock, looked down on the canal fed by a tributary of the Frene as it meandered towards the marshy lands bordering the Severn. A huddle of great elms leaned together at the back of the house, protecting it from the prevailing south-west winds. In these trees, year after year for as long as living memory could remember, a colony of rooks nested. In the Seventies the trees succumbed to the great epidemic which killed so many millions of elms throughout the country, and the Colonel was forced to fell the crumbling and infected timber; but on the morning when Miss Harris visited Gatt's

Rise the trees still stood, and the black harbingers of spring announced their reproductive intentions with loud persistent cawing which echoed through the house.

Gatt's Rise and Gatt's Crossing, in ancient times a ford, where now a lock interrupts the steady surface of the canal, are both mentioned in the deeds of the house, which was once owned by a certain Jacobus Gatt. His tombstone, cut out of the local reddish iron-containing rock, lies in the nave of Frenester church, protesting from under the feet of all who tread on him: 'He departed this earthly life February 10 in the year of our Lord 1620. He lieth down in God's green pastures until the Last Trump shall call him to return unto his own.' Whenever Mary walked over him she wondered if this declaration didn't indicate a certain disappointment with the afterlife. Could he possibly be finding the fields of paradise less fertile than those at Gatt's Rise?

Miss Harris was also impressed by the hard useful work in progress. The low-lying land was not suitable for arable crops, but it made good pasture on which the Colonel fattened sheep and young beef. The farm also produced quantities of potatoes. All this Mary explained to Miss Harris as she showed her over the house, the stableyard and fields.

As soon as Miss Harris met the Colonel she was charmed, as many women were, by his stern good looks, his upright commanding figure, and the old-fashioned courtesy which belonged to his public face, though she could not have imagined the complexity of his character, the many different layers of desire and discipline of which it was composed, nor guessed that he was not really a Christian at all. His ancestors had been Huguenots, and, in spite of the racial and cultural mixing that inevitably took place from living in England for three hundred years, traces of the old Calvinist iron and elitism had been handed down to him. He still attended church to celebrate the main festivals of the Christian year, but he no longer believed in Christian theology. He used to quote Diderot to explain his position: 'The first step towards philosophy is incredulity.' He didn't love his neighbour much; nor was he much liked in the neighbourhood, although he was everywhere respected. He believed that he, and to some extent his daughter too, belonged to a special class of person whose responsibility it was to protect and improve as far as possible the moral quality of life as well as the physical well-being of the rabble. *'Noblesse oblige . . .'* he used to say. It was not altogether a social snobbery, nor was it entirely a feeling of intellectual superiority. It was more a conviction of self-worth of which altruism was a necessary part, but altruism without folly: a beneficence of a calculatedly useful kind.

Mary thought of him as an ancient Roman; and he himself looked back towards the Augustan era of the Roman Empire as the Golden Age of man: a society well organised, he thought, orderly, rational and prosperous, their engineers making good roads and building good centrally heated villas, expanding the empire and bringing civilisation to the barbarians. When Mary reminded him of the cruelties and slavery that went with it he used to say: 'Every civilisation has been built on slavery.' He loved honour, face, or reputation more than anything. He believed he lived by reason, disliking any emotionalism, distrusting enthusiasm and people whom he described as bleeding hearts: do-gooders whom he blamed for their sloppy, unthinking kindness. He despised all those who belonged to what he thought of as the lunatic fringe of society: idle young men with long hair and dirty fingernails, conscientious objectors to war, hunting, nuclear armaments and the battery-farming of poultry; and he feared artists, whom he classed as more or less mad and, apart from those safely dead, usually a menace to established order. 'Colly's rather old-fashioned, you know,' said Mary as she led Miss Harris into the kitchen for a cup of tea after her investigatory tour of the premises.

'Why, if I may ask without being too nosy,' asked Miss Harris, 'why do you call your father Colly?'

Mary shrugged. 'Heaven knows! I always have. Perhaps it was a kid's way of saying Colonel. Or perhaps,' she laughed with uncomplicated amusement, 'it's something to do with his being like a sheep-dog, always nosing other people in the right direction.'

And no doubt into pens as well, thought Miss Harris, but did not say so, since in the circumstances she considered that no bad thing. The old sheep-dog would provide a safe home for Hannah where she would certainly not be allowed any licence, where she might learn to lead a useful and orderly life and not be too unhappy. An added advantage was the fact that she would be able to return to her old school in Frenester. Miss Harris presumed that Mary would supply the necessary feeding and affection. She left, pleased and satisfied with her visit; and in due course she brought Hannah to her new home at Gatt's Rise.

The few weeks' interval needed for all the enquiries, reports and decisions to be made gave Mary time to prepare one of the attic bedrooms for Hannah's use. With the help of Mrs Wiltshire, the Frenester seamstress, she installed curtains, bedspread and dressing-table cover, all matching in a white fabric scattered with small pink and blue flowers; and in spite of the extravagance she had the wooden floorboards covered from wall to wall with a carpet in crushed strawberry pink. She was delighted with the result. 'It's just what I would have liked when I was a schoolgirl,' she told Mrs Wiltshire. 'So I hope Hannah will like it too.'

'If she don't she'll be an ungrateful little minx!' said Mrs Wiltshire, who thought all this fuss over that trashy kid Hannah Batherswick (who before she ran off the rails was in the same class in school as her Kevin) was proper daft.

Colonel Chicon took much the same view, although he did not oppose his daughter absolutely. He knew he must respect her decision, a consensus decision made by all three magistrates. He must abide by it, although he thought it was a mistake.

'You're wasting your time, Mary,' he warned her. 'That girl will be working in a brothel by the time she's twenty.'

'I've got her for three years,' argued Mary. 'Till she's eighteen.'

'The good anyone can do is always very little,' he said. But he made up his mind to accept Hannah's presence in his house. That didn't mean he would alter his routine in any way for her. Far from it. He continued to rise early, spend his days in supervising the farm, sometimes on horseback (which was his way of consoling himself for the fact that on doctor's orders he'd had to give up hunting a few years ago after a heavy fall), and his evenings alone in his study rereading his favourite classics: Virgil's *Georgics* in the original Latin for the pleasure of it, and the *Maxims of Marcus Aurelius* for common sense. Virgil he referred to as the Mantuan Swan – though why poets were called swans Mary as a child could never understand, since the only noise swans uttered was an occasional ugly honk. Sometimes he read Gibbon's *Decline and Fall of the Roman Empire*, probably for the sheer horror of it, in the way that other people read the tabloids.

He was a fastidious drinker, though not entirely teetotal, but he was bored by local society. He would not allow television (whose values he considered stupid, false and brash) into the house. Mary had to confess to herself that she dreaded the evenings with Hannah and no telly to amuse her.

When Hannah first saw the attic bedroom that was to be her own her eyes opened wide. She flitted from one object to another, touching the frilled cover of the dressing-table, lightly stroking a fold in the flowered curtain as if to make sure these things were real. She leaned on the dormer windowsill to gaze down on the paddock below, where Mary's old horse Rollo had been put out to graze as best he could the poor grass of early March, and at the fields beyond intersected by hedges still as transparent as veils.

'Cor!' she breathed softly. Then turning she saw Mary in

21

the doorway, and immediately her delight shrivelled to suspicion. 'What you doin' this for?' she demanded harshly. 'You religious or something?'

'No,' said Mary. 'Not really. Hardly at all, as a matter of fact.' She could read in those cruel young eyes surveying her the thoughts: she knows nothing about men. She's a poor sex-starved spinster and a frump. She won't ever understand my sort. How could she, living in a place like this?

'Why d'you take me on then? You're a beak, aren't you?'

'I am human too, you know.'

Hannah stared at Mary as if she doubted it. 'I shall run away!' she threatened. 'You know I'm a bad lot!'

Mary sat down on the edge of the bed. 'I don't think you're a bad lot,' she said. 'I think you've got a lot of good in you. You've certainly been unlucky, as well as wild and silly. I'm going to be your foster mother for a time. It's for your care and protection.'

'Protect me from men, I suppose?' Her tone was one of withering sarcasm.

'Well, yes – until you're old enough and wise enough to protect yourself. Did you ever think you might have a baby? And then what would you do?'

'Course I did. I got myself on the pill, see? – when I ran away – as soon as I got to Bristol and could find the clinic. I've got that much savvy.'

She stood on the other side of the bed, glowering. Her fingers played with the end of a cord she wore as a belt round the waist of her jeans. Mary was reminded of a wild, terrified Dartmoor pony she had once broken in.

'It's what my dad's blondes used to say to me: "I'll be a mummy to you, dear!"' She wriggled her shoulders in imitation of her dad's women. 'But they never was. People tells lies. All the time.'

'I'm not that sort of a mother,' Mary said.

'I should hope not! Bloody sluts! They were all the same, them blondes. They used to come down to breakfast on

22

Sunday mornings with their hair hanging all over their smudged make-up, cigarette dangling; but they never seemed to eat anything. That's what sex does to you: spoils your appetite. Never stopped *him* eating, though. He used to have bacon, egg and fried bread, the lot – fried it all himself. The blondes never lifted a finger, except to flick ash all over the butter. Sluts! And liars too.'

'I don't think I'm that sort of a mother at all.' Mary's cool voice broke into her soliloquy. 'No one can ever replace your own mother. I know that, because I lost mine too.'

'You did?' Hannah was interested, but Mary did not pursue that subject. 'I'm going to give you a home here till you're eighteen, where you won't have problems to trouble you, where I hope you'll be safe and happy. We must both try to make it a success.'

'OK,' said Hannah. 'I'll give it a go.'

'And perhaps you can help me as well.'

Hannah made no comment on that, but fiddled very fast with the unravelling tassel on her belt.

'Did you know I once knew your real mother, Hannah?'

The girl suddenly became very still. Then she sat down on the other side of the bed. She touched Mary's arm timidly, her hungry eyes searching her face.

'What was she like, my mum?' she asked.

'Very like you,' said Mary. 'Very like you about the eyes.'

'I can't hardly remember her,' Hannah murmured.

Mary suddenly realised that Fate had after all dealt her a few trump cards in these memories she had of Maeve Delaney. 'We sold your grandmother a pony for Maeve to ride,' she said. 'It was a Dartmoor pony that I'd broken in myself.' Hannah's eyes were glued to Mary's face now as if every word she spoke was of vital importance.

'Could my mother ride, then?' Hannah spoke dreamily, her voice surprisingly soft, quite unlike the truculent tones she'd just been using.

'I actually taught her to ride. And yes, she did look good in the saddle.'

'Gran never told me that,' said Hannah. 'Perhaps she didn't want me to know, because I kept on at her to buy me a pony. "When you're old enough," she used to say. But she died before I was old enough.'

Mary was surprised at the girl's sudden change of mood, and dealt with it awkwardly. 'But now you must wash your hands and come down to the dining-room for lunch with my father,' she said briskly.

Hannah did more than wash her hands; she combed her black luxuriant hair carefully, and put on some scarlet lipstick which Mary feared would make Colly see the girl as a painted Jezebel. She followed Mary downstairs, moving in a clumsy rush like a young colt; but at the door she hesitated.

'What shall I call him?' she whispered.

'Just call him Colonel.'

While Colonel Chicon stood stiffly at the head of the table Hannah sat down and stared at him. To her he must have seemed an alien being from another planet. She was fidgety during lunch; she was afraid of using the wrong fork, and of dropping food on the white cloth, but most of all she feared the old man's steady glare returning her sidelong glances, and his abrupt, harsh voice which stopped her fluttering display of charms and made her sit at last crouched over her plate like a winged bird.

In spite of this first uncomfortable lunch it all proved easier than expected. For one thing Hannah had to go to school. She caught the school bus at the corner where the farm lane met the Frenester road; and she had her lunch pack with her. She returned for a high tea in the kitchen with Mary, after which she did her homework there. Hannah liked reading, rather to Mary's surprise, so she was persuaded to join the Frenester public library. After finishing her homework Hannah went to bed with a book. Sometimes she was surly, occasionally rude; but she was docile enough to seem willing to fit into the farm routine. Colonel Chicon she avoided as much as possible.

In order to avoid her he had, in spite of himself, to make some changes in his habits. 'You'll have to excuse me from eating with her, Mary,' he said. 'She does cramp the conversation at table, you know.'

'Does she, Colly?'

'Well, she takes up so much of your attention that you have no time to listen to me.'

So Mary made some alterations too.

Her father already ate his sandwich lunch from a tray in his study while Mary cooked and served the midday meal in the kitchen for Tom their regular farm worker, who lived in the tied cottage at the gate, and old Mikey the gardener who lodged with a landlady on the Frenester road and did a few hours' gardening when he felt like it. They were joined three times a week by Beryl who cycled down from Frenester to clean and do the washing. On Thursdays when Mary had to appear in court they ate cold meat and salad, which Beryl served and presided over. Mary decided to shut the dining-room (thus saving a little space heating in winter) and to serve dinner for her father and herself on a folding table in his study by the big log fire.

'It's like living in a camp,' he grumbled. 'That's what that girl is driving us to: camping out in our own house.'

'It's more sensible,' said Mary. 'And it does save me work.'

On Sundays Mary didn't have to feed the workers, but Hannah was at home, so she served Sunday's main meal at midday in the kitchen for the three of them. It was always an anxious time for Mary, because if she wasn't very careful the atmosphere became full of flying darts. Having spent all her life with her father she knew him so well, his hobby-horses, prejudices, likes and dislikes, and also the signs he gave of approval and the warnings of impending sarcasm, that she was adept when alone with him at deflecting the conversational ball from the danger-

25

ous corners of his irascibility; but in Hannah's presence it was more difficult. Hannah, who didn't know the Colonel, was quite unaware of what might trigger his underlying hostilities into anger. Although she had often quarrelled and indeed come to blows with her own father, she had never learned to hold her tongue, so that as her new surroundings became familiar and she began to relax she spoke blithely at mealtimes about whatever came into her head.

'Glint Gloss is what my friends at school are using now,' she said. 'But I can't seem to get it in Frenester. Frenester is that old-fashioned.'

'What,' asked the Colonel, 'is Glint Gloss?'

She looked pityingly at him, 'It's shampoo,' she explained. 'Supposed to be the best. Makes your hair soft and gleaming, like the adverts says.'

He gave her a baleful stare. 'It's silly to believe adverts,' he said. 'Adverts don't tell you the truth. They're trying to sell you something, get money out of you. So they tell lies to do it.'

'My friend Sandra has tried it,' argued Hannah. 'She says it's fab. And she's not an advert.'

'We all have hair,' he said, his voice rising as it tensed to a tone Mary recognised only too well as signalling his attempt to control his temper. 'We all have hair, more or less. You have a great deal more than I have. And we all have to wash it. The matter is of no interest or importance. Vanity of vanities, empty and trivial. What's more, the subject is boring.'

Hannah was astonished, but silenced.

But one Sunday in May when Mary announced at lunch that the Reverend Brown was driving over from Mudcott that afternoon to see Hannah the girl suddenly laughed, exclaiming, 'You mean Disability Brown?' And the Colonel unexpectedly laughed too. 'I've always thought of him as Good-for-nothing-but-Mudcott-Brown,' he said, 'but Disability's rather good. He certainly has no capability to speak

26

of.' It pleased Mary to hear him laugh. She relaxed her vigilance, and encouraged Hannah to talk by asking why poor Mr Brown had been given such a nickname.

'It was my gran who called him the Reverend Disability,' said Hannah. 'That was when I was living with her at the mill. He wasn't very popular in Mudcott. My Aunt May said that was because he was a bachelor. "What's wrong with being a bachelor?" I asked. I was about nine then. They exchanged looks over my head, so I knew they were keeping a grown-up secret from me. "Well, in his case it's a disability," said Gran. I didn't know that word, so I kept on badgering them with questions: "What's a disability then?" Gran smiled, and stroked my hair, as she often did. "Well," she said, "might be a wooden leg. That 'ud be a bad disability. Might be only a stammer. That 'ud be a small one." When I asked if he had a wooden leg under his cassock they both laughed. "Now don't you be asking him now, and making him blush," Gran cautioned me. But they never explained.'

There was a long pause after this little speech. Hannah reddened, thinking she had somehow put her foot in it again; but both Mary and her father were silenced by Hannah's revelation of earlier days, of a brief happy childhood spent with her own relations, and by her loss.

'Well, I like him, disability and all,' said Hannah defiantly. 'And I'm glad he's coming this afternoon.' But she looked sad.

Mary offered her a helping of apple crumble, which Hannah took without noticing what it was. Her thoughts were suddenly far away. 'It hasn't exactly purified me,' she said.

'What hasn't?' asked Mary.

'Suffering,' said Hannah. 'That's what Disability talked about.' Tears spurted down her cheeks, and she couldn't eat her pudding. 'Excuse me!' she gasped, and noisily pushing her chair away from the table she ran from the room, out into the yard and across the paddock, trying to cope

27

with the sudden rush of painful memories which assailed her.

It was while she sat in class listening to Miss Poole droning on about King John and Magna Carta that Gran must have had her stroke. I was eleven then, she thought, staring across the field but seeing only the long slope of tarmac road down to the mill at Blissy Brook as she free-wheeled happily home. November it was, dry but cold. She liked to hear the crackle of fallen leaves under her cycle wheels and often steered into a pile of them just to hear it. Not knowing at all about what was happening to Gran. . . .

By the time she got home Gran was unconscious. Still breathing but she didn't know me, Hannah remembered. She thought Gran must have a headache, because she kept groaning and shaking her head, and every time she groaned Hannah felt a stab in her belly. So she put a handkerchief soaked in eau-de-Cologne on Gran's forehead, and held her hand.

When Dr Marten arrived Gran wasn't groaning any more but snoring. He stood over her; he moved her legs; he shone a torch in her eyes, lifting her eyelids with his thumb because she couldn't do it herself. Then he ordered Hannah to bed; but she wouldn't go, and Auntie May, fluttering about in her distress and indecision, couldn't make her obey.

Gran died later that night. Hannah held her hand while it grew cold, and Auntie May whimpered like a dog locked out, till first light broke through the bedroom window, when she left the bedside to make a pot of tea.

Hannah remembered what the death certificate said: 'Cerebral haemorrhage.' And underneath: 'arteriosclerosis and hypertension.' These long dignified words were a bit of comfort to her. They seemed to respect a special person so unexpectedly laid low. Dr Marten put his arm around Hannah's shoulders and hugged her. She was grateful for that, though she never said a word. The Reverend came later. Auntie May, who was tearful and trembling by this time, ushered him into Gran's room, where Hannah still sat.

'Hannah hasn't cried at all,' she complained.

'How long has she been sitting here?' he asked.

'All day and most of the night. I can't get her to go away.'

He knelt down beside Gran's calm face. Beautiful she was, like a marble statue. He shut his eyes and prayed silently. Afterwards he took Hannah by the hand and led her outside, where they walked about on the wet grass without speaking. It was so still and cold she knew there'd be a frost that night.

'She is with God,' he said at last.

'Do you think so?'

'Of course. Jesus died and rose again on the third day. She will rise again in heaven too. God loves her, you see.'

After a long pause Hannah said, 'I don't think God loves me very much. He took my mother from me, and now He's taken Gran.'

He had the sense not to bombard her with theological arguments, but his hand tightened over hers. They walked on into the walled garden where Auntie May's strawberries grew. Hannah distinctly remembered the feeling of its warmer air on her cheeks as she followed him along the clinkered path.

'Life is hard,' he said. It was no comfort to her to hear what she knew already; but she respected his honesty. Then he took her hand again, and spoke gently: 'God loves those who suffer. It is like fire, suffering. It may destroy you; but if you are brave enough and have faith enough you can come through purified.' As they turned back to the house he said: 'Remember God.' And putting his arms round her he hugged her.

That Sunday afternoon at Gatt's Rise Hannah put on

her best behaviour like a Sunday dress. She prepared a tray for tea in the sitting-room; she cut slices, not very thin ones it must be admitted, of brown bread and butter; she spread strawberry jam and blobs of whipped cream on scones Mary had made; and she asked were there any little tea-table napkins they could use?

'You sit down Miss Chicon,' she said. 'Let me get the tea. You work so hard all week you should have a rest sometimes on Sundays.'

Surprised, Mary sat down, examined her idle hands, and watched Hannah.

When Mr Brown arrived, to be greeted by Mary and led into the sitting-room, the Colonel joined them. Hannah bustled in with the teapot, which she held out stiffly before her, spout in one hand, handle in the other. She felt important as she put it carefully down on a pottery tile on the round tea table. Then she sat nervously on the edge of a small chair. Conversation, which was polite and desultory, alternated with awkward silences, so when at last the Reverend Disability suggested Hannah should take a walk with him down to the lock and along the canal she jumped up immediately, delighted to be let off the hook.

Hawthorn hedges in full bloom lined the canal banks. Sunshine and shadows of poplars fell across the calm water like colours woven into silk. Hannah was filled with happiness. She ran about in short spurts of irrepressible energy, stopping to smell the May blossom or pull off a few sprays.

'Like snow!' she cried. 'Only it don't melt. Magic really. Ouch!' sucking her thumb which a thorn had pierced deeply enough to draw blood. 'I do love the month of May, don't you? All this blossom – it's like a wedding!'

He glanced at her sideways. He supposed that was what girls thought of all the time: weddings. He walked on steadily till she fell into step beside him.

'Are you settling down here all right, Hannah?' he asked.

'OK,' she admitted. 'Bit boring sometimes of course. I

don't like *him*, the old man. What happened to her mother, then?'

'She disappeared long ago. Nobody seems to know much about her. They say she ran off with another man. And the Colonel never speaks of her, I'm told.'

'The Colonel is an old dinosaur, extinct really, but not buried yet. She's all right.'

'You get on all right with Miss Chicon?'

'She's nice; but she's always trying to please *him*. Can't understand it. I think she really loves him. It's funny. . . .'

'He is her father, Hannah. Children do love their fathers, sometimes even when they're grown up.'

'Seems strange to me. Can't remember a time when I didn't hate mine.'

'Why did you run away from him, Hannah?'

She stopped to look at him. 'You know I couldn't stop on at the mill when Gran died. Auntie May was too ill to look after me. That hive of bees she kept in the garden, and all that honey which she thought was healing, and all the stings which she thought would cure her, never did. Her arthritis got worse after Gran died. So I had to go and live with Dad.'

'And it didn't work out?'

'It wasn't too bad at first. He could be quite nice at times. I remember when a boy at school gave me a bottle of perfume as a birthday present – silly kid he was, too! Dad had forgotten my birthday of course; but when he smelt the perfume he asked: "What's that lovely pong then?" "Picadilly Nights is what it's called," I told him. "Well, I never smelt any of them sort of nights in Frenester," he said, and tickled the back of my neck. I was sitting doing my homework in the kitchen.'

He let her talk. He guessed she was feeling bottled up at Gatt's Rise and needed a listener.

'Yeah. He could be OK sometimes. But I hated him all along. He killed my mum, didn't he? by his reckless driving in that rotten old sports car with its smelly exhaust. And he never cared about me, did he? All he cared about was his fag-end blondes. They was all the same, you know; dyed hair falling about and fag ash falling on the toast at breakfast. Well I didn't mind them so much. It was when I said I wanted to go to college and learn to be a teacher, and that I wanted to be a lady like my mother, that he got mad. "Your mother was no lady!" he shouted at me. "She was the same as any other little bitch!" And then he told me: "I fucked her behind the brickworks and that was the beginning of you. I had to marry her then. And that was the beginning of all my troubles." I flew at him then, trying to scratch his eyes out, screeching, "She was much too good for you! All you're good for is them fag-end blondes! And none of them will have you for keeps, neither!" He pulled me off him as if I was a crazy cat, and he hit me so hard I fell on the floor, where he kicked me once or twice before he left me alone. Next morning when I woke up I could hardly open my eyes, and my face was all black and blue, and my ribs ached. So I didn't go to school. I was too ashamed.'

She stood still on the path and stripped all the leaves off a spray of hawthorn she was carrying.

'I didn't speak to him all that week. I locked myself in my bedroom. I came downstairs and got myself some grub when he'd gone to work. And on Saturday morning, after he'd gone to the pub, I went into his room and found where he'd hidden his wages. So I took a five-pound note. Then I put on my best clothes – no mac, 'cos I thought that looked too much like school uniform – and no high heels, but strong trainers, 'cos I knew I'd be doing a lot of walking. And then I left.'

The energy suddenly seemed to fade from her face, and she looked tired. She walked on ahead of him quickly.

He said nothing, respecting her silence as they walked back; but as they reached the paddock and began to climb the slope to Gatt's Rise he asked his last question: 'Do you still want to be a teacher?'

32

'That's what I'm working on. With her help.' She nodded towards the house. And then as an afterthought: 'Why d'you think she took me on? I can't figure it out.'

'I think she's the sort of person who wants to help others,' he said. And perhaps help herself, he thought, but did not speak his guess aloud.

Mary was relieved when her guest took Hannah for a walk across the fields and her father retired to his study to read the Sunday papers and, she suspected, fall asleep in his chair, though that was something he didn't admit to. She always felt shy and tongue-tied in Mr Brown's presence. He had probably forgotten what caused her embarrassment. Why, it was a quarter of a century ago! But Mary still felt awkward when they met. The explanation of why she'd left his choir so abruptly, when she'd been his best soprano, the one he relied on most just when he was planning to schedule a special mass for Christmas Eve, still after all these years lay unspoken between them. It was silly, she knew. She was a middle-aged woman now, and at her age should have had the sense, the *savoir-faire* to be able to give him, quite lightly and jokingly, the apology she owed him; but she couldn't bring herself to do it. Nor could she forget the matter whenever she saw him.

Hannah was right. She did feel tired that afternoon. She decided to hide herself in her bedroom, to put one or two of her favourite cassettes in her tape recorder and listen to some music, relax, perhaps even fall asleep. She left the teacups and the crumbs, hoping that Hannah's good mood would last long enough to make her clear the table.

Oklahoma . . . she let the corn-fed, sunsoaked music pour into her ears. She was eighteen when she saw that show. David had the tickets in his pocket when he drove her up to town in his battered red MG. They took the old road across Salisbury Plain. It was a bright, clear morning, she remembered, unusually warm for September, so they drove with the hood rolled back, wickedly fast it seemed to her, as the wind rushing through her hair blew all the grips out. She knew she'd look a mess by the time they reached London, but she didn't care. David wore a flat tweed cap with the peak pulled well down to shade his eyes, and a long green woollen scarf round his neck. They passed through Devizes, along the wide market street of Marlborough with its solid old brick houses, to the outskirts of Reading, where he pulled in to the roadside to unwind his scarf. 'Too hot!' he gasped. Looking at her pink, wind-whipped cheeks and her bright, trusting eyes he smiled: 'You all right?'

'Rather!' she said. And again, 'Rather!' It was a good thing she was sitting in the car because the little wisps of fair hair, which the unwinding had exposed on the nape of his neck, were making her feel weak at the knees.

It was a matinée they watched. Mary was a bit woozy owing to the gin and tonic he'd given her at lunchtime, and which she'd never in her life tasted before. 'Do you good,' he explained. 'Loosens up the joints. Flexes the muscles and all that!' So she was suitably loosened and flexed to enjoy all the high spirits on stage. And oh! the music! – that sweet, warm, persuasive voice of Curly the Cowboy stroking her ears! And she agreed with him absolutely that it was a beautiful day, and everything did seem at last to be going her way, Mary was convinced of it. The war was over, and everybody was moving into a bright new post-war world.

'A candy-floss musical,' said David during the interval, as they sucked ice-cream, 'but nice.'

He'd booked dinner for two at the Rendezvous in Soho. Rationing was still in force, but they were able to order a good, well seasoned spaghetti Bolognese and enjoy it with a bottle of tangy Valpolicella. Their little table was beside a gallery overlooking the dance floor, so they leaned over the edge to watch the dancers as they ate. They danced later. It was just before rock 'n' roll burst on the scene, with its rhythmic thump which jerked you out of the hum-drum and into possibilities of wildness, when everybody did his or her own thing. Before rock 'n' roll people danced in couples sedately, which Mary and David did, to a senti-mental foxtrot. David didn't talk at all; but Mary knew by the way he held her elbow to swivel her round a corner, and pushed his hand against her back when they achieved a neat sidestep, how he felt about her.

'You're a good dancer, Mary,' he said, as they climbed into the car for the journey home. 'Who taught you?'

'Oh, school!' said Mary. 'We all had to learn dancing at school. You're good too.' But of course he was! He was so good at everything.

It was terribly, terribly late when they got back that night. Mary knew her father would be angry, but she didn't care.

'We must do this again,' said David, squeezing her hand as he helped her out of the car.

'Oh yes, please!' said Mary. She smiled happily at the prospect. She could still, after all these years, smile happily at that prospect which was never fulfilled.

They stood for a moment at the front door while Mary fumbled in her handbag for the key, but before she had time to use it her father opened the door. He was fully dressed and icily polite; but he didn't invite David inside.

'Thank you for bringing my daughter home,' he said. 'I was beginning to fear you might have kidnapped her.'

'Only wish I could!' grinned David cheerily.

'I don't think you'll get another chance,' said the Colonel.

A great stony pillar of righteousness, he towered above them. David seemed to shrink like a deflated balloon. Mary forgot the curls on the back of his neck, as well as the tender look in his blue eyes. She saw an unimportant young man cringing. She shook his hand formally. 'Good-bye,' she said. 'Thank you for a lovely day.'

'So long! he muttered, keeping his eyes on the ground;

and then he scuttled like a beetle away to his car, without a backward glance.

'I'm sorry we're so late, Colly,' she said. 'I'm afraid I rather lost track of time. You shouldn't have waited up for us.'

'Go to bed now,' he said. 'We'll talk in the morning.'

THREE

Colly used to say that every effect had a cause, though some causes produced very small results. As the tape recorder ran on for a few seconds before switching itself off Mary considered that both these statements were undoubtedly true; and as she let her thoughts run back silently into the groove of her remembered past she told herself it was really her father who had set in motion that whole chain of events.

When she left school at seventeen without having passed any exams, because the boarding-school she attended did not take exams for young ladies very seriously, she was sent to a secretarial college in London to learn book-keeping, shorthand and typing. Colly arranged it all. He told her these skills would make her a very useful farm manager. He would be grateful, he explained, for her help in relieving him of some of the great burden of work he carried since her mother's departure. She understood, though he didn't exactly spell it out, that he had undertaken all this work in order to be able to send her to a good school, which would bring her up well, protect her from her mother's influence, and perhaps keep her happy too. In London she was able to stay in the house of the widow of an old Sandhurst friend. It was this widow who introduced Mary to the cordon bleu cookery classes attended by debs and other smart girls. Mary spent several hours each week learning how to cook while laughing and larking about with some of these girls. Sometimes she truanted from shorthand lessons to sneak off with one of them to a cinema, and on one or two occasions to devour tea and toasted teacakes at a Lyons' Corner House. She found she liked preparing tempting dishes a great deal better than shorthand; but she managed to achieve a moderate speed in typing, and was commended in her final secretarial college report for neatness in accounting and presentation. Her father seemed satisfied when she came home with this report.

She was always an even-tempered girl who took everything as it came along; but she did feel some dismay when she began to realise that for the foreseeable future her life would be spent on the farm with Colly who, apart from his hunting acquaintances, had few friends and was known in the district as a bit of a recluse. She found she missed the cookery classes and the slightly wicked expeditions with the girls. When in the evening after dinner she sat with Colly in his study in a profound silence, broken only by the crackle of the fire, the turning of a page as he read on steadily, and the thump of her dog Buzzby's tail on the carpet when he caught her eye, then she did feel lonely. 'Dear Claudia,' she wrote her letter on her knees sitting by the fire, 'you have no idea how quiet it is here after the noise and bustle of Lyons' Corner House! I miss you all. I even miss the squeals of dismay we used to utter when our sponge cakes came out of the oven all soggy in the middle! I am having a nice new hacking jacket made for me for the cubbing season, a present from my father. I look forward to that – cubbing I mean, as well as the jacket.'

It wasn't so bad in winter when there was always the hunting to look forward to each week. Riding to the meet on a crisp fine morning was when she felt truly happy. The excitement of the chase, the slight risk she suddenly took at every jump, and the final gallop after the hounds in full cry filled her with exaltation that satisfied and exhausted her to the exclusion of all other feelings; but in the summer months when the country all around was at its best, adorned in its full, unashamedly luxurious greenery, the days often seemed too long. There was no one to share her feelings with but Buzzby. To his delight she often chased across fields with him in a frenzy of pent-up longings.

She knew she would have to go out and make friends for herself, but how? At school she had often been told that she had a pretty singing voice, so she decided to join a choir. Which choir? The Frenester Bach Choir met in the church hall every other Tuesday evening, so she plucked up courage and marched in at the right time one Tuesday. As soon as she entered she saw she was the youngest person present; there was no one else remotely near her in age. A robust lady wearing stalwart brown brogues, a tweed skirt and a jacket which was finding it difficult, even when buttoned up, to cage her rambling bosom, spoke kindly to her.

'Are you a new girl, my dear? Well, come and sit by me. Let me take you under my wing.' Upon which she raised an arm in greeting and released such a gale of scents from under it that Mary immediately resolved that it was one wing she would certainly not shelter under. It may have been what put her against the Bach Choir.

There were, however, other reasons which prevented her joining. The Bach Choir, though a secular club, was affiliated to St Jerome's Church, whose vicar, the Reverend Peter Bliss (commonly giggled over by his church ladies as 'Heavenly'), had recently had words with her father. Peter Bliss was a tall handsome man with a mane of greying hair, and although in his late forties was still single, so he could be relied upon to fill the missing male's chair at local dinner parties. This was one of his assets which endeared him to the ladies. It did not endear him to the Colonel.

Their quarrel began over a pamphlet describing the life and times of one Christoferus Twigge, a monk who had

39

been foolish enough to get involved in a local revolt of peasants against feudal landlords in 1371. In those days before the Dissolution of the Monasteries by Henry VIII, an Order of Contemplatives was attached to the church of St Jerome, and Christoferus was one of these. Before his notoriety and disgrace he spent much of his time in a tiny cell two stone spirals up inside a tower where, alone and in complete silence, he drew in elegant Latin calligraphy and illuminated with much originality and skill a text from Isaiah. Although isolated from the world, Christoferus was still able to hear the grumblings of the hungry poor, which after three wet summers and bad harvests turned into such loud lamentations that at last their sufferings made him speak. Moreover he had seen a vision in a dream; and in this dream God had spoken to him so clearly that he knew he must break his vow of silence in order to tell the world what God wanted to be done. So he penned in his beautiful script a treasonable declaration on vellum which was passed secretly from hand to hand:

> No good will come to England,
> No peace will England see
> Till all her land in equal parts
> For equal men divided be.

At first his religious superior tried to protect Christoferus, whose work on the manuscript he admired and knew was not yet finished. He begged him to recant, to give himself time to complete his work, to save his body and, more important still, his soul. But Christoferus remained true to his vision. So obdurate was he that he was at last taken off in chains to a dungeon and, after the necessary legal processes of torture to extract the truth, was found guilty of treason by the state and blasphemy by the Church. He was then hanged, drawn and quartered.

His unfinished manuscript was kept in a glass-lidded box inside the tower. When Mary was still only a child her father told her the harrowing story. He took her up the dark, curving stone staircase to peer at the strange old parchment book. He read aloud and translated for her the last passage written by that monk's hand: 'Yea. They are greedy dogs which can never have enough, and they are shepherds that cannot understand. They all look to their own way, every one for his gain from his quarter.' The upright of the capital Y of Yea was shaped into a bone, and a pair of crouching dogs, one on either side of it, bared their teeth.

During the last years of the nineteenth century an artist of Fabian sympathies and William Morris enthusiasms had written, illustrated, and printed at his own expense a little history of poor Christoferus Twigge's life and unhappy end; and for generations this pamphlet had been sold along with others from a shelf near the ancient, creaking, hobnailed oak door of the church. But when the Reverend Bliss arrived in Frenester and wanted to modernise things a bit he swept out this pamphlet along with a lot of other dusty objects and outmoded rituals.

It was some time before the Colonel missed it. When he did he asked the vicar where it was. 'It's an interesting piece of local history, you know,' he said.

'Local history it may be,' said Bliss. 'But judging by the small sales it had I don't think it was of great interest. And as a matter of fact I thought, after this recent wave of arson and vandalism in the district, that it might give a bad example to the young.'

'Do you mean to say you've silenced him? Excommunicated him, in a sense, from the Church?'

He had. Trying to remove the look of horror from the Colonel's face he murmured gently, 'The end does justify the means in this case, Colonel, I do believe.'

Colonel Chicon took the argument home and continued it with his daughter over the dinner-table.

'That man Bliss is a fool,' he said. 'How can rubbing out a piece of history stop crime? The sort of vandal who

41

sets a barn alight for fun doesn't bother to read history. And certainly wouldn't go into a church to do so.'

'He probably can't read anyway,' said Mary.

'Quite so.' He made an impatient gesture, dismissing her suggestion as one accepted long ago when in fact the thought had only entered his mind when she expressed it. 'And this pamphlet was illustrated by that chap – friend of William Morris, connected with those silversmiths in Chipping Campden, wasn't he? That's another piece of local culture we should prize.' He cut a piece of chicken rapidly and speared it fiercely on his fork. 'But that wouldn't interest that philistine. Ends and means indeed!'

'You mean Bliss?'

'Who else?'

They finished the chicken in silence.

Meanwhile Peter Bliss had also taken the argument home, and because he had nobody to listen to him over a cup of tea he continued the discussion angrily in his head. Chicon really was a bit of a fanatic – creating a fuss about a miserable old pamphlet nobody wanted to read, and certainly nobody bought. To get more copies of it now he'd have to have it reprinted. And the church certainly couldn't afford that. It occurred to him he might ask the man to pay for a new edition. That was quite a good idea. He might follow it up. But instead of doing so he locked the little door to the tower where Christoferus Twigge had once worked with such patient dedication, and removed the notice telling the public about the illuminated manuscript in the cell above the spiral staircase. He hoped that in this way in time his troublesome priest would be entirely forgotten. There might even come a day when the old manuscript might be sold quietly to some cranky museum curator, or some arty-crafty collector for a large sum which could go towards the cost of maintaining the church roof.

It was when the Colonel discovered that the door to the tower was locked and the key removed that he had words with the Reverend Bliss; these words became hotter and more acrimonious each time they met, until one day when they stood face to face just inside the church porch their argument exploded into ungodly wrath.

'This man Twigge was a communist!' cried the vicar. He had often practised using his voice to good effect in the pulpit. He now threw his indignation up towards the vault, which reverberated magnificently. St Jerome's was famous for its excellent acoustics.

Stung by the accusatory echoes the Colonel, who was not by any means such a gifted orator, spoke quickly. 'Has it come to this?' he cried, 'that in England now a man's name can be erased from history because of political bias?' He was annoyed to notice that indignation was making his voice squeaky.

'He ignited the ignorant poor to violence,' said Bliss in sonorous tones.

'Whatever he did it's a historical fact you are obliterating.'

'He was a criminal, Chicon.'

'So was Henry VIII.'

'Well, he was not hanged, drawn and quartered.'

'Exactly.'

'And he was a King.'

'That is undeniably true. But he was a butcher and a murderer. And though he retained his title of Defender of the Faith he was undoubtedly a fornicator and an adulterer as well. I believe his form of married life is called serial monogamy nowadays. He gives a very bad example to the youth of England; but *he* has not been obliterated from history.'

Bliss heard him out with rising irritation. 'Henry VIII is neither here nor there,' he said. 'What we're concerned with is the malign influence this man Twigge might have on the young today. Are you a crypto-socialist yourself by any chance?'

This sharp dig made Chicon redden. He tried to control his anger, but his voice rose another decibel or two. 'Certainly not! But I do find it interesting that this rural riot in our small town preceded by a decade Wat Tyler's rebellion of 1381. This obscure Twigge fellow's ideas actually antedated Marx by five centuries, you know.'

'That's what makes him so dangerous today, Colonel,' said Bliss, mollifying his tone a little as he remembered the man's reputation as a loner, who probably lived surrounded by his musty volumes of history and was undoubtedly protected from the realities of present-day living by a screen of printed pages.

'You know what, Bliss? What you're doing is censorship of information – lies of omission for the sake of selling moral order. Anyone would think you were an advertiser.'

'It is not for mercenary considerations at all, as you well know.' In spite of himself the vicar was getting angry.

'This is a form of Anglican Inquisition you're about, Bliss – a burning of the books,' insisted the Colonel.

'That is absurd, Chicon! I've burned no books. This wretched pamphlet is now out of print, and I haven't had it reprinted. That's all.' He felt his face blooming to an uncomfortable purple as rage burned in his heart. In his undergraduate days he had been a rugger blue; he now felt an urgent desire to tackle his opponent, to bring him down and hit his head smartly on the stone floor; but instead he turned away without another word and nobly stalked up the nave towards the altar.

Colonel Chicon shouted after him: 'Bliss! You're a clerical fascist, Bliss!'

The Reverend Bliss savoured in imagination the coals of fire his silence must be heaping down upon the Colonel's head. He knelt down, bowed his neck and prayed for patience. Meanwhile Chicon, stamping triumphantly down the churchyard path, was congratulating himself on having had the last word.

At the next rehearsal of the Bach Choir Mary cleverly avoided the lady with the powerful wing; but she felt acutely uncomfortable. As soon as she entered the hall silence fell and twelve pairs of eyes were fixed on her. Her father had quarrelled with Heavenly Bliss. Everybody knew; everybody was talking about it. Mrs Beccles, who had been arranging a pyramid of flowers around the base of the pillar nearest to the door had heard it all. In her agitation at the angry words being shouted in the house of God she dropped a scarlet gladiolus. Mercifully she was able to stoop to pick it up, thus hiding her embarrassment when Colonel Chicon spat out those rude words about Henry VIII. Mrs Dobbs, who had been polishing the brass but stood at some distance from the combatants, said 'butcher' was the word he used, 'butcher and murderer'. She added stoutly, 'Which is what he was!' (referring to Henry).

'He did say "fascist",' said Mrs Beccles.

'I think he was meaning the vicar then,' said Mrs Dobbs. 'Frightened me to death he did.'

What nobody could understand was why the Colonel got so excited about ancient Tudor history, which everybody knew anyway. Sadly Mary was too young and too shy to be able to explain that it was not Henry her father was upset about but the suppressing of truth in historical records. She of course knew her father was absolutely right, and the Revd Bliss was quite, quite wrong.

Within a week Frenester was polarised into Heavenly and anti-Heavenly factions, and echoes of the tumult soon reached Gatt's Rise.

'I hear as how you've set the cat among the pigeons, Sorr,' remarked Mikey as he led the Colonel down the garden path towards the greenhouse, where a sprawling vine, which had for many years produced grapes for the table, rather sour ones in England's cloudy summers, looked unmistakably sick. 'They're all at each other's throats now over the Rebel, Sorr.'

Echoes from the Emerald Isle rang through his speech occasionally even after thirty years of exile in England, fifteen of them as gardener to Gatt's Rise. 'You mean Christoferus Twigge?' Chicon laughed. 'It's all a storm in a teacup. That rebel died six hundred years ago, you know.'

'Ah! but 'tis the principle of the thing!' argued Mikey. 'The vicar's got the wrong end of the stick entirely, hasn't he now?' The Colonel's private opinion of Ireland and the Irish came from the time of the original Troubles when his own father had been stationed in Dublin Castle. He considered that the main difference between our countries was that the Romans never got as far as Ireland; but he had enough tact not to express his views before Mikey. He said nothing to encourage him; but he continued: 'In Mr Bliss's book heaven is full of happy Tories. And getting there is a matter of politics now, and nothing to do with religion at all.'

Chicon was pleased with Mikey's support, but said nothing, considering it wiser to refrain from adding fuel to the fire. In the town, however, plenty of fuel was flying about. One ardent Bliss supporter, who was also a keen gardener, referred to him while phoning a friend, as Heavenly Blue. She had read the up-to-date plantsman's guides and liked to call plants by their proper names. 'Ipomoea, my dear, beautiful big blue trumpets. I saw it in Madeira before the war growing to thirty feet. It's a sub-tropical weed really, that convolvulus. But of course over here it's little me who's the clinging one!' They both giggled. Other people were calling him Tory Bliss and True Blue Bliss. One wit in the Ring o' Bells described him as Blue Rinse Bliss, which raised a laugh, encouraging him after another pint to change the vicar's name to Blue Bastard. This produced the loud laugh that spoke the vacant mind in Goldsmith's Deserted Village but in Frenester denotes the addition of a full beer belly.

For a time Chicon was labelled the Red Colonel. Even as far away as Frenton Byways, four miles downriver, someone heard him referred to as 'one of them Red Devils', and Mikey, when he walked along the canal towpath to the Moorhen, as he liked doing when the weather was fine, picked up that rumour.

'I don't know about Red being right for the Colonel,' he

46

said judiciously. 'Although sure enough there's reds under
the bed up at Gatt's Rise all right. There's that bleeding red
setter dog of the young lady's sleeps under her bed and
won't be budged.' He uttered a shrill cackle. 'That's a red
maniac all right. Didn't he bury a bone in the middle of
me carrot seedlings, and then dig them all up to get at it?'

Sally, who had spent her Sunday off with her mum in
Frenester, reported to Mary on Monday as she piled the
washing into the machine: 'Mrs Dobbs is talking. Well, she
always does, don't she? That's all she's good for: talking
and polishing the church brass.'

'What did she say, Sally?' asked Mary.

'She's saying he's a foreigner, and what can you expect?'
Mrs Dobbs's actual words were: 'Got Frog blood in 'is veins,
baint 'e?' but Sally expurgated her account to save Mary's
feelings. Even the expurgated version was enough to make
Mary explode.

'That's disgraceful prejudice, Sally! His Huguenot fore-
bears took refuge in England long before the French
Revolution. We've been British for three hundred years!
And he's lived at Gatt's Rise for twenty.'

'I know, Mary,' said Sally kindly. 'I know. I know. But
you try telling her! Ignorant cow!'

'It's racism!' declared Mary; and immediately decided not
to do any shopping in Frenester for at least a fortnight. She
cringed physically when she thought of it. But the Colonel
was enjoying the excitement of being the centre of this
battle. His step was brisker and his eye brighter for a few
weeks because of it.

As a result of this tiff with the vicar the Colonel shook
the dust of St Jerome's off his boots, and Mary did too,
although she was sorry to do so. She loved that church, so
richly and tenderly decorated in the days when Frenester
had been a wealthy wool merchants' town. She loved the
cool, calm, stone-bound spaces, the long high nave, its
pillars embellished above her head with garlands of oak
leaves and acorns; and she was amused, and in some way

comforted by the strange beasts with gaping mouths and the rude peasants' faces which leered at her from arches, and the carved-in-wood animals which pranced on light fantastic toe for ever around the choir stalls. She stopped going to the Bach Choir rehearsals too.

It wasn't long before she found another choir which welcomed her small, clear, reliable and seldom out-of-tune voice in the church of St Luke. It was within easy cycling distance in the almost deserted village of Mudcott. The Revd Theodore Brown, who was vicar there, was a gentle, considerate man, and Mary felt safe with him. She actually loved singing in his choir on Sunday mornings, and willingly attended Wednesday evening choir practices together with his motley crew of one elderly soprano spinster, one aggressive farmer's wife contralto, two tenors who were shopkeepers in Frenester, and the bearded bass, who was known to live in Upper Coldacre with one of the tenors in unisexual sin. Mary was pretty sure Theodore Brown didn't care how they lived so long as they sang in tune. Nor did she, though she sometimes wondered how exactly they did whatever it was they did.

She began to notice things about the other tenor, who was a young man not much older than herself. He was shy, and seldom addressed a word to her, but she found him standing beside her quite often, offering her a share of his hymn book, or pointing out the place on his sheet of music. Sometimes they exchanged smiles, even giggled over jokes the others didn't seem to grasp, and once, when he accidentally brushed his hand against hers he blushed. She noticed, too, the clothes he wore, which were neat and attractive. He wore a jacket of fine grey woollen cloth, less flabby than flannel, less harsh and hairy than tweed. It was, she learned in due course, Cotswold woollen cloth, a fabric which had for generations before the war been woven in the district, but was now gradually disappearing. She learned his name: David Wetherley. If it hadn't been for the quality and cut of his coat she would never have believed it possible that he was the son of old Wetherley the Frenester tailor. That such a tall, straight-limbed, fresh-skinned fair young man could be a sprig from that withered old gnome of a tailor was a miracle. Mary supposed David's mother must have added something to his grace. She hadn't seen David in the shop when Colly took her in to be measured for the new hacking jacket, because at the time David was sitting in the sixth form of Frenester grammar school studying for his A levels. Old Wetherley was celebrated all over the Cotswolds not only for his shrunken stature but on account of his craftsmanship. An article about him had recently appeared in *Country Life*, David told her. He cut and stitched expensive clothes for gentlemen, he created hunting coats in appropriate colours for several West Country hunts. At the back of the shop he kept three apprentices sitting with bowed heads as they stitched and finished garments by hand. He ruled them with a rod of iron, physically as well as metaphorically, for Colly had once caught him hitting one of his apprentices across the shoulders with the rod he used to measure out lengths of cloth. Of course Colly had protested. 'I say! you can't do that sort of thing here! Not in this day and age. This is Frenester, Wetherley, not Turkey, you know!'

'Lazy lads they are, Colonel,' said Wetherley, not a bit abashed. 'A bit of stick keeps them up to standard.'

But in spite of his fame and his standards his business was falling away. Men were buying cheaper ready-made clothes. The demand for the beautiful local cloth was less, and Wetherley's craft was in decline.

One Wednesday evening after choir practice David asked her if she'd like a drink at the Waggoner, which was the only pub in Mudcott.

'What'll you have?'

She shook her head. She had no idea what she should ask for. 'Why not try a port and lemon?' he suggested. 'That's a good old-fashioned barmaid's tipple.' She sipped it, liked its sweetness, and burst out laughing at the sheer audacity of what she was doing. She enjoyed herself so much that it seemed the most natural thing in the world to accept his invitation to tea the following Wednesday before choir practice.

'You can leave your bike at home,' he said. 'I'll drive you to Mudcott for choir practice in my MG.'

'I'll walk up to Frenester then,' she said. 'And I'll bring Buzzby if I may.'

'OK,' he agreed. 'He can sit in the car and listen to the singing from outside when we get to church.'

'But don't park too near,' she begged, 'or when he hears the singing he'll howl.'

Messrs Percy Wetherley and David S. Wetherley Bespoke Tailors occupied splendid premises in the middle and on the sunny side of Frenester High Street. A pair of big bay windows bulged from the Georgian façade on to the pavement. In one were displayed bales of cloth and a length of russet-coloured fabric draped over a stand; in the other, which was Mrs Wetherley's private front parlour, lace curtains screened the interior of the room from the inquisitive passer-by. Mrs Wetherley seemed anxious as she invited Mary into the room and it had, Mary noticed, a musty smell as if it was not much used.

'Sit you down. Sit you down,' said Mrs Wetherley, patting the back of an armchair, and fussily shaking a cushion. Mary sat down gingerly on a small balloon-backed chair with pieces of mother-of-pearl glued into its woodwork. She was quite peckish after her walk, and eager to taste all the delectable scones and cakes displayed on a three-tiered cake-stand. A low table, on which were spread fine porcelain cups and stiffly starched napkins, stood on fragile bowed legs by the empty grate.

'I'll go and make the tea,' said Mrs Wetherley. Mary saw her as a stately woman with a white marble profile.

As soon as she disappeared Buzzby approached the food in his friendly way, and sniffed. Then he looked up at David with trusting eyes, and with two swishes of his handsome tail he swept all the fine porcelain off the table on to the carpet.

'Oh my God!' said David, 'Mum will be that upset!'

Detecting tones of displeasure in the strange man's voice Buzzby approached him with even greater friendliness and more vigorous tail-wagging, and in a moment the cake-stand was hit sideways, and all the delicate fancies which Mrs Wetherley, sacrificing precious rations, had cooked with her own hands, were spilled across the floor.

'Bad dog! Bad dog,' said Mary, pushing the animal away from her as she crouched on her hands and knees in a desperate effort to pick up the pieces, to lay the table again, and set the cake-stand straight before her hostess reappeared. The stupid animal kept licking her face in an attempt to pacify her anger, which was not very terrible anyway, because she was finding it difficult to stop giggling; but he did have the sense to snatch a scone before she had time to grab it.

When Mrs Wetherley came in with the tea the young couple were seated sedately and in silence; but she caught sight of Buzzby eating half a scone and thought: that dog's spoiled rotten, that's for sure. She sat down in the armchair and drank a cup of tea. Buzzby was making this difficult by pushing his nose between her knees; and as her hands were too occupied with the cup and saucer, she was unable to shove him off. All she could do was tighten her knees together.

'Colonel well?' she asked.

'Very well, thank you.'

'Potatoes clamped up yet?'

'No, not yet. It's been a bit too wet.'

'Ah, well, let's hope we get a few more of these fine days.' She put down her cup and, pushing Buzzby's nose away, she rose. 'I'll leave you two young people together a while then,' she said.

David blushed up to the roots of his hair, but Mary didn't notice. She was watching his mother go through the door and thinking: he gets his good looks from her. She was wondering, too, what Rachel Wetherley had looked like as a very young girl, only twelve, when she left the flat wetlands of Somerset where her father cut willow shoots and bent and wove them into withy baskets for a living, and her mother kept house in a wooden bothy built on stilts above the marsh. Rachel had travelled north into Gloucestershire to a great house high up on the Edges above Frenester, where her aunt was housekeeper. Her aunt kept an eye on her in her tweeny days, checked the clumsiness in her movements and picked out the country burrs from her speech, and gradually, as she said, 'made a lady of her'. In the town people spoke of her as 'always one for bettering herself', which was why, after fifteen years of service she'd married a tailor, not for the cut of his coat to be sure, nor for his looks which weren't up to much even in his youth, but for the look of his bank balance. Whatever people said about her she'd made a good job of her son, was what Mary thought.

'What does S stand for, David?' she asked, when the door closed.

'What S?'

'The S before your name on the board outside?'

He paused, blushing again before he replied: 'It's Sibelius.' And as if to excuse the irrevocable baptismal act he added, 'My dad was always keen on music.'

Mary burst out laughing. 'Sibelius!' she echoed, her mouth full of Victoria sponge roll. 'That'll take some living up to!'

'You're not easily daunted,' he said. 'And I'm glad you don't mind too much. Dad put up that notice last year to tempt me into the business; but he won't succeed. I'm not going to be a tailor.' He sounded truculent.

Buzzby's bad behaviour at that tea party and Mary's laughter chased away the remaining shyness between them, so that afterwards they sometimes held hands surreptitiously at choir practice, and once or twice when they parted, if nobody was looking their way, he kissed her cheek.

She said nothing to her father about David. Why should she? She was no longer a schoolgirl. He was a respectable local boy, and a member of a church choir. So when she informed Colly she'd been invited to go to London to see a matinée of this new musical *Oklahoma* with one of Mr Brown's voices he presumed, poor man, that her companion was a soprano. It must have been a bit of a shock for him to see David Wetherley standing with doffed cap at his front door at 2 a.m. that morning.

She knew that like the vicar of St Jerome's she was guilty of a small omission of the facts. She expected to be hauled over the coals for not coming home at a more reasonable time, but instead of reprimanding her the Colonel reserved his censure for David. The assault began at breakfast next day while Mary was feeling decidedly not her fittest on account of all the excitement and the alcohol she'd consumed the evening before.

'Wherever did you pick him up?' her father asked.

Mary, who was just about to bite off a piece of toast, dropped it on her plate.

'You mean David?'

'Is that his name? Yes, David then. How did you meet him?'

'He sings in Theodore Brown's choir down in Mudcott. He sings tenor.'

'Well, I hope his voice is better than his conversation, or his contribution to the music will be thin indeed.'

'You didn't give him much chance for conversation.' Mary defended her young man bravely. 'You didn't even ask him to come in.'

'I should think not. At 2 a.m. in the morning? He wasn't thinking much of you, was he? And certainly not of me.'

'It's a long drive from London,' she said, hearing the lameness of her excuse. 'And we danced a bit after dinner.'

'Can he dance?'

'Rather well!' she affirmed, brightening a little.

He paused for a moment, remembering his own youth in the dancing-crazy Twenties when he'd sometimes wished he could Charleston as well as Flora did, before saying, 'Even if he were as good a dancer as Nijinsky was that wouldn't excuse his late-night habits. You're not yet old enough to stay out with strange young men, dancing till all hours of the morning.'

'Sorry,' she said, and bowed her head. She found she couldn't finish the toast.

He said no more then, but returned to the attack at lunchtime. 'This young man of yours, he's Percy Wetherley's son, isn't he? A counter-jumper, Mary, a tailor's son, that's not good enough for you, you know. And he doesn't seem up to much to me. Rather soft, I think. He hasn't got the old man's grit. Bit of a wet rag, isn't he? And anyway he's *trade*.'

Mary said nothing. What on earth was a counter-jumper? She managed a mouthful of potato mashed with melted margarine.

'He's probably got it all worked out with his parents that there's a nice bit of capital coming to you when I die.'

'Of course not, Colly!' Mary was at last stung into speech. 'I'm sure such a thought never entered his head!'

'Well what are his motives then?' he asked. He delayed a little before continuing: 'It's not as if you're a beauty like your mother. Every man chased her because of her looks, but that will never be the case with you. So I'm driven to the conclusion that it's your money he's after.'

Mary looked down at her hands clasped together tightly in her lap. She hated his speaking about her mother; she knew that when he did his talk became nasty and coarse. She managed to blurt out: 'He's not mercenary at all. I'm sure of that!'

'How can you be – a child of your age? And if it isn't money, what is he after? Rolling in the hay with you like any common lout?'

Mary sniffed once or twice.

'There's something you've got to learn for your own protection, my dear,' he warned her. 'Young men have got this highly active animal between their thighs, which stands up on the slightest provocation from any female. They can't really help it, you know. That's why girls must be so careful to keep a certain distance between themselves and the boys. Man is a filthy thing from the moment of his birth. *Inter faeces et urinam nascitur*, as Augustine briefly and for all time put it.'

Mary wept silently. Big tears rolled down her cheeks and plopped into the mashed potato on her plate. Everything is spoiled now, she thought. It won't be fun at all now.

'We won't say any more about it,' her father said, wiping his moustache with a napkin. 'I trust to your good sense to put this young whipper-snapper in his proper place.' He hit a little bell on the table beside him to summon Sally to clear away the dishes. Mary hastily pulled a handkerchief from under the cuff of her blouse and blew her nose. Sally threw her a sharp look over her shoulder as she left the room. She was not deceived. As soon as she reached the kitchen she informed Cook that the old bugger was putting a damper on poor Mary's romance.

For a month she tried to avoid David. It wasn't too difficult, so she wondered if perhaps he was trying to avoid her too. Her thoughts about him veered wildly from an image of him as a hangdog browbeaten little fellow scuttling to his car under her father's Olympian gaze, and her fantasy of him as a knight in armour who might seize her one morning from under the elms and gallop off with her lying across the saddle of his palfrey. She hesitated over the word palfrey. It wasn't quite right somehow. A palfrey was a light pony, wasn't it? A knight in heavy armour with a girl of her size would need a stronger animal to carry them both. A farm dray perhaps. . . . But the image of David astride a dray was not entirely attractive. And anyway she doubted if he could ride.

That October was a wet month, but towards its end, at the time of what the old country people called St Luke's summer, they were blessed with a few glorious days when the poplars lining the road to Upper Coldacre shone as if hung with gold medallions. So bright were they in the slanting sun that afternoon when David drove Mary up the hill to the Edges in his MG that they seemed to be lit by footlights on a stage.

'Look, David!' she cried, pointing to them. 'Like Oklahoma!'

'It's a bit of all right,' he agreed. He was taking her to tea at the Copper Kettle teashop. He had arrived unexpectedly at Gatt's Rise one Thursday afternoon when Wetherley's shop was closed for the half-holiday and he knew the Colonel would be in court all day.

Mary was worried that they might be seen by the tenor and his friend the bearded bass.

'They might come in here for tea,' she said, looking round at the olde worlde beams and the cramped windows with leaded panes.

'Of course they won't,' said David. 'They've got their own place. So why would they want to come here?'

She chose a table in the furthest corner. There was another couple sitting under a window, so he dropped his voice to a conspiratorial level: 'It's nice to talk to you again.'

Her hand shook a little as she poured out the tea.

'I don't think I can meet you like this any more, David,' she said.

'I was afraid that might happen.' He sounded resigned. He was resigned. When he'd told his mum about his abrupt dismissal from Gatt's Rise, and the hatchet-faced expression on Mary's dad's face she'd said: 'You won't be able to stand up to the Colonel, son. If he's against you there's an end to it.' Mrs Wetherley did not sound too unhappy either.

'It's because you're a tailor,' explained Mary. She was

56

still innocent enough to be tactless. She remembered the way Colly had said that one word: *trade*.

'I'm a hopeless tailor,' said David. 'Though my dad did try to teach me. But I can stitch a good buttonhole. I finish off a lot of buttonholes for him, like the mice in the *Tailor of Gloucester.*'

Mary felt a warm rush of affection for him. 'That was always my favourite of the Beatrix Potter books when I was little,' she said.

'Mine too,' he sighed, thinking how blue and kind her eyes were – not at all like her father's. They smiled at each other over the rims of their cups, sharing, as if it was some precious secret, their childhood pleasure. Mary thought: however many buttonholes he stitches I shall always love him. But she knew it was a hopeless affair.

He suddenly spoke up with unexpected spirit: 'I'm not going to be a tailor for ever, you know. You don't think I'm going to spend the rest of my life stitching coats for grandees like your father, do you?' He sounded so belligerent her fantasies began to escape again to parade in her imagination. They would elope; they would run away from Mudcott one Wednesday evening after choir practice, and drive terribly fast to London, where they would live in a garret, poor but ecstatically happy, like that artist and that girl whose tiny hand was frozen in the opera the music class was taken to see during her last term at school. Her romantic flight of fancy faded as she remembered that that opera came to a sad end, and that frozen-fingered girl died of TB, though she did somehow manage, in spite of her badly damaged lungs, to sing a famous aria before pegging out.

'What will you do, David?' she asked.

'I want to be a jazz musician. I'm learning to play the saxophone. I practise every day, you know.'

She could almost hear the slightly off-key notes bleating like lost sheep in some back room of old Wetherley's house;

and her heart sank again. Learning to play the saxophone would not endear him to her father.

'I practise in the warehouse,' David explained. 'Mum can't stand the noise at home, so I go in there. The bales of cloth do deaden the sound a bit.'

When he took her home he drove into the yard at the back of the house. As she was climbing out of his car he caught her hand. 'I'll never forget you,' he said.

'No,' she murmured; but before her feet touched the ground she leaned towards him and kissed him on the mouth. Then she fled without a backward glance. He sat quite still for a moment before starting the ignition. The elms stood, silent witnesses slowly dropping their leaves. The rooks had all left months ago, and would not return till February.

And that was the end of her little romance. Had she cried when it was over? Of course she had. Many, many bitter tears were shed on her pillow at night; many sobs not entirely smothered by the bedclothes were heard by Buzzby lying under her bed. Every time she uttered a sob Buzzby, poor beast, unsure of the meaning of the sound, tried to tell her that he heard her voice, that he was near her, by thumping his massive tail on the floor. Sometimes she held out her hand, and he emerged from under the bed to lick it.

She slept badly; she lay awake trying to think of ways to break down the wall of the inevitable. If only her father could see things the way many other people did. . . . If only he could understand that the dividing lines between the classes were beginning to be blurred. . . . If only he didn't use those strange Edwardian words about David. . . . If only David were not dependent on his father, if only he were a rich banker with a house in London. . . . Her love was a hopeless one, she knew, and she must hide it away.

It was Aunt Dot who rescued her. Dorothea, the elder sister, she of the strong opinions and very big nose, before whom even Colly quailed, came to visit them in December.

She had been a deb in her youth, and was presented at court in the days before the war when debs were brought to London for a season of parading in front of all the available and eligible bachelors, and presented to the ruling monarch as part of the ritual ceremonies ('a sort of elite cattle market for upper-class landowners on the look-out for good breeding heifers,' was how Colly described it). And Aunt Dot did find a rich banker for a husband.

She took a brisk look at Mary's peaky face, the dark circles round her eyes, and the dowdy skirt and jumper she was wearing, and decided to speak out. She waited till after dinner when Colly retired to his study before remarking, 'You don't seem to care how you look, Mary. How much dress allowance does your father give you?'

'Oh, I spend about thirty pounds a year on dress,' said Mary. She sounded weary.

'You cannot *dress* on thirty pounds a year,' said Aunt Dot severely. 'You can merely clothe yourself.'

'I don't live in fashionable circles like you,' Mary defended herself. But Dorothea was not satisfied. It was obvious the girl must be rescued before she sank into the irretrievable frumpishness of colourless country ladies in clay-coloured clothes who looked old before they were forty.

At breakfast the following morning she attacked her brother. She didn't beat about the bush. 'What have you been doing to your daughter, Frank?' she demanded.

He put down his copy of *The Times* and looked at her over the tops of his bifocals. 'What do you mean, Dot?' he asked.

She was in no way diminished by his use of her nursery pet-name. 'She's lost weight, Frank,' she said accusingly. 'You've only to look at her to see she's pining. I suppose,' she added, rapidly spreading home-made marmalade over toast, 'it must be some unsuitable follower she's fond of, and you've put your foot down.'

'Well, he's certainly not one of us!'

She cast a quick appraising glance at him before launching into her attack. 'You know, Frank, times are changing. Class distinctions are getting blurred. The fact is the walls of Jericho are tumbling down before the armies of the newly educated and the new rich. All that one-of-us sentiment is a bit out of date, you know. It will be a classless society before you know where you are.'

'Classless society!' he scoffed. 'That's the sort of phrase that sounds good in an after-dinner speech when the listeners have all drunk more than enough wine. It's what journalists love: high-sounding and meaningless rhetoric. You know as well as I do that it isn't a fact of life.'

'It might be one day, Frank. And anyway what do all your distinctions matter?'

'They matter to me. I couldn't eat with a man who slurps his gravy.'

'How absurd you are!' she laughed. 'That sort of thing – table manners can be learned. And times *are* changing, Frank. Why, only last season Lady Billoughy-Crease's gel ran off with the chauffeur. And instead of cutting her off without a shilling they welcomed her back into the fold like the prodigal daughter, and even offered the chauffeur a slice of the fatted calf, followed by a splendid wedding at St Margaret's. But let's hope it won't come to that. In any case the best way to heal a gel's broken heart is to give her a change of air.'

'The young man hasn't a penny,' he grumbled. 'He's hardly more than a schoolboy.'

But Aunt Dot pursued her advantage. 'Do you mean to keep her out here in the sticks for ever? She has no friends of her own age, and her own kind, no society at all. You'll never get her married that way, you know. Or is that your intention?' She had always had a suspicion that he was that sort of carnivorous father.

'What are you driving at, Dot?' He was indignant. 'I shall always do my best for Mary. You know that. I've left her everything in my will. And as to marriage . . . that can be a snare and a delusion, you know, sometimes even a hell. Once they've done the necessary procreation most couples would like to get divorced if they could afford it. Marriage is rather an overrated sport, in my opinion.'

She regarded him speculatively. 'You never divorced Flora, did you?' She had always wondered what had happened to Flora. There were a few unanswered questions there.

He turned his head away from her. He stooped to pick up his napkin which had fallen from his lap before replying: 'I couldn't divorce her because I had no idea where she was. Couldn't trace her. She disappeared into thin air with that fellow. And she couldn't divorce me because I gave her no cause for it.'

Dot regarded him steadily. Of course he could have traced her if he'd wanted to. He knew the name of her family solicitor, didn't he? In her opinion he didn't sue for divorce in order to punish her, to keep her in the slightly shady twilight zone of the unmarried. Marriage was in the eyes of all right-thinking people the normal proper goal. And it was her intention to thwart his selfish plans to keep his daughter single.

'I shall take Mary back to London for Christmas,' she announced. 'What she needs is a good time. Morever I shall buy her a few glad rags, and push her off to a few parties with Vicky.'

To all of which he agreed surprisingly meekly.

FOUR

Aunt Dot's mansion in Eltham Square was big. The rooms
were large, the ceilings high, the mahogany doors heavy;
enormous expanses of thick carpet swarming with flowers
covered the floors, and a splendid staircase twisted itself
upward from the wide, well-lit hall to the cooler, darker
bedrooms and bathrooms above. The holly and the ivy
hung and twined at every vantage point to celebrate the
Christmas season, and even the running deer made its
appearance in the form of venison for dinner on that first
evening of Mary's visit. The huge table created to carry
gargantuan meals for Victorian feeders, and for the dis-
comfort of those unlucky sitters with skirted knees who
encountered the bulbous table legs, was heavily laden. This
surprised Mary, because although post-war rationing was
still in force there seemed to be no shortage of anything
on Uncle Bertie's board. She supposed he must have his
own special sources of supply. There was smoked salmon
from Ireland, and oysters from heaven knows where,
which Mary had never tasted before, and which she was
urged to swallow. As she added a squeeze of lemon and a
few grains of pepper, tilted her head back, and threw the
glistening thing straight out of its shell into her mouth
the whole family watched in silence; but when she laughed
and declared it was delicious everybody clapped, and the

butler, who had escaped conscription during the war because his hand was too shaky to hold a gun, let alone fire it, refilled her champagne glass, spilling a few drops and wiping the neck of the bottle ostentatiously with a very bleached white napkin. Then Uncle Bertie lifted his glass to toast her, and she felt she'd passed some kind of test.

The drawing-room on the other side of the hall was furnished with vast sofas and chairs, their chintz surfaces spread with pink roses in fuller and larger bloom than any seen at horticultural shows, their upholstery so opulent that Mary feared as she sank into it that it might prove impossible to struggle out again. Each armchair was equipped on one hand with its own standard reading lamp and rose-coloured lampshade with the spread of an umbrella, and on the other with an ashtray balanced on a burnished brass pedestal. A slight and not unpleasant scent of cigars hung about the place. It was certainly all very different from the ascetic style of living at Gatt's Rise with its uncovered oak beams, stone-flagged floors, and the draughts which whistled in under rafters and ill-fitting doors whenever the wind was high, as well as Colly's essentially simple, though fresh and plentiful food, consisting chiefly of home-grown vegetables and lamb from the farm.

In retrospect it seemed to Mary that the remains of her youth were taken over by Aunt Dot that Christmas and immersed in her cleansing round of entertainments: shopping, parties with dancing and robust party games, being nice to fat, taciturn, cigar-smoking Uncle Bertie after dinner ('Talk to your Uncle Bertie, there's a dear,' Aunt Dot imposed the duty on her), a visit to the theatre, and a trip to the ballet at Sadler's Wells. It seemed everybody – her aunt, her cousin Vicky, Uncle Bertie and the gangling twin boys, who looked so alike with their buck teeth and high foreheads that Mary couldn't tell one from the other – was conspiring to give her a good time. The good time was so arduously and persistently pursued that she had hardly a moment left in which to feel miserable. Every night she fell into bed too tired even to comb her hair, let alone think; every morning she rose conscientiously determined to repay her aunt's kindness by enjoying all the activities planned for the day ahead. In this way the memory of David and much of her heartache were being sponged out of her mind.

On Christmas Eve they all walked to their neighbourhood church to take part in a carol service. Mary sang with a surge of joy the old remembered songs; but suddenly, in the middle of Christina Rossetti's verse she began to cry.

> In the bleak mid-winter
> Frosty wind made moan,
> Earth stood hard as iron,
> Water like a stone.

She didn't really know why she was crying. The words made her think of the stables at home and the frozen troughs of water in the fields, and then of David singing, as he should have been, beside her in the choir at St Luke's in Mudcott. Aunt Dot, looking down her formidable nose was shocked to see tears on her niece's cheeks. Good heavens! The child really is morbidly sensitive, she thought. She stopped singing, and fumbling in her crocodile leather handbag she produced a handkerchief which she passed to Mary without a word, after which she quickly picked up her place in the hymn book and carried on.

Mary was ashamed; she felt she'd let Aunt Dot down, and determined to try harder than ever to fit in and enjoy this Christmas.

On Christmas morning she phoned Colly.

'Happy Christmas, Colly!'

'Is that you, Mary? The same to you, my dear!'

'Are you all right?'

'Of course I'm all right. As a matter of fact I'm off to eat the traditional bird with the Brig.'

'Oh good!' She was relieved to find she had no need to worry about him. Colly always said the Brig's cuisine was Saxon-primitive; but she knew the two old soldiers would be happy together cracking jokes and walnuts and reminiscing over a bottle of port. Brigadier Flower, who lived with a shadowy wife (known by Colly as Fading Flower) in a vast cold house up on the Edges above Frenester, was one of the few friends Colly still had. 'Give them my best wishes, won't you?'

'I'll do that. Now see you enjoy yourself up there in London. And give Dot and that hedonist husband of hers my Christmas greetings.'

She sat beside Uncle Bertie after the turkey and Christmas pudding and thought about Colly's description of him. Bertie, deep in his own thoughts (rummaging through the money markets of the world?) patted her knee, smiled a complacent cat-like smile at her, and then continued sucking on his cigar. He made no attempt whatever to converse with her, which she found restful. In fact it was the only interval of peace and quiet she was allowed during the day.

There was a spare ticket for the ballet on Boxing Day, so she was allowed to invite her friend Claudia to join the party. They sat together in the stalls listening to Tchaikovsky's music and watching *Swan Lake* danced in its full classical perfection. During the performance Mary was lifted out of herself, out of the Christmas season, out of time into the beautiful myth of love's power to transform. If only . . . if only . . .

'Your friend Claudia didn't have much to say for herself,' was Aunt Dot's comment afterwards. In Dot's world, bright but not necessarily intelligent conversation was an essential attribute for a young lady.

'I think she was struck dumb by the grandeur of your house and hospitality,' said Mary.

Dot shot her a questioning look, though questioning was not a habit of hers. She wasn't sure if Mary was simply stating a fact or whether there was some underlying criticism she couldn't quite catch. To Mary, Claudia had described the atmosphere as one of philistine opulence, 'more money than taste', but to save Dot's feelings Mary edited those remarks a little. Claudia, who had a degree in the history of fine arts and had just written an article for some connoisseur's journal she secretly intended one day to edit and direct, was a bit critical.

'But she did enjoy the ballet,' Mary hastened to add. 'She simply loved it. She said the balletic precision of the *pas de deux* created a state of metaphysical exaltation in which the craft of dance was transfigured into high art. And of course I loved it too.'

Aunt Dot pursed her lips. She had an uneasy feeling that Mary might be, in the words of her old Irish nanny, 'taking the mickey'; but she wasn't quite sure, so she let the matter rest with: 'What a mouthful of words!'

'She has a penchant for polysyllables,' Mary conceded. Hearing her own voice she was suddenly aware how like Colly she must sound.

No uncertainties interfered with Aunt Dot's programme for Christmas holiday festivities, which continued relentlessly with charades after dinner on the following evening. Claudia was again invited. It was while the girls were standing in the hall beneath a stained-glass Tiffany lampshade, suspended from the ceiling and hung with so much mistletoe that the light was dimmed, confessing to each other that neither could discriminate between Mary's male cousins that the boys burst out of hiding behind the dining-room door and pounced on them. It took a little time to disentangle the foursome. Afterwards Claudia confided in Mary: 'It was rather like being bitten by a rabbit. Did you enjoy it?'

'Not much. Which one did you kiss?'

'I have no idea. Which was yours?'

'God knows. I don't.'

On New Year's Eve Uncle Bertie took them to a night-club, where they danced and watched the cabaret and listened to the band playing Noël Coward's songs. The great performer had appeared there in person earlier in the year, but had retired to his winter quarters in a warmer climate some weeks ago. His songs seemed to hit a resonant chord in Bertie's soul because, during the chorus of 'Mad Dogs and Englishmen' he joined in with such gusto that Aunt Dot raised her reprimanding eyebrows at him, to no avail. He continued fortissimo, stamping his feet and waving his cigar about, dropping an inch of ash which landed on the white tablecloth and fell apart. When Mary heard the music of *Bittersweet* her eyes filled with tears. Goodbye David, goodbye . . . She would never see him again except in the bitter sweet sensations of memory. This time it was Bertie who passed a handkerchief to her.

The old year was passing away, and the new one was erupting in an explosion of applause, hoots, whistles, crackling of paper streamers thrown across the room, popping of corks and scraping of chairs as people rose to hug each other, or leaned over tables to kiss, with squeals of laughter and all the wishes suddenly spoken out loud of men and women wanting to put the past behind them and begin again. Mary found the noise had brought her to her feet; but she stood silent and lonely recalling Noël Coward's haunting tune. Beside her Bertie put his fat arm round her shoulders and spoke in his deep grating voice: 'They say he wrote that song in a taxi while stuck in a traffic jam in New York. Now that's what I call genius. Pure genius!' It was the longest speech she ever heard him make.

A few evenings later Aunt Dot took a party to the Dorchester for a ball in aid of some pet charity of hers. Bertie did not attend, but in his place there was a stranger. Although Mary's thoughts still clung to David she couldn't help feeling a flicker of interest in this handsome, confident, godlike man sauntering across the room to shake her hand. She felt herself blushing, and was furious with herself for doing so, furious with Fate, too, for making any man so good-looking. It really wasn't fair. She became so confused she missed his name. When she caught his eye he was watching her with an expression of amusement, which made her blush even more. He looked foreign, she thought, his dark hair cut close to his head, the skin over his forehead smooth and more deeply tanned than an Anglo-Saxon skin could be. His large dark eyes were bold and challenging, and when he walked his chin lifted with a distinctly arrogant tilt.

'Blasé,' was how Vicky described him when they were powdering their noses in the ladies' cloakroom after supper. 'And very rich.'

'I didn't catch his name. Something Spanish, was it?'

'Pedro,' said Vicky. 'South American, actually. Bolivian or Colombian or somesuch. Father's a friend of Daddy's. His family own mines.'

'Gold mines?'

'No, not gold. Tin or coal or something.'

Mary was disappointed. Gold would have more in keeping with Pedro's appearance, romance being attached to the word gold but not to mines, still less to coal mines where men smeared with black dust and smelling of sweat laboured underground for long back-breaking hours and died young. Though Pedro would hardly be one of them. . . . As soon as they emerged into the ballroom he was at her side. He didn't ask her to dance, he didn't speak, he simply took her elbow and steered her on to the floor. Mary thought crossly that the effort to keep up that disdainful expression on his face left him no energy for conversation; but he danced divinely. So she abandoned herself to the music, letting her body swing and sway to it and her feet perform the neat sidesteps and the easy turns her partner required of her. The band was playing a nostalgic pre-war melody; and in her mind Mary sang with it: 'Lady be good!'

When the music finished and people clapped Pedro spoke at last: 'Unforgettable Gershwin! And you follow in his footsteps.'

'Do I?'

'You've got rhythm too.' In Mary's ears his foreign accent added a little exotic glamour to his speech.

He led her off the floor in search of orange juice. 'Maria!' he said softly, looking at her over his glass. They drank in silence. He was, she noticed, the same height as herself. 'Can you tango, Maria?'

She could hear the band beginning to play one. She recognised the tune but couldn't put a name to it. There were very few dancers on the floor this time. Not many were risking making fools of themselves; it was not after all an Anglo-Saxon dance. She was nervous, guessing that he would dance it supremely well, and feeling that whatever happened she must not let him down. It was while he was poised like a hawk, bent over her in a mock-romantic Fred-Astaire-and-Ginger-Rogers sort of position, that he whispered in her ear: 'I will tell you my secret.' Surprised, she straightened up. 'I think I am les-bi-anne.' Whatever could he mean? And when they took off again with a rapidly aggressive tapping of heels he added: 'I think I must be because I love women so much.' She laughed suddenly, and his proud face relented into a smile, though he did not drop the tilt of his chin one little bit. 'Especially you – at this moment,' he added graciously. When he looked at her his gaze was almost tender, though his claims were false in more ways than the obvious one. The truth was he needed women more than he loved them. Secretly he despised them, less because they responded so readily to his need than because they didn't fulfil it for long. And this failure he blamed not on himself but on them.

Dot sitting at her table watched him. That rich young dago has certainly taken a shine to Mary, she thought. And my goodness! What a great little dancer she is too! Dot had no idea . . . Flora of course had always been crazy-mad on dancing in her day. That particular talent must have been handed down by her – certainly not by Francis.

For Mary the rest of the evening passed like the scent of

roses caught briefly in a garden and lost almost at once. 'I hope this will not be goodbye,' Pedro said as he took her hand when she stepped out of the taxi at the door of Dot's house.

'I'm afraid it may be,' said Mary.

'Why? How so?' He sounded alarmed.

'Tomorrow we catch the Golden Arrow Snow-Sport Express at Victoria. We're all going skiing.'

He looked at her directly and, she thought, anxiously. 'Such a rough sport for so beautiful a dancer!' he said. 'Take care of those ankles on the slopes. Promise me.'

'I promise.'

Mary delayed getting into the train for as long as possible. She knew it was silly to hope he'd come to see her off; but she couldn't help hoping. And sure enough he arrived with about three minutes to spare. She spied him threading his way through the crowd, clutching a little twist of white tissue paper in one hand, and running. He was quite breathless when at last he found her.

'I was afraid I might be too late!' he gasped.

She smiled with sudden delight. 'Oh no! You're just in time!'

He thrust his little offering into her hands. 'It is for you. It is a rose. White for innocence. . . .' And as she grasped the tissue-paper-wrapped flower he seized her fingers and kissed them one by one.

Aunt Dot, already seated in her corner of their reserved carriage, saw all this through the window of the train and was startled. This was something unexpected; but at least this Pedro, whom everybody in their set knew to be a philanderer, would push the tailor's son out of her niece's mind.

Mary climbed into the train, but stood leaning over the edge of the window.

'Such a good beginning for the New Year!' she sighed smiling down at him. As the train began to move he ran along the platform beside her. 'Write!' she called out urgently above the clatter of rolling wheels. 'Poste restante, Grenoble! That's where we'll be after skiing!'

'Poste restante!' he echoed, running, smiling and waving, and at last standing still and waving till she was out of sight. Mary was smiling too, blushing and looking happy for the first time since she had left Gatt's Rise. As she settled back into her seat opposite Aunt Dot, the Golden Arrow Express gathered speed between the bleak and blackened buildings of that part of London, and then streaked out into the countryside, bleak too, and grey on that sunless January morning; but Mary was not daunted by her surroundings. Her imagination was filled with images of yesterday: little warm rushes of remembrance of words spoken, of hand pressures, of dark eyes glowing under bright ballroom lights; and her heart was in a turmoil with flutterings of hoped-for love and with small warnings about hoping for too much. Dot's loud clear voice broke through the romantic fog of her thoughts. Mary withdrew her gaze from the winter landscape outside the train window and tried to focus on her aunt's commanding voice.

'Don't let yourself be carried away by Pedro, handsome though I must admit he is. He has quite a reputation, you know – and not a good one. A bit of a lounge lizard, Mary, that's what he is. My generation would have called him a sofa cobra. In polite terms a flirt – in plain words probably worse.' Dot thought the snake image being definitely phallic might be warning enough. Mary might not have heard of Freud, but she would certainly be familiar with the story of Adam and Eve and the Serpent in the Garden of Eden.

Mary shook herself. 'Oh! Aunt Dot!' she cried. 'Why! I hardly know him! I only met him yesterday. He's a marvellous dancer. That's really all – '

'He's certainly that. You both are. I had no idea you were so good. But I'm just uttering a few alarm chirps in case you are having thoughts of nest-building. He flirts madly over here in England; but when it comes to marriage I think he won't be allowed much choice. There'll be a whole hierarchy of blackrobed women over there on the other side of the Atlantic: mother, grandmother, aunts and even cousins if they're rich, with perhaps a priest or two as well, gathering together to plan his marriage. And the bride chosen will be some good Catholic *señorita*, preferably with an inheritance from a neighbouring *estancia*.' She thought but did not say so that a simple country lass like Mary of no great beauty, with no dowry, a foreigner and a Protestant to boot, wouldn't stand a chance.

Mary was kept busy in the first week of skiing. There was hiring of skis and boots to be done, instruction for beginners on the nursery slopes from a jolly old ex-mountain guide, the climbing up the slippery snow with gritted teeth and prayers that the uncertain hold of your skis would somehow inch you up to the top of the slope before you had to stand up in order to slip, slide and tumble back to the bottom. In the second week there was the slow drag up on the one and only ski lift that resort possessed in those days before the wooden seat hit you smartly behind the knees and felled you face down into the snow. But at the end of the fortnight Mary was able to ski down the least demanding of the pistes without a fall. In the evening there was *après-ski* and the drinking of disgusting hot spiced *Glühwein*. That didn't matter much because by 5 p.m. she was so sleepy she didn't care what she swallowed.

Aunt Dot, wrapped in a voluminous fur coat and wearing purposeful knee-high boots, presided from a distance over all the heavy exercise. She spent her days moving in a calm and stately progress from meal to meal with a break for coffee and cognac for elevenses and another for tea and *pâtisseries* at 5 p.m. and after dinner she sat at a table drinking more cognac and watched over the *après-ski* frolics, thus ensuring that it was kept within the bounds of innocent snow-white fun. Uncle Bertie did not share in it.

72

He was in London having retired into his own world of financial juggling on the telephone.

At the end of this holiday Mary was sent off to Grenoble with Vicky to study French at a college suitable for English girls. 'It's in order that you can learn to speak French properly,' said Dot. 'After all, it is the language of your ancestors. And it might come in useful one day.' Somehow, by telegram and long-distance phone Aunt Dot had persuaded Colly to agree to it.

It was a pleasant enough six months, but not a period of much significance in her life. It was more a marking time, a waiting for real life to begin. At first she went regularly every week to the poste restante to ask for mail, but there never was any for her to pick up. Slowly she realised that Pedro was not going to write to her, that he had forgotten her. They had been acquainted for a mere twenty-four hours, and she was after all just a girl he'd met and flirted with briefly, who must have faded from his memory as quickly as the white rose he'd given her had withered inside its ephemeral tissue-paper wrapping. She was tempted to write to him, but did not know his address; and the thought of Dot's blackrobed coven presiding over Pedro's fate prevented her from asking her aunt to forward a letter. By the time spring was shining through the valley of the Isère Mary was forgetting him too.

She shared a room with Vicky in the students' hostel. When they washed their hair and tried to dry it in front of the single-bar electric fire they used to confide in each other their loves and hopes and their feelings of embarrassment at the old-fashioned ideas of their parents.

'What happened to your mother, Mary?' Vicky asked one evening.

'She ran away. It was during the war. They used to quarrel, she and Colly,' Mary said. She began to describe the event, stumbling a little at first with her own shyness at revealing her secrets. 'I must have been about ten at the time. Their voices woke me up one night. They were so *angry.*'

She was wearing pink winceyette pyjamas, she remembered, sitting up in bed listening, pulling the bedclothes up to her chin and shivering. She could hear her mother screaming, and her father shouting, but she couldn't make out what they said.

'Oh God! Make them stop!' she prayed. And as if her prayer had been answered the noise stopped. She got out of bed and crept down slowly, holding the banisters to guide her because it was dark except for the rectangle of light thrown across the hall through the open study door. The shouting began again as she approached. She stood in the doorway as Daddy threw a book which thudded against Mummy's shoulder. Mummy was holding one of her high-heeled shoes. She began to shriek, not in fear, not in lamentation but in rage. She pointed the shoe at him, accusing him of some crime; and Mary, who the evening before had been reading a children's book of stories from Homer, saw her as Clytemnestra about to murder her husband Agamemnon for sacrificing their daughter for a fair wind. Or was it because he had returned from the Trojan War with Cassandra the daughter of King Priam on his arm? This confused impression of his return from Troy must have been coloured by the fact that Daddy was wearing his uniform and looked every inch a soldier. He was holding a second book against his chest like a shield. Such violent feelings were roused in Mary by this scene that she began to tremble; and when Mummy raised her arm as if to hit him with the shoe Mary cried out: 'Don't! Don't!'

Mummy turned in surprise. She stopped yelling and dropped the shoe. 'Oh my poor little girl!' she said. She opened her arms as Mary ran to her. She was crying, and Mary could feel her wet cheeks. 'Now go back to bed my darling, and I'll come up and tuck you in. I promise!'

But she didn't come, though Mary waited for her a long time before she fell asleep again.

There were no more quarrels, or no more that Mary heard. Next day they behaved as if nothing had happened. 'Daddy went back to his camp after the weekend,' Mary said. 'I was living alone with Mummy at Gatt's Rise. "It's safe here," Mummy said. "No bombs here." But when Daddy went overseas to Egypt to fight the Germans in the desert I was sent away to boarding-school so that Mummy could do war work to help win the war.'

'Poor you!' said Vicky. 'It must have been beastly for you.'

'I was thirteen at the time I heard she'd left us – Colly and me.'

Mary and Vicky became great buddies, and went everywhere together. They spoke to French people in the town, gradually learned a little French, and developed a liking for French food. Their college was not part of the university, but they were allowed to attend some of the 'open' lectures given there. In the spring they went for mountain walks and picked (for Mary's later developed environmental conscience) far too many wildflowers, which they tried to identify in a French botanical book in the university library. In summer they explored the old town hemmed in between the River Isère and the mountains, or sat with other students drinking wine or coffee at pavement cafés and discussing Grenoble's most famous son, Stendhal, and his novel *Le Rouge et le Noir*, which they were struggling to read and translate for themselves.

'It's an annoying book,' said Vicky. 'I can't bear the hero, that Julien Sorel. He's a social climber, and so conceited too.'

'Oh can't you?' Mary felt rather sorry for him: a clever, uncouth lad from a dull provincial town who was thrust into high society where he wanted to shine but didn't know how to move or when to speak. 'I know just how he felt.' Admiring his honesty, though admitting he could be a bit harsh sometimes, she saw him as a young Colly might have been.

Sometimes they listened to French students telling of the exploits of fathers, mothers, uncles and cousins, who all seemed to have been members of the French Resistance during the war. Sometimes they simply sat in pavement cafés enjoying the warm bright air and watching the world go by.

At the end of six months Mary no longer thought of Pedro. She recognised that the glamorous Pedros of this world were not for her, that indeed all that hectic London life Aunt Dot had treated her to with the best of good intentions was not and could never be her scene, because she was at heart a country girl, out of place and ill at ease in Eltham Square. She sometimes still dreamed of David, so she had not quite forgotten him; but she knew now he belonged to the past which she had shed like a snake's skin and left behind her.

Buzzby hurled himself at her as she stood in the doorway. He thrust his paws against her chest and licked her face; he was beside himself with transports of delight at her return. He loves me, she thought. 'There now Buzzby boy, down Buzzby!' she protested, patting his head and stroking his silky neck as he tried to wind himself round her knees.

'I'm glad to be home,' she said.

'Not as pleased as I am,' said Colly smiling one of his rare beautiful smiles and folding her in a brief embrace.

It was more than conventional gladness that she felt. A wonderful happiness welled up from deep inside her as she knew she loved Buzzby, Colly, and Gatt's Rise, and recognised that this place, filled with memories of childhood joys, was home. The old house with its surrounding fields and the whole green vale of Frenester in which they nestled were where she belonged. She became aware, however, that a number of changes had taken place in her absence, or perhaps it was that Dot's wealth and organisational abilities combined with the clear mountain air of Grenoble were somehow blowing away the cobwebs from her vision. She saw that the house was dark and unkempt, and looked as if it hadn't been cleaned for months. Cleaning had in fact been very perfunctory for some time. Cook had reached retiring age and had retired, Sally had left to be married, and Colly had been unable to replace them. Resident domestic servants were becoming an extinct species it seemed, so Colly had been managing with a char who came for a few hours daily and left behind her a rather nasty meal for him to heat up for his supper. Every morning, still in his pyjamas and dressing-gown, he made his own breakfast in the kitchen.

'This won't do, Colly,' Mary said. 'This won't do at all. You're living in a mess.'

'I know, I know,' he agreed with surprising meekness. 'But how can I help it?'

She knew how. She looked at him silently and thought: I know how to make a success of Gatt's Rise. And I could make it pay too. Vicky of course would stay at home in Eltham Square until Mr Very-Rich-Right came along, and Claudia had a career already mapped out in journalism. Mary could imagine no Mr Right for herself in the foreseeable future, nor had she any degree to help push her into an interesting career; but now suddenly everything was falling into place like a jigsaw puzzle whose pieces she could fit into one whole grand design. Gatt's Rise would be her career; and all her faculties would be used to the full in the endeavour. She would manage the whole place, farm and house and garden, all on good business lines. Of course she would have to take over the accounts, and no doubt make sweeping changes; but she would take advice from both Colly and Tom until she understood things better. It was a job she knew she could do, and do well. She was filled with excitement at the prospect.

'You've got to listen to me, Colly,' she said when they met over breakfast next day.

'I'm listening,' he said; but he did not lower his newspaper.

'I intend taking command of the house. I shall be your Cook General in the real meaning of the title. You'll have to pay me a salary of course; but you needn't get your own breakfast any more. And there'll be no more pigging it for supper in the study. We'll eat dinner in the dining-room in a civilised manner.'

He lowered his copy of *The Times* then, and looked at her attentively, wondering what else besides French she had been learning.

'I'd like to learn about all aspects of the farm too, so that I can be useful there as well.'

'You really have grown up, Mary!' he laughed. 'I seem to have lost a little girl.' But he was glad he had a real soldier's daughter to work beside him now. Cook General indeed!

Yes, she was determined to make a success of Gatt's Rise, and she would make Colly happy too. She paused for a moment as she climbed the stairs. Was Colly not happy then? He seemed unchanged; but had he perhaps always been unhappy, and she hadn't guessed it before? Well if so, that was one of the things that had to be changed.

In the evening she walked down to the tied cottage, and knocked at the door. Marjorie seemed flustered as she invited Mary in, but she shouted to Tom to come in out of the garden where he was tending a bonfire. He came in sheepishly, and stood in his own kitchen awkwardly twisting his flat cap from one great red hand to the other. He was a bit suspicious of Mary's intentions at first; but it was not long before he realised that her youth and energy, which were what she was offering, might actually prove assets on the farm. Then when Marjorie made a cup of tea and they all sat round the kitchen table sipping it Tom told himself the great thing about Miss Chicon was that she wasn't stuck up. She was willing to learn, and probably wouldn't be such a skinflint as the old man over new enterprises and expenditure. Marjorie was pleased, too, because Mary suggested she might like to try working up at the house. She could bring the little boy with her, Miss Chicon said, which would be a great convenience.

'I don't want Gatt's Rise to be just a hobby farm in order to claim tax refunds on losses,' Mary said. 'We've got to pay our way, and make a profit too.'

Tom stood in the doorway gazing out over the fields where sheep were quietly nibbling the short autumn grass. 'We'd need another two hundred acres to make real money,' he said. 'This size of farm will never make more than a subsistence.'

'We'll make it a good subsistence then,' she asserted. 'For a start we'll have to take up all the subsidies we can.'

'Government wants us to grow wheat to reduce the amount of imports,' he argued. 'How can we grow wheat down here? It's too wet. We might try a bit of oats, or barley maybe. Then there's the orchard. . . .'

Mary flushed. The orchard was a painful subject for her, and for Colly too. A subsidy was being offered to farmers who cut down old unproductive cider-apple orchards to make way for more useful crops; but that apple orchard to the south-east of the house was so much part of her childhood that she hated the thought of losing it.

'I'll think about it,' she said.

When she mentioned the matter to Colly a spasm of pain crossed his face. He had always felt a special attachment to the recurring beauty of apple blossom. 'I know it's useless from the agricultural point of view,' he admitted. 'Wasted land I know, since we don't make cider here any more; but it's a thing of beauty, and a joy.'

'But not for ever,' Mary said firmly. 'Only in May.' The orchard was part of her growing up. One of her early recollections was of standing at an upstairs window with her mother who was pointing at the great clouds of apple blossom below. 'It's a rose pink sea!' her mother cried; and Mary pressing her nose against the glass tried to see the pink waves breaking. When you opened the window and leaned out you could smell the elusive perfume coming in gusts from the blossom, and you could hear the buzz of bees, like distant factory machinery at work. Every May it was a joy, a foretaste of paradise; but her rational self told her the trees were old, unproductive, diseased and full of canker, and were withering slowly where they stood. Was it sensible, was it right to sacrifice three to four acres of good land for the sake of a glorious flush of beauty every year for a few weeks in May?

'I remember how Mummy used to love it,' she said. She was aware of how she was manipulating Colly. Any mention of her mother's liking the orchard would harden Colly's determination to get rid of it, since, as Mary well knew, it had been his desire for years to cut Flora's memory root and branch from their lives.

'Well, I'm not going to make a Russian fuss in four acts over an orchard,' he said. 'I can see it will have to go.' Mary knew then that she could assure Tom the trees could be destroyed.

'I had in mind getting rid of the old trees and planting raspberry canes in their place. They would provide a profitable crop in summer,' she suggested. 'We could keep a small area of orchard for our own use – plant some good new disease-resistant dessert apples for the table.'

He thought that a good idea but warned: 'You'll have to get expert advice about your choice of apples. See you order varieties that flower at the same time in order to get cross-pollination. I'll look into the subject. Lord Lambourne's my favourite for colour and taste, though I know most people prefer Cox's Orange Pippin.'

'And James Grieve is mine,' said Mary. They were both smiling as their enthusiasm for the fruit they intended growing overcame their sadness for the blossom to be lost.

Mary discovered other changes in Frenester had taken place during her absence. For one thing the Reverend Peter Bliss was not Heavenly any more. He had installed a Mrs Peter Bliss at the vicarage, and was therefore no longer available to fill the vacant male chair at dinner parties. 'The new Lady of the Vicarage may improve the Rev's mind in time,' said Colly, 'but meanwhile I have transferred my patronage to St Colm's in Upper Coldacre.' Mary felt a spasm in her stomach as she remembered driving to the teashop there in David's battered red MG.

She resisted the temptation to make enquiries about David; but in due course she learned that he had left Frenester, that he had done very well in his exams and won a scholarship to a redbrick university in the Midlands. She wondered what he was studying there. 'The law,' she was told. 'Or something like that.'

On Thursdays Colly spent the day in court as chairman of the bench; on Wednesday he rode with Mary to the meet whenever it was held within reasonable riding distance, he on his bay gelding Garibaldi, she on her five-year-old mare Friska. Garibaldi was not young even in those days. When he went the way of all horse flesh, ending up in the green pastures of memory, Colly acquired another hunter, Romilly. He liked calling his horses after great men, especially reformers, though, as he hastened to explain to Mary, Samuel Romilly was never gelded, 'not until he came to commit suicide, poor man! when all his faculties were cut away'.

'How awful! Why did he do it?'

'Who knows? He was a moody man of great talents, of Huguenot descent like ourselves – like many of our best refugees – and wore himself out backing good causes and trying to change the law about such things as Catholic Emancipation and the Abolition of Slavery. Then when his wife died he shut himself up in his house and cut his throat with a razor blade.'

Mary was thankful that Friska had nothing that needed to be cut away. It was this mare which in the following year she took to Lady Abersyllt's stallion, and it was Friska's foal which she later sold for Hannah's mother to ride.

Hunting days were long, lovely, happy days. The horses had to be groomed and saddled before riding to the meet in the crisp morning air. Mary always felt proud beside her father as they rode, he so handsome in the saddle, and looking as if made for it, and she herself comfortable and at ease in her hacking jacket and jodhpurs. The meet was held in some prearranged place, a cross-roads or the yard of a village inn. Then the horses moved off to a nearby copse and waited, shuffling the fallen leaves under their hooves while the hounds snuffled in the covert for the scent until the fox was found. Then began the baying of the hounds, and the excitement of the chase: a wild gallop across fields with the added thrill of the risk taken at each jump over hedge or ditch. She didn't like to be in at the kill too much, as Colly did; what she most enjoyed was the quiet ride home in winter's early dusk. It was then that she relished her friendship with her father. It was a simple animal closeness, an absence of thinking, and a contented acceptance of simply being. But sometimes in the deep relaxation that follows heavy exercise of the body their minds floated easily towards each other and they shared their thoughts. Once when they had enjoyed an exceptionally long chase and were later than usual riding home darkness fell. It was a very cold clear January evening. They stopped for a moment before the descent into Frenester, and looking northwards above the top of the hill they located the Great Bear and the Pole Star, while arched over them the Milky Way streamed through the heavens like a great torrent of ice falling, a great glacier slowly falling unimaginable distances for ever. Colly broke the silence.

'The Greeks called it the path to the palace of Zeus.'

Romilly whinnied suddenly and shied, taking fright at something stirring in the hedge till Colly spoke softly, patting his neck, and the horse stood still.

'It's the immensity of the universe that's so difficult to imagine,' said Mary. 'And then when I do I feel giddy from feeling how small I am . . . unsupported like a speck of dust falling. And then I think that thing that people call the soul. . . . Why should such a speck of dust as each one of us must be in infinite space and time be of any importance in the mind of God? Why should He care about us at all?'

'Why indeed?'

'When I look at the Milky Way and all those far-flung galaxies the notion of a personal immortality does seem rather absurd.'

'We can only speculate about what happens after death, we can never know because nobody comes back from after it to tell us.'

They moved off down the hill, Mary watching the distant glow on the horizon indicating the lights of the city of Bristol, but Colly, like a hound nosing the fox's scent, pursued and worried at her thought. He quoted Pascal, who confessed to being terrified of the eternal silence of the heavens. ' "Man is only a reed, the weakest thing in nature; but he is a thinking reed." We are important to ourselves,' he asserted. 'Not of course from the perspective of the eternal, but in the here and now. We do possess something different from other animals, and that's our ability to think. Mind, soul, brain, call it what you like, does give us the ability to foresee a little. And that, I think, does grant us some sort of will, free or not so free, which can, I believe, alter, if only infinitesimally, the course of events. I do believe that can happen sometimes. And that does give us an importance, an identity quite apart from the consciousness of self, you know.'

Mary made no reply. She was tired, and her horse was too; they were both jaded and moving slowly after the long day's hunting, but Colly continued to think aloud. 'Your kind of thinking – about being a speck of dust and so on – is fear really, fear of the unknown, of being deserted, unsupported as you say. But in the here and now you are not alone. You have me to give you strength.' He spoke firmly, tying to reassure what he thought of as her anxiety.

He is so certain, Mary thought. Perhaps he is right, he must be right; but in reality she was not at all anxious. The idea of personal annihilation after death filled her with very little terror. She had faced this possibility much earlier in her teens and had then locked it away in a remote cupboard of her mind, dismissed it from the present because she had only thought but not felt it. At twenty death was too far away to touch her.

Buzzby barked as they entered the yard. He followed feverishly first one and then the other as they watered, fed and stabled the horses before going into the kitchen of the unlit house to eat a supper of cold meat with apple chutney and bread and cheese. Colly drank beer, Mary water. Neither spoke while eating. As Mary left the table to take the empty plates to the sink she said: 'I do so love our hunting days.' And Colly, following with the glasses said: 'Just heaven for me too!'

When she went upstairs he called after her: 'Goodnight, my dear!' She hardly heard him; she walked in a trance of physical fatigue. She lay in a bath for a while letting the hot water soak the aching out of her muscles, relishing the luxury of that easing. Then she climbed into bed and fell immediately into opiate ponds of sleep as profound as any drug-induced oblivion.

In the ensuing years Colly wondered occasionally at his luck. Sometimes as he opened a gate, or crossed the bridge at Gatt's Crossing to the path which in ancient times before the building of the canal was the main cart track to Coldacre, four miles away, he paused and was amazed at how well it had all worked out. After the excitement, then the uncertainty, anxiety and desolation, and finally the resentment and hatred of marriage, after the noise and blood, the terror of armoured skirmish, the long-drawn-out tense alertness of the desert war, and finally his own injuries and helplessness, it was really a miracle that he had survived, recovered and floated down into this calm lake of happiness with Mary at Gatt's Rise. That his girl had proved such a wonderful partner in work, and such a companion, too, was an amazing blessing, a reward perhaps for his stamina and will in all those bad years. And moreover she was happy. Anyone could see she was contented and fulfilled in spite of being single still. He was sometimes surprised, when he remembered Flora, that Mary was so unlike her mother: she did not want nervous stimulation, bright lights, parties, sexual encounters, social dangers; she didn't even seem interested in men. Once or twice when his conscience lurched against his will, upsetting momentarily the balance of his life strategy, he asked himself: am I selfish? Am I using up the years of her youth? – exploiting this good gentle daughter who is too trusting to see any evil in me? And he did from time to time consider what might happen to her in her lonely old age when he himself was dead. She would own Gatt's Rise, that's what would happen. She would be a wealthy woman, independent and safe, unless some quite undeserved catastrophe lay waiting in the future. He was old and wise enough to admit that even his will couldn't protect her for ever; but he thought of the farmer in Frenton Byways who not many years ago while ploughing dropped suddenly into a cavern below his barley field and uncovered a Roman villa full of Roman treasures. Well, that proved to be good fortune for him and no disaster. Colly was enough of a historian to understand that the past, like that Roman villa buried under centuries of accumulated soil, had a way of coming unexpectedly to the surface of the present. And Fortune, it seemed, hides good as well as bad luck in her pockets.

When his conscience pricked him he would decide Mary must have some social life, must meet more young people. He would buy tickets for the annual hunt ball, the Young Conservatives' ball or the Young Farmers' get-together. Mary would pull out from the back of her wardrobe the evening dress bought for her by Aunt Dot, which was growing steadily more old-fashioned as the seasons passed, and Colly would squeeze himself into his dinner jacket, and neatly tie his black bow-tie. Neither of them enjoyed these outings much. He spent most of the evening at the bar discussing hunt matters, politics or farm prices and yields as the occasion demanded, but he managed to keep an eye on Mary from afar. If he noticed any of her partners dancing with her too frequently or paying her too much attention during the supper interval he made a point of dropping some derogatory remarks on the way home: 'Did you see his *boots?* Fancy anyone coming to a dance in boots! What a clodhopper!' Or: 'Not too much chin to that young man. But I dare say the cows don't notice in the milking shed with their backsides turned to him.' And once he burst out laughing as he described the son of Smithers, who was a big pig-farmer in the district, as resembling a side of smoked ham. 'Did you see him leaving the floor with his arm round his partner? – his great red hand slung across her shoulder like a packet of sausages!'

'There's no need for you to accompany me to these dos,' said Mary. 'Now that I've passed my driving test I can perfectly well take myself there and back.'

'O but, my dear,' he explained,' I can be useful simply by being there to rescue you when you're a wallflower.' He could at least come to her side when he saw her standing on the edge of the floor wistfully watching the dancers. The few males in the district who could dance well never seemed to come her way. It was, he knew, the longing to dance as much as the desire for a partner that smeared her face with sadness.

Mary winced. Her diffidence, which rendered her dumb and awkward with young male strangers, her fear of being left a wallflower, that most humiliated of females, did make her grateful for her father's presence; but she was well aware that people laughed at him behind his back when he guided her over the floor in a stately slow foxtrot or the old-fashioned waltz. Her own shyness and Colly's derisive comments afterwards turned these social events into a form of torture to be endured but dreaded. It all came to a head at the Young Farmers' midsummer romp held to celebrate the longest day of the year. Nearly all the hay was cut and baled, the corn not yet ready for harvesting, so there was a brief pause in work which allowed for the party to be well attended. It was held in a big field on the plateau above the Edges. A marquee had been hired to protect band, dancers and drinkers in case of rain. This didn't seem likely to Mary, who thought it was one of the most beautiful days she could remember, warm and sunny all day and cooling towards evening. She discarded her old evening dress and wore a simple short dress of lime green with a full floating skirt. She felt relaxed and happy for once as they got into the car. Summer, too, was wearing her most gorgeous apparel. By the side of the road elms, oaks and horse-chestnut trees, heavy in leaf, cast long shadows interrupted by patches of sundrenched hedgerow through which the briar rose struggled to display the perfect shape, the innocent simplicity of its frail, transient flowers. Just to catch glimpses of them from the car as they drove past made Mary's spirits rise. Colly, looking sideways at her from the steering wheel, remarked: 'You look happy, my dear, and quite pretty, too, this evening.' At which, as near a compliment to her looks as she would ever receive from him, she smiled without speaking.

It was Jerry Trotter who caused the trouble. He was the son of a neighbouring farmer, who, in Colly's opinion, coveted the ten-acre field on their northern boundary. Jerry Trotter made a beeline for Mary as soon as she arrived, danced with her frequently, and took her off into the supper tent at half-time. Colly, hearing the music stop, turned away from the bar, and not being able to see Mary on the floor felt a sharp stab of alarm. When at last the pair emerged from supper he pierced the unfortunate Jerry with angry glances. He hated seeing the young man's great red hands steering his daughter's body, and his stupid face cracking with braying laughter which resounded even above the noise of the band. He was greatly relieved when at last his ordeal was ended and he had Mary safely back inside the Rover.

'What a jackanapes that son of Trotter is! I'm afraid you

must have had a very boring evening,' he commented at the wheel.

He was surprised at the sarcasm in her voice when she spoke: 'Is jackanapes another of your erudite Edwardian terms of abuse?'

'No, no!' he replied. 'It's much older. Shakespearian. "I will teach a scurvy jackanape priest to meddle. . . ." '

'Well, he's not a priest anyway,' she said crossly.

'That must be the only thing in his favour.'

They completed the journey home without another word. He was telling himself that Jerry Trotter coveted not only the ten-acre field but the whole of Gatt's Rise, and was beginning a campaign of courtship in order to acquire it. Mary was angry because Colly didn't seem to understand that of course she cared nothing for Jerry Trotter with his ham hands and his donkey laughter, but it was better for her to dance with good-humoured jackanapes than to remain a miserable neglected wallflower. She was aware of Colly's jealousy, and she was beginning to recognise and resent the tactics he used to destroy any man who dared to admire her. Midsummer's day had passed and was no longer lovely; and in the darkness she couldn't see the wild roses still blooming in the hedges.

The young man tried to phone Mary a few days later. Fortunately she was outside working in the raspberry field when the phone rang, so Colly was able to intercept the call. A letter in an unknown scrawl did arrive then for Mary. Colly noted its arrival; but he was of course too honourable to open it. Mary said nothing about it, and for a few days his mind was torn with surmise and uncertainty; but no further development took place.

She didn't tell Colly, nor anyone else what Jerry Trotter had written. It was a love letter of a sort, and it contained the nicest thing, the prettiest compliment she'd ever received. 'In your green dress so airy and light,' he wrote, 'you reminded me of the willow trees on the banks of the Frene in springtime.' She recalled his sweaty face beaming at her over the rim of his glass at supper, and the shower of pastry crumbs clinging to his chin and black bow-tie. Appearance can be deceptive, she thought. Poor Jerry hid some delicate feelings behind his red bucolic mask. She thought kindly of him as she tore his letter into small pieces which she dropped into her wastepaper basket; but of course she knew, in spite of the shimmering willow trees which stood along his stretch of the Frene, he would not do.

When the subject of dances came up again Mary said: 'Do we have to go, Colly? I'm afraid I find them rather terrible, really. What about you?'

'Excruciating, my dear. Shall we sacrifice them?' His eyes gleamed happily at the prospect.

They soon resumed their quiet routine of work, eating, talking and reading. Mary made an effort to take part in the communal activities of the town: she became leader of the Girl Guides, she joined the WI and taught the local members a few tips on how to make soufflés, she learned from them how to dry rose petals, lavender and scented geranium leaves to make pot-pourri; but she was not a very regular attender at meetings, and gradually over the years other duties and interests replaced the attractions of the Frenester WI. So the years passed contentedly, and with a frightening speed, Mary thought, when on her fortieth birthday she looked in her mirror and wondered where they'd all gone. As far as she could see her skin was as smooth and unwrinkled as it had been at thirty. People always told her she looked young for her age, and she gave credit to her active open-air life for her youthful appearance; but there was no denying the fact that she was forty now.

Forty is a significant milestone in any woman's life. She hadn't thought much about it till that moment when she stood staring into the mirror above the washbasin in which she was washing her hands, soaping them mechanically and remembering a poem of Auden's:

> O plunge your hands in water,
>   Plunge them in up to the wrist;
> Stare, stare in the basin
>   And wonder what you've missed.

> The glacier knocks in the cupboard,
>   The desert sighs in the bed,
> And the crack in the tea-cup opens
>   A lane to the land of the dead.

A feeling of loss as sudden as it was unexpected surged up into her throat from deep down in her consciousness. Perhaps because she had considered the matter so little before the grief was so poignant that it made her gasp. She lifted her wet hands and clutched her neck. She sat down on the edge of the bed and wept. She knew now she would probably never bear a child. To hold her own baby in her arms had always been her secret heart's desire. It would certainly not now be granted to her. The means, the necessary man was nowhere to be seen in Frenester nor on any imaginable horizon. Was this why she wept? she asked herself. Well, then, it was foolish, despicable self-pity. She scolded herself, counting her blessings, telling herself that she was luckier than many, than most women. She should be grateful for the gifts the gods bestowed, not least the beautiful new improved-performance-engined Mini Cooper Colly had bought her for her own personal use. She must not let him see tears on her face, for that would spoil his day, so she went again to the basin and washed her face, added a little discreet make-up, and went down to the kitchen to serve lunch.

It was a special birthday lunch which two of Colly's old buddies from Sandhurst and their wives were coming to eat with her. She had prepared that morning from a Greek recipe a boned joint of lamb and stuffed it with a clove of garlic, chopped onions and dried apricots, added a sprinkling of thyme and a scattering of flaked almonds, and placed it to cook in the lower, cooler oven of her much prized Aga. She had bought and installed that ten years ago when she was thirty, when she had at last brought Gatt's Rise out of the doldrums, had made the farm pay, and believed she owed herself this reward for her efforts.

The Aga held for her the dignity of a sacred fire. It was the core, the warm heart of the whole house. She looked after it conscientiously and seriously: she cleaned out the flues every six weeks to keep a good draught blowing through it; she riddled out the ash and fed the flame twice daily with the small hard, high-quality anthracite beans which were dug in a colliery in South Wales and brought by rail direct to the siding at Frenester station, from where Minnie and her mother delivered them to Mary's back door.

Minnie was a great gaunt woman with a coal-smudged face and blackened arms, who with her wizened mother were the local coal merchants in the old days. It was said in the district that the man of that family used to beat his womenfolk with a knob-ended elm cudgel; but they escaped his wrath by outliving him, and for a time ran the business themselves. Minnie's ma, who drove the bedraggled horse, sat with a sack over her head and shoulders to protect her from the rain, and Minnie swung her black-stockinged legs from the side of the cart, ready to jump down, heave a hundredweight on to her back and stagger forwards to discharge it into the coalshed. After the load was delivered she came to the back door fluttering a bill. Mary used to offer her a mug of tea, which she drank standing.

'I won't sit down, Missus, thank you. I might blacken your chairs. I'll drink it standing if you don't mind. Plenty of sugar, yes. And I'll take a mugful out to Ma.' Ma never stirred from her position in the yard in charge of the old nag. The only concession she made to comfort was to pull out a clay pipe, into the bowl of which she tamped the tobacco with a hardened blackened forefinger, and which after some lighting and puffing, relighting and puffing, gave her the solace of a brief smoke with her tea.

Mary reflected, as she opened the oven door and smelt the appetising scent of her well-cooked dish, that these colourful albeit black figures had disappeared from her life, relics of ancient Frenester vanishing as the town and its inhabitants moved into the Seventies.

When the guests said nice things about the food Colly explained that Mary was his Cook General.

'Not so!' objected one, who was himself a General. 'She is Generalissimo!'

'Well, if this is the sort of fare your Generalissimo provides for you here,' said the other, who was of slightly lower rank, 'you'll soon have the Ministry of Defence enquiring into your expenditure.'

'We don't eat like this every day,' said Colly. 'Today is Mary's birthday.'

'Birthday? Oh! happy birthday!' chorused the wives.

And they all toasted her birthday in glasses of Colly's six-year-old claret St Emilion. It was, Mary remembered, in spite of those tears earlier in the day, a birthday which ended in a haze of happiness. Although she was forty and still unmarried she knew she was loved, appreciated, and gilded with praises.

Voices in the hall dragged Mary back to the present. She glanced at her watch wondering if Hannah and Mr Brown had got as far as that bargees' pub, the Moorhen. They would, she guessed, have chosen the towpath going west, as that was the prettier way. She remembered uncomfortably that she owed Mr Brown an apology because all those years ago she'd let him down without an excuse or even an explanation when she suddenly stopped singing in his choir in order to avoid meeting David again.

She went downstairs as her father emerged from his sanctum to offer Brown a drink; but the vicar politely refused, explaining that he had to hurry away to Frenton Byways to hold an evening service there. Mary saw him to the door.

'If I can be of any help,' he said, 'to Hannah, or to yourself, please do call on me. Any time.'

'Thank you,' said Mary. She couldn't bring herself to call him Theodore, and Mr Brown seemed too formal, so she simply repeated: 'Thank you. Yes. Thank you.'

Hannah pushed past her, and seized the vicar's arm.

'We had a lovely walk, didn't we?' she asked anxiously.

'We did indeed,' he agreed. 'And we must do it again.'

'We got as far as the Moorhen,' she explained to Mary, 'but it was closed – seeing as how it was Sunday.'

FIVE

Hannah was moody after Mr Brown's visit, which made Mary fear that the girl might break out and do some foolish impulsive act. She wondered how on earth she was going to keep her occupied in the long summer holidays looming ahead. She suggested Hannah might like to join the local Girl Guides. Mary was no longer in charge of them herself. She had resigned her leadership when Colly had that bad fall and injured his hip, but with the naivety of desperation she hoped Guiding might amuse Hannah and so help to fill some of the long evenings to come.

Hannah laughed at her openly.

'Oh I couldn't! See me in that uniform? Not bloody likely!'

But she was eager to learn to ride. Mary had sold her own hunter when after Colly's accident they both abandoned hunting but his old hunter, Romilly, was still kept at grass. He had grown lazy with age and retirement, and was quite safe for a beginner. Hannah was soon able to persuade him into a brief canter across the paddock. She enjoyed grooming him too, and even cleaned out his stable willingly. She liked working outdoors, but Mary knew she was often bored and restless, even resentful, inside the house.

One Saturday morning after they left Romilly grazing in the paddock and were approaching the lock gates in order to cross the canal and walk over into the further field, Hannah kicked a tussock of grass savagely.

'What's the matter?' asked Mary.

'Browned off!' scowled Hannah. 'Fed up!'

'Why?'

'Bit tame, en' it?'

'Most happiness is tame.' Mary was suddenly conscious of her prim voice. 'Passion and violence crack you open like boiling water in a glass. It all leaks away.' Hannah turned away her scornful face, but Mary continued patiently: 'Happiness is stored up bit by bit, like honey in the long summer days.'

Hannah didn't laugh at this as Mary had expected she might, but said thoughtfully, 'It was like that at Gran's: the bees buzzing, and the lovely heat in the garden. My aunt kept bees. I was stung once.'

They stopped to stare at a barge chugging slowly towards the lock. 'My aunt grew strawberries,' said Hannah. 'I remember the smell of strawberries in the garden on a hot day.'

'Have you ever smelt cowslips?' Mary asked. 'There are some down there near the canal.' But Hannah stood still, entranced by her memories, as the barge slowed down and stopped. 'Let's pick some cowslips,' Mary suggested. 'They smell so heavenly in the house.'

When Mary stooped to pick a flower Hannah waved at the barge. The man who had jumped out on the bank to work the gates waved back at her, the other one standing at the rudder sounded a hooter in greeting. She laughed suddenly, snatched Mary's proffered flower and sniffed it greedily.

'Cor! What a scent! Better than Piccadilly Nights any day, I reckon!' She flung out her arms and ran wildly about the hillside, still holding her single flower, while Mary watched her wondering what on earth had come over the girl.

When the barge, loaded with stone chips from the quarry at Coldacre below the Edges, disappeared on its slow journey to the old docks on the Severn, they picked a bunch of cowslips. Hannah was singing happily as they returned to the house.

> 'Believe me if all those endearing young charms
> Which I gaze on so fondly today . . .'

'Why, what a good voice you've got, Hannah!' said Mary. 'How does it go on? Can you remember the words?'

> 'Around the dear ruin each wish of my heart
> Will entwine itself verdantly still.'

Hannah smiled happily as she sang. 'I get the words a bit mixed up. I used to think the old mill was the ruin. I never thought of Gran as an old ruin at all, in spite of her white hair and her voice cracking when she sang that song.'

'That's one of Tom Moore's Irish airs; but your gran wasn't Irish, was she?'

'Oh no! But Dan Delaney was. And it was he who sang it to her first. She used to call him her Irish bog-trotter; but I knew by the way she said it that she loved him. He was my grandad, but of course I never knew him.'

On the following Saturday morning Mary drove Hannah to the open-air livestock market held in Frenester's station yard. Hannah was immediately fascinated by the auctioneer, who was standing on a box and gabbling incomprehensibly at a semicircle of dour, secretive faces below him. Now and again one of the silent men jerked up a stick, or pulled on the peak of his cap, or simply nodded suddenly. They were bidding for groups of sheep penned by hurdles up against the station wall. Meanwhile Mary bought a dozen day-old Aylesbury duckling chicks. Hannah was flushed with excitement when they packed the squeaking cardboard box into the boot of the car.

Hannah helped to feed the chicks with a mixture of mash and milk. At night they huddled together round a small slow-burning paraffin lamp inside the coop; but as soon as daylight woke them they emerged on to their grass patch, which was covered by a wire netting run, and cheeped loudly, demanding breakfast. The run was placed outside the back door so that their calls could easily be heard from the kitchen and their hunger quickly satisfied. All that weekend Hannah had to give them two-hourly feeds to stop their deafening clamour.

'Love 'em!' she said tenderly as she stood and watched them gobble. 'Who'd a thought such little balls of fluff could make such a hell of a row?'

'See you move the run on to new ground as soon as the grass looks trodden down,' said Mary. 'That way you'll keep a fresh floor under their feet.' She herself attended to the lamp.

Hannah didn't lose interest in the birds after the weekend. She rushed back every afternoon after school, threw her satchel on the kitchen table, and hurried to prepare the evening meal for her voracious brood. Only one was lost, trampled to death by its brothers and sisters inside the coop; eleven survived and grew fast. Very soon they were no longer pretty babies covered with yellow down but sturdy young birds growing their adult feathers, and by ten or twelve weeks they were ready for the table.

Mary couldn't bring herself to wring their necks. Tom did that for her; but she and Hannah sat in the sun on the stone step below the kitchen door and plucked the carcasses. Then Mary drew out their innards before packing them for the deep freeze. Two were kept for Sunday dinner: one for themselves, and one for Tom's wife. Mary was afraid that Hannah might be upset when a good fat duck appeared cooked on Sunday, so she took the trouble to praise Hannah loudly in front of Colly for her good work in rearing the birds. He cast a short approving glance in her direction, and nodded. Mary needn't have worried. Hannah's appetite for food cured her nostalgia for baby

97

chicks, especially as Mary served the duck with slices of orange, peas and roast potatoes.

The Colonel and Tom used to drive off in the Land Rover towing an empty cattle truck, to view and buy from neighbouring farmers, or the Frenester cattle market, promising baby calves, which were then handed over to Mary's care. When the next batch arrived she took Hannah to the sheds to inspect them. There was one little Hereford heifer with a red-brown face and white eyeliner round one big brown eye that Hannah fell in love with. She cooed over it, trying to stroke its head, but the calf shied away so Hannah sang to it instead:

'Jeepers, creepers, where'd you get those peepers?
Where'd you get that big brown eye?'

Mary laughed, and promised they would call that calf Hannah, and it would be hers to rear.

It was Mary's job to teach the calves to drink milk out of buckets, sucking upwards, which the poor little creatures don't do instinctively, since in nature they suck downwards from their mothers' udders above their heads. Mary showed Hannah how to make them drink. First they washed and scrubbed their hands carefully because, as Mary explained, calves were prone to pick up infections from dirty hands, then they mixed the powdered milk with warm water which they took to the stalls. Here each bewildered calf had to be seized by the head and its nose pushed down into a bucket where Mary's fingers, dipped in milk, presented themselves to the calf's lips. The young creatures soon learned their lesson. Hannah was delighted when her own baby began to suck from her hand.

'She's a bit thick,' she said. 'Slow in the head. I suppose my fingers aren't as good as cows' tits. But she's learning.' Hannah loved this work, and did it eagerly. She didn't grumble about scouring the buckets, nor at having to scald them with boiling water after each feed; she willingly carried bales of straw to spread over the byres, with a little hay for her new babies to nibble. She was sorry when they were old enough to be handed over to Tom's care and were driven out into open pastures. Mary and Hannah watched them as they ran in short spurts foolishly, disorientated by the space around them and by the feel of cold earth under their feet. After a while they stooped towards the fresh grass and began to pick at it.

'Do you know what, Mary? I shall miss the calves,' said Hannah.

'Will you, Hannah? Yes, I always do at first.' It was the first time Hannah had called Mary by her first name.

They walked into the orchard where apples were ripening and the trees ridding themselves of superfluous fruit in the June drop. Hens wandered freely there, picking at the fallen fruit. Hannah bent to enter one of the hen-houses and emerged a minute later with her hands full of brown eggs. 'None fresher than these,' she said. Free-range eggs were sold at the kitchen door to passers-by.

'People like to think of hens enjoying freedom of movement in the open,' said Mary. 'But I'm not so sure the hens like it all that much themselves.' It was all right in the summer in fine weather when the birds could pick up a variety of food from the ground and a good supply of natural grit to help harden the shells, but in the winter months they were often miserable outside. On wet days they chose to remain semi-comatose inside the huts for a large part of the day. When they did venture forth they moved slowly, picking their claws disdainfully out of the mud and trying to shake their dripping feathers dry. Poor bedraggled wretches, they looked like refugees far from their native climate.

'Last year we had a visit from Mr Fox,' Mary said. 'One fine spring noonday when the hens were all outside enjoying their freedom a big dog fox strolled into the orchard as calm as can be. And before anybody could stop him he'd slaughtered four hens and left another two dying from deep wounds in the neck. Tom was in the yard when he heard the terrified squawking. He seized that gun he keeps in the tool shed, but by the time he got to the hens Mr Fox, carrying one in his jaws, was walking scornfully out under the far gate. I think he intended coming back for the others. Tom had been so enraged he chased across the paddock after the thief, but without success. It was only several weeks later he discovered a vixen's lair with young down among hawthorn roots along the canal bank.'

'Did he shoot them?' asked Hannah.

'I'm afraid he did,' Mary admitted. 'Sad, really. . . . The little foxes are so pretty.'

By the end of June soft fruit was ripening in Mikey's walled garden. This was Hannah's favourite place to be, so she used to find excuses to go there. She soon became Mikey's pet, perhaps because she listened to his talk, perhaps because she seemed willing to do odd jobs for him which his stiff joints found difficult. He sat when it was warm enough on an ancient straddle-stone at the gate between the yard and the fruit garden, his knees spread out and one gnarled hand balancing on a twisted branch of elm polished by long usage into a smooth walking stick. From this position on his gardener's throne he could order her about. Their friendship ripened with the strawberries. She told him about her aunt's strawberry garden at the mill, and how careful she used to be with her plants, never letting them fruit for more than three years.

'The virus gets them, you know,' she confided, 'as they grow old.' Auntie May used to peg down the side shoots into little pots and bury them between the rows. When the suckers had made strong roots she snipped them, as if dividing so many umbilical cords, and pushed the baby plants into new ground.

''Tis the way of it,' said Mikey. 'The old die off, and the young take over.' He nodded his head solemnly, but his eyes gleamed wickedly. He pointed towards the base of the wall at a clump of primroses in need of dividing and planting out. 'An' did you know that if you was to plant them primroses upside down they'd come up polyanthus?'

'Go on!' exclaimed Hannah. She opened her eyes wide, and watched him as she waited for his gleeful cackle.

When the strawberries were ripe at last Tom's wife Marjorie joined forces with Mary and Hannah for the picking. Each had two baskets, one for perfect berries, the other for fruit damaged by birds or slugs. Sometimes a blackbird caught in the nets screeched, fluttering frantic with fear as Hannah approached it, pecking fiercely at her hands as she tried to free its wings and feet from their entanglement. Bending over the plants to pick made Hannah's back ache, but she didn't mind that. At the end of each row she stood up and stretched, sighing with contentment at the heat trapped and reflected by garden walls, and the all-enveloping strawberry smell. Frequently she popped one of the less than perfect berries in her mouth before bending to the next row. She could hear the distant sound of the tractor from the field beyond the canal where Tom was busy cutting hay. At the end of the picking session they all carried their baskets into the kitchen. As they emerged from the enclosed garden into the yard the smell of new-mown hay drifted in gusts towards them on an easterly wind. Hannah's face lit up. She took several gasps of breath. The mixture of scents from the hayfield and the fruit she was carrying was almost overpowering.

'Ooh! The scent!' she cried. 'It makes me go all over queer with joy!'

Some strawberries were sold in punnets at the kitchen door, but most were taken by Mary to the greengrocer in Frenester for sale in his shop.

By the middle of July strawberries gave way to raspberries, which were less tiresome to pick, because you could do it standing, but had to be handled with even greater delicacy because they were so easily crushed.

Hannah on one side of a row of canes could see Marjorie on the other side through the leaves.

'You don't come up to the house much,' said Hannah. 'That's why I only see you when we're picking fruit.'

'No,' said Marjorie, looking from side to side over her shoulder to make sure Mary was out of earshot. 'I works at the old folks' home. But I does shifts, see? That way I can do night shifts when there's summer fruit picking to be had here.'

Hannah picked faster than Marjorie, but sensing intuitively that Marjorie wanted to say more, she slowed down and lingered over the canes.

'I worked up at the house once,' Marjorie confided. 'About fifteen years gone.'

'Didn't you like it there?'

'Oh, I liked it all right. And of course I liked *her*. Everybody does.' She bent her head in Mary's direction. 'But well . . . things do 'appen unexpected sometimes.'

'What things?' Hannah stared at her through the canes.

'Tom liked his work here. It was a good job for him, see? And having the cottage an' all, with the kid just starting school in Frenester, and the school bus stopping to pick him up at the gate. I knew it wouldn't be easy to find a place like this again. So it was up to me to put up with things.'

'What things?'

'Lord knows I'm too fat now; but in them days I was but a slip of a girl.' She dropped her voice, her eyes wide as an owl's at twilight. 'The Colonel . . .' she whispered.

'Never!' gasped Hannah. 'Got fresh with you, did he?'

'Fresh? He was sex mad! He chased me into the broom cupboard under the stairs, and caught me once in the bathroom as I was bending over to clean the bath. It wasn't safe to be alone with him in a room. In the end it got so bad I had to look for another job.'

'I wouldn't have believed it,' said Hannah. 'That old cliff-face!'

'Oh yes,' Marjorie assured her. 'Cliff-faces do 'ave a way

of crumbling sometimes. And then all sorts of ancient savage beasts come crawling out of the wreckage.'

'Dinosaurs,' said Hannah scornfully, 'stuck in the stones.'

'So I found this job at the old folks' home. Said the hours suited me better. Told them it fitted in with the kid's time at school. But don't you go blabbing all this to *her* now. *She* don't know nothing of it. I'm just telling you as a warning, that's all. I dare say he'd think you easy meat because of . . . because of what happened to you, see?'

'I don't care what he thinks of me,' declared Hannah, tossing her head, and tangling a few strands of hair in among the twigs. 'He can keep his deep thoughts as well as his hands to hisself. Anyroads,' she added, pulling her hair free, 'he don't like me. Nor I him. So you've no need to worry.'

'Well, just mind he don't turn you into his doxy-rose.'

'Not bloody likely!' Hannah picked up her basket and moved quickly along the row. 'That old fossil!' She tossed her head, freely this time.

After that day Hannah often spent the evening with Marjorie at the cottage where they watched television together. Mary was pleased at their friendship. It relieved her a little, demanding less watchfulness from herself. She calculated that Marge's son, now a strapping lad in his twenties who still lived at home, would be no threat to Hannah since he was going steady with a girlfriend of his own. Moreover Hannah's absence from the house in the evenings made the atmosphere less irksome for Colly.

One hot afternoon in August Hannah and Marge cycled down to Mudcott to see the old mill where Hannah had spent the years between her mother's and her grandmother's deaths. They leaned their bikes against the wall of the bridge over the Frene and stared at the building. There it stood silent and deserted. The great wheel hung motionless, no splash of water fell from its cracked wooden paddles, and only a trickle oozed out from under the sluice gate to join the river beyond the bridge.

'That great wheel must have made a hell of a racket when it turned,' said Marge.

'Suppose it must have,' Hannah agreed. 'But that was years ago – before my gran's time even. It must have worked the loom for weaving the cloth. But I never saw it turn.' She explained that when Gran's father inherited the mill he threw out all the old machinery and put in new. He took to grinding corn and mixing it for cattle and pig feed. Later he installed electric power. 'The noise of the electric grinders and mixers was bad enough. And the dust from the chaff was something terrible,' said Hannah. They wandered round to the back. 'It was nice though, in the evening when the grinding stopped. And sometimes in bed at night when it was very quiet I could hear the water running away for ever under the house.'

They stared at the millpond whose surface lay unmoving, unruffled under its green algal coat. A neat black moorhen shot out from under the bank as they approached. She jerked her little red head and chattered in alarm as she broke in urgent zigzags through the smoothness of the green weed.

'How long has it been empty?' asked Marge.

Hannah made no reply as she tried to push open a door. Finding it locked they peered into the murky interior through the broken panes of a lower window. Inside rusting machinery stood still, the dust of idleness settling thick upon it, cobwebs hung everywhere, greyish fungus thrust itself upwards from the base of the wall, and the whole place seemed under the bad spell of its own immobility till a rat suddenly scuttled out from under a pile of rotting sacks and disappeared down a hole.

'It smells sort of mushroomy,' said Hannah.

'Who does it all belong to, Hannah?'

'Gran left it to Auntie May for her lifetime, and after that to me.'

'D'you mean to say this'll all be yours one day?' Marge found it difficult to believe.

'This ruin – yes, maybe. Maybe not.' Hannah explained that Auntie May was ill in a nursing home. 'Last time she wrote to me for my birthday she told me she was trying to sell it to pay for the home. But who's going to buy this ruin anyway?' They fell silent as they walked back to their bikes.

Hannah knew that just below the bridge the river fell dramatically over a weir, and below this there was a pool to one side and out of the main current where it was safe to bathe.

There was nobody about when they reached the place, so they wheeled their bikes along the riverside path and rested them against some young birches struggling to grow in the poor soil between boulders and brambles. Here they stripped off their clothes and wriggled into swimsuits.

'This is where Gran taught me to swim,' said Hannah, though truth to tell there wasn't much teaching about the affair. Here it was that Gran tied orange-coloured balloon bags to her arms and watched her wade in, and as she lay on the water, finding to her immense surprise that the water-wings actually did keep her afloat, Gran and Auntie May, neither of whom could swim, stood on the bank making pushing-away gestures with their arms and shouting instructions which she couldn't hear because of the noise of the weir. She remembered the glorious day when she threw away the orange lifebuoys, and trusting her body to the pool had found herself jerking through the water like the frogs she'd often watched in the millpond at home. She was so proud of her achievement that she ran up and down the footpath waving her arms and shouting: 'Bim! Bim! I can swim!' And Gran, catching her with a towel and rubbing her wet hair remarked, 'You'll never sink, Hannah, that's for sure. Your high spirits will keep you afloat if nothing else does.'

Hannah and Marge placed stones on top of their clothes. Then they walked gingerly into the cool water uttering little cries of shock and pleasure, and soon they were both plunging about making the hollows and rocks echo with their shouts.

Their voices attracted the attention of a group of teenage boys walking across the bridge. They stopped to watch Hannah's hair streaming out over her white shoulders as she performed her best breaststroke.

'Hey! Look at the mermaids!' shouted one. 'Roll over, Mermaid and let's have a look at your boobs!' shouted another.

Hannah couldn't hear their words because of the crashing of the waterfall behind her; but she could see their faces laughing and their fingers pointing. When two of them left the bridge to run down along the bank she was afraid they might seize her clothes and run off with them. So she scrambled out as quickly as she could and picked up a stone. Giggling, the boys halted. They hesitated, glanced sideways at each other, and then one of them picked up a handful of gravel which he threw at Marge, who stood waist high in the water laughing at them.

Hannah lifted her stone. 'Clear off, you buggers!' she shouted. As soon as she took a step towards them they fled, laughing. Marge watching from the safety of the water thought: She's a tough little so-and-so. She don't need all that care and protection. I reckon she can look after herself. And just fancy! She might one day own that property in Mudcott. . . .

'Where's this home your auntie's at, Hannah?' asked Marge when they were drying themselves.

'It's called Meadowsweet.'

'Sounds all right. Shall us go and visit her one day?'

'That 'ud be nice,' agreed Hannah. 'But it's a long way. Grovesend on the Bristol Channel.'

'It must be lonely for her, Hannah. I know how they feels in places like that.'

Hannah nodded. 'I do write to her sometimes.' She thought of Auntie May stamping up the garden path in her padded wellies. She used to wear thick woollen stockings on the hottest days. It made Hannah feel faint even to imagine those feet steaming away inside the wellies, but Auntie May thought the heat was good for her painful joints, Hannah remembered, as she rubbed her own toes with her towel.

SIX

Pick-yourselfers were admitted to the raspberry field by the beginning of August. Although they sometimes broke the canes and trampled on good fruit Mary tried to look the other way and be grateful because their picking relieved her of a lot of work, giving her more time for other necessary tasks such as delivering the fruit. A greengrocer who had opened shop in Upper Coldacre agreed to take four dozen punnets on a trial run. So Mary packed the punnets into the boot of her Mini one Friday morning; and Hannah went with her for the ride. As they drew up to the shop Mary realised it was on the site of the old Copper Kettle. 'This used to be a teashop. I came here once with a young man,' she confided to Hannah as they left.

'You did? What was his name?'

'Guess! I'll tell you when you guess right.'

Hannah suggested Tom, Gerry, Kevin, Barry, but for some reason David eluded her. 'What happened to him?' she asked.

'Oh! We were very young at the time. He went away from Frenester and I lost track of him.'

Mary moved the car down the main street to St Colm's church, where she parked again.

'There's a very interesting tomb here,' she said. 'And quite a story attached to it too.' She didn't tell Hannah that she had other reasons for stopping there. When Wetherley the tailor had died earlier that year Mary heard that his widow was selling the business and buying a cottage near the church in Upper Coldacre. She looked about till she caught sight of a terrace of stone cottages: Colm's Walk. The door of one of them was open, and a pile of builder's rubble occupied the front lawn. Mrs Wetherley was having alterations made. Máry intended visiting her one day to offer her condolences, but to Hannah she said: 'Did you ever hear about the bold bad baron Bruno of Coldacre who kidnapped a local girl? She was known as Blanche the Fair. He's buried here in the wall of the church.'

It was a small, mainly Norman building with thick walls. The wool wealth of the Cotswolds in the Middle Ages had not spilled over to Upper Coldacre to decorate St Colm's church, but it had its own austere beauty of quiet spaces between high stone columns and plain strong arches. In the north wall she found Bruno's tomb with the effigy of half a knight, his head and armour sliced so that only a hand, with the tip of its forefinger chipped off, and one foot resting on the hind-half of a dog were visible.

'Why is he cut in half?' asked Hannah, her voice echoing in the empty nave.

'He sold his soul to the Devil in exchange for the power to bewitch people,' Mary explained. 'Especially fair young damsels, both high born and of low degree. They probably swooned when he smiled at them.'

'Go on!' said Hannah.

'He must have had what we call charisma. He was a sort of medieval film star.'

Bruno the Bold, known as Blinkenstern owing to the effect his bright eye had on all who fell under his gaze, was guilty not only of snapping up young girls but also of carrying off other people's property, so he was an outlaw and an enemy of the Church. He couldn't be burned at the stake for sorcery, however, because he was after all a man, and rather a powerful one too, since he commanded his own private army. It was really only poor feeble-minded females possessed by the Serpent who needed to have the evil of witchcraft scorched out of them. So for many years he operated with his own private army, a medieval Mafia in the district of Frenester, and although he was a thorn in ecclesiastical flesh and a terror to local matrons and their daughters he got away with it, hiding out in the oak forests which then still covered Severnvale. But at last old age and sickness overtook him, and he knew the time had come to confess his sins. Not only did he make the sign of the Cross over his breast, thus dismissing the Devil within, but he threw a bag of gold into his confessor's hand, demanding with his last breath that a mass be said daily in perpetuity for his soul. He could not have foreseen that a day would come when the celebration of mass would be forbidden by law and his investment would prove to be a complete waste of cash. The clerics after much argument decided to bury him in the wall of the church, where he was neither fully admitted nor entirely cast out. 'It was a fair compromise for the times,' said Mary.

'Serve him right,' said Hannah shortly. 'That Bruno sounds a bit like my dad – only *he* wasn't much cop for young damsels. I hope his joints ache with being cramped up in half a coffin all those years!' she added spitefully.

'My joints will be aching next week when I begin cutting down the old raspberry canes to make room for the new ones,' said Mary.

'You never do it all by yourself, do you?' Hannah was dismayed by the prospect of so much stooping and cutting and carrying away of canes.

'Marge will give me a hand. And Mikey always helps.'

'How can the old sod manage it?'

'On his hands and knees, creeping along the rows.'

After tea they sat out on the lawn in the shade of the elms. One stood dead and leafless, some were already shedding their leaves, but the rest, though infected with disease, still

110

held enough foliage to throw long evening shadows across the grass. Colly sat with his newspaper, Hannah with her copy of *Lord of the Flies* from the public library open on her lap, and Mary with an embroidery frame, stitching meticulously a tapestry design for the seat of one of the dining-room chairs. Hannah watching her asked at last: 'What's that dog doing?'

'It's a heraldic wolfhound,' said Mary. The beast stood with one paw on a shield, his head turned back to face his upturned tail.

Colly laughed suddenly. 'It's the Chicon crest,' he explained. For centuries we've been trying to make both ends meet.' This amused Hannah, and she laughed too. Perhaps it was her laughter at his joke, or perhaps it was simply the warm summer evening which put him in a good humour. At sunset, when it became too chilly to sit outside, he asked her if she would like to learn to play chess.

'OK!' was her response.

He opened the door of his study and invited her to step inside. She stood for a moment on the threshold in awe staring around at the walls lined with shelf upon shelf of books.

'Cor!' she breathed. 'So many books – !'

She picked up a leather-bound volume from his desk and the book fell open where his bookmark lay. 'It's Latin, isn't it? What does it say?'

He took the book from her and translated a passage describing how to plant a garden for bees with wild thyme, savory and violets growing in a damp place, with a stream running close by. 'It's from Virgil's *Georgics*,' he said, adding, 'The garden must be sheltered from high winds.' He then went on to explain how when the hive began to swarm around the King the Romans used to clash cymbals together to make the bees clump and settle.

'My auntie used to clang a bell,' said Hannah. 'And it wasn't a king you know; it was a queen which led the flyaway swarm.'

Colly laughed. 'Well, yes,' he admitted. 'The Romans weren't great feminists. And they hadn't read Fabre, who described the social structure of the hive. They were nineteen centuries before his time.'

They sat down at a small table near the window, and Colly emptied a box of red and white chessmen over the board. It made Mary smile to see all the books, silent referees, looking down upon the players so unevenly matched, as Colly slowly taught Hannah the rules of the game. Now and again Hannah glanced up at the shelves as if daring the dead authors in their leather-bound tomes to speak.

One wall was devoted to Greek and Latin classics and to works in French. Voltaire, Corneille and Racine, Montaigne and Pascal stood beside French historians and the novels of Victor Hugo and Zola, and even Rousseau, whom Colly referred to as a Johnny-come-lately with his head full of half-baked dangerous ideas, had his own parking space. On the opposite wall books in English were classified under appropriate headings; philosophy, history, biography, poetry and fiction. Apart from spy novels which he sometimes read for light entertainment Colly had no interest in contemporary fiction; but the nineteenth-century novels he'd read in childhood and adolescence were allowed houseroom. Dickens, whom he condemned as mawkish at times, stood there, there were a couple of Thackeray's novels, and one, *Middlemarch*, by George Eliot; but Trollope, whose warm-hearted treatment of human foibles he criticised as 'pandering to his public', was not represented. Conrad stood there in force, and most of Hardy, towards whom Colly felt ambivalently but who fascinated him. The great Russian novels of the last century stood with the French. A few modern historians had crept into the room. Churchill's *Second World War* and Shirer's *Rise and Fall of the Third Reich* were present, and Elizabeth's Longford's *Wellington* had been admitted. Her style pleased him and her wit made him smile as he turned the pages; and of course he revered the Iron Duke.

Each book, Mary knew, had its proper place. It annoyed Colly greatly if a borrowed book was replaced wrongly. She remembered wryly that time in her teens when she had borrowed Aubrey's *Brief Lives* in order to find out where exactly Raleigh had smoked that first pipe of tobacco and had been doused with a bucket of water by a maidservant who thought he was on fire. She replaced the book in a space vacated by a life of Richard III Colly was reading, so her mistake was quickly discovered. 'If Aubrey had got in Richard III's way,' he said, glaring at her over the tops of his bifocals, 'his lives would have been even more severely curtailed.'

'All those books . . .' said Hannah, gazing at the shelves and carelessly letting Colly take her knight. 'Have you read them all?'

'Quite a lot of them. Yes. Of course I don't remember all I've read exactly: but I do know where to find what I want to read, or reread. Reading leaves an overall impression on the memory, not always an exact photograph. But if the books are near you you can always refer to them for the quotation needed.'

After that first initiation into the mysteries of chess Hannah was frequently invited into the study for a game. It wasn't long before she was an enthusiastic player. Whenever she took one of Colly's pawns she used to rock herself to and fro with pleasure, and if she managed to capture any piece of greater value she squealed with triumph. Colly remarked to Mary that Hannah was a good deal more intelligent that he had been led to suppose. 'A natural aptitude for chess,' he said. 'Really quite quick thinking. Remarkably logical for a girl. And there's male chauvinism for you!' he added with a rare inward glance at himself.

Potato-picking was late that year. It had rained so much during October that it was impossible to clear the big field till early November, when it was already quite cold. The work began on a Friday, when the weather forecast was promising. Colly did not take part but left Tom to supervise the team. Tom drove the tractor, two casual labourers were hired by the day, and Marjorie, dressed in dungarees and boots, came to lend a hand. On Saturday Hannah, throwing aside her school uniform in favour of jeans, a pullover and wellies, joined them. It was back-breaking work, stooping to pick potatoes as they lay mixed with lumps of dirt and chits of stone in the grooves dug out by the spinner, and collecting them into baskets to be loaded on to a cart; but Hannah enjoyed it. She liked the company of men, too, and it wasn't long before she was exchanging banter of a kind that some folks might condemn as sexual harassment, but which she obviously found amusing. She even broke into song after she had tipped a load into the cart and was strolling back along the row swinging her empty basket. She sang in a strong challenging voice:

'Hand me down my old banjo.
Hand me down my old banjo.
Oh hand me down my old banjo,
Get out of my way and watch me go
For all my sins are taken away!'

One of the labourers asked her as she passed him, 'Where be goin' then, Hannah?' Tom, who had just switched off the engine and jumped jauntily to the ground, answered for her: 'Right to the top of the charts, I shouldn't wonder.'

Mary came to the field with Thermos flasks and poured tea into mugs, which steamed in the cold air as the workers standing round the tractor drank slowly, blowing away the steam.

'These spuds have pink skins,' Hannah remarked, sipping thoughtfully. 'I never seen pink spuds before.'

'They're Desirée,' one of the casuals explained. 'Desirée do always have pink skins.' The other man laughed and said: 'I reckon they be blushing 'cos your 'ands is stroking them, my dear!'

'Get off, will you?' Hannah said, with what she thought was withering contempt; but Mary could see she was not at all put out. A few coarser suggestions were then made as to what Hannah could do to make them blush even pinker, which Mary pretended not to hear. As she turned away she couldn't help reflecting that Hannah seemed to have become one of the boys a good deal more easily than she ever could.

That evening over supper Hannah was too tired to talk much. The cold air and exercise had whipped up the colour in her cheeks making them glow, making her luxuriant black hair, which fell untidily around her face, seem glossier than ever. In the relaxation and contentment of her young body she was radiantly pretty. Mary caught her father glancing more than once across the table at Hannah, with almost a shock of surprise.

'No chess tonight,' said Hannah as soon as she finished her meal. 'I'm too sleepy. I'm going up to have a bath.' Mary took her embroidery into the study where Colly sat staring at the fire, his newspaper spread out over his knees unread.

'Conrad writes somewhere that beauty in women is a kind of genius,' he said. He spoke in an uncharacteristically dreamy way.

Mary felt a sharp pang of anxiety. Talk of beauty in women always made her feel uneasy. It reminded her of her beautiful but false mother, and what she believed to be her own plainness. And she knew from past experience that any such reference by Colly was sometimes the prelude to an unpleasant harangue about Flora's wickedness.

'Does he?' she asked.

'I think it's in the *Outcast of the Islands*. That's the one where the beautiful Malay girl utterly destroys the trader.'

Mary folded her needlework quietly. 'I'm going to bed,' she said. 'I'm tired too.'

'Yes, yes, you go to bed, my dear. Is Tom pleased with the crop?'

'So far, yes. He thinks it will be good. Surprisingly, no blight in spite of all the rain we've had.'

'Well, there's still a lot to be done,' he said, trying to keep her with him a little longer. 'Any blight will become obvious in the sorting.'

Cartloads of potatoes dumped in the barn would have to be passed over the mechanical riddler, through which small ones fell along with chits, but any damaged or diseased had to be picked out by hand before the rest were dropped into sacks. There were coarse hessian sacks for hundredweights to be sold to wholesalers, and thick layered paper bags for half-hundredweights to be sold on the premises.

'It'll take a bit of time,' said Mary. 'Let's hope we'll have a few days free of frost.'

She climbed the stairs slowly. She lay in her bath for a longer time than usual, letting the hot water ease her aching muscles. When she sat down at her dressing-table and slowly brushed her hair she stared at her reflection in the mirror. What Colly had said about the beauty of women disturbed her peace of mind. It made her think of Flora, the lovely frivolous mother who had deserted her. She wondered where was Flora now?

Mary was not at all unhappy at school at first. She was an only child who longed for friends, so she revelled in the company of other little girls. She made friends easily, partly because she was good-tempered and adaptable, partly because of the tales she could tell about Gatt's Rise and all the animals on the farm, especially as she had some photos of her Shetland pony, Belle, to show them. Every week she received a flimsy little airmail letter from Daddy in Egypt, and she was proud to show it off to her new friends. Sometimes Mummy came in a car to take her out on Saturdays, once for a whole weekend.

Mummy always came in the same car, an open Humber

the colour of polished mud, driven by the same man, who was called Sandy owing to the colour of his hair and small moustache. They were always laughing and larking about. As soon as they got back to the house, her sister Vi's house, Mummy threw her coat and hat and handbag over the back of the sofa in the sitting-room and rushed to the upright piano. She pulled out the piano stool and sat down; she lit a cigarette and held it between her lips. The smoke made her eyes blink, and ash fell steadily over the keys as she played abrupt neat snatches of jazz, humming in a low voice made husky by chain-smoking. Sandy joined her to sing in his light tenor: ' "Life is just a bowl of cherries!" ' With one hand he beat out the rhythm on the top of the piano while the other dropped cigarette ash on the carpet at his feet.

' "Smoke gets in your eyes..." ' he warbled. Mary thought his voice was sweet and tender. Hearing it was like being gently stroked. Then he suddenly turned and seized her and danced her across the room till she overbalanced and fell on the sofa, laughing. 'Not in mine!' she cried. 'I'm not tall enough!' She meant: to get your smoke in my eyes.

It was Vi who took Mary upstairs and showed her where she was to sleep (not with her mother, but alone in the attic on a camp-bed), who gave her tea, and explained things.

'Flora's left Gatt's Rise, you know. It's full of evacuee kids now, and your father has put a manager in charge of the farm. So that's why your mother is staying here with me. Flora and Sandy have joined a professional concert party. They have to travel about the country to various camps, giving shows to entertain the troops.' This was interesting information for Mary to file in her portfolio of stories to tell the other girls at school.

When she went back to the sitting-room, Mummy was bending over a pile of black records and Sandy was winding up the gramophone. 'Here's an old favourite!' Flora cried; and as the record spun they performed a quick foxtrot to the music, singing as they danced: ' "Happy feet!" ' over and over again: ' "Happy feet!" '

When they took Mary back to school Sandy didn't go inside. He sat in the open car smoking and thinking about the child, for whom he felt some affection tinged with pity: a thin, quiet, lonely little girl with fair hair cut in a long bob and a long fringe above frank blue eyes. She was shy, but not afraid. An aura of innocence surrounded her, a certain goodness, which Sandy knew you didn't often come across, shone from her. You knew she wasn't the sort who would manipulate you for her own purposes, she would never harm you, would always try to take the best, the reasonable course. He felt rather guilty too, 'in a fit of the futures' as he later told Flora, that he was carrying off Flora for himself, because he knew that without a mother, with no brothers or sisters to protect her, Mary would be overcome by her father's powerful personality, imprisoned, possibly swallowed up entirely by him. Sandy sighed. He supposed Flora knew what she was doing. . . . Perhaps during adolescence Mary might escape? In any case it was not really his affair. At least the child must have made friends at school. . . .

Flora seemed to be taking a long time over her goodbyes, so he sounded the horn. Immediately a group of older girls rushed to the big window in the hall to stare at the car and at him. He was wearing a flat tweed cap, but they caught a glimpse of his moustache and could see his broad tweed-covered shoulders behind the wheel. He was dressed in civvies, but that was no disgrace when you knew who he was. Mary, still clinging to her mother, who was talking to the matron, heard the girls' excited voices: 'I say, it's – must be – Sandy Boston! You know – that singer on the wireless. Isn't he gorgeous? He's that crooner with the Big Band. . . .' And Mary relished the little bit of stardust that his celebrity showered over her.

Flora began to rush about the hall, picking up her hand-bag, hunting for cigarettes and squeaking out messages of love and farewell to everybody present, leaving lipstick kisses on Mary's cheeks before she ran out of the front door. The watchers at the window heard the car burst into life, and saw Sandy Boston grinning as he took off his cap and waved it at them. He pushed his foot down on the accelerator, and the wheels of the Humber skidded as it disappeared up the school drive.

It was the last time Mary saw them together. She always remembered them as cartoon figures on a flickering cinema screen, jumping, jigging and singing, as ash fell uninterruptedly from their fingers.

When the bad news came it was not Mummy who comforted her. Mummy was on tour with ENSA, playing the piano for Sandy Boston while he crooned. It was Auntie Vi, with Matron and the headmistress who told Mary her father had been seriously wounded in the battle of El Alamein, who put their arms round her and assured her that he was safe in hospital, that he would soon be cured, and when he was well enough he would come back home to see her. All the girls in her class were very kind to her because her father was a wounded hero, covered with medals and glory, and Beryl Plympton, whose mother saved her sugar ration to make sweets for Beryl, gave Mary some of her lovely home-made fudge.

It was more than a year before Daddy could come to visit her. All that time he was undergoing operations in hospitals and recuperating, first in Egypt, then in England. He used to write telling her of his progress, with gossip about the nurses, and some of the funny things the other patients said, cheerful letters asking her what she was learning and reading, and suggesting books that might interest her. Flora also wrote throughout Mary's school years, mostly on postcards with views of seaside places. Sometimes these were funny and a bit rude too, which made the other girls laugh when they were passed round from hand to hand; but Flora didn't visit her. She was too busy, and always away travelling, and they had no petrol coupons left over to spare for the long journey, and the nearest railway station was so far from the school, and trains so unreliable in wartime anyway. . . . It was Vi who visited her and picked her up for the holidays all the time Daddy was away.

Mary was terribly excited on that Saturday afternoon when Daddy came at last. She stood on the drive in front of the school waiting for his car to arrive. When it did she rushed forward eagerly; but her heart sank when he took so long to open the door, and longer still to ease his body out, to stand up slowly and stiffly and hobble towards her with the aid of two sticks. He embraced her calling her his little girlfriend, and thanking her for all the sweet letters she'd written to him while he was in hospital. He drove her to a big red-plush hotel where he was staying for the weekend, and gave her a splendid tea in front of a great open wood-burning fire. He made her feel very warm and comfortable, and compassionate towards him because of his injuries. She told him how she spent the holidays either with Vi, or sometimes with Auntie Dot in a country house in Dorset. 'Dot's left her London house for the duration, you see,' she said. He did not tell her his bad news till Sunday morning.

They were walking along a hedge beside a ploughed field where wheat was growing through the furrows. He insisted on going for a walk in spite of his lameness. 'Both legs broken in that blow-up,' he explained. 'Right one at the hip, left one below the knee. But they're mending now.' It was a cold March day with a biting wind, but primroses were peeping out here and there from the bottom of the hedge.

'Quite a lot of celandines too,' said Mary. She knew the names of lots of wildflowers, which she collected, pressed and dried, and fixed into an exercise book. She was shivering, but she couldn't walk fast to keep warm because he was crawling along so slowly behind her.

He stopped suddenly, and balancing himself on his sticks

he said, 'I'll have to tell you, Mary. Your mother has deserted us. She's run off with another man. Bolted.'

She turned back to stare at him. In her mind's eye she saw a terrified mare bolting through a stable door left carelessly open, her eyes staring, nostrils snorting, long tail streaming out behind her with the speed of her escape. Mary didn't ask which man; she already knew.

'My poor little girl,' he said, when he saw the tears running down her cheeks. He hobbled up to her and put his arms hesitantly round her. 'We'll have to look after each other now, won't we?'

Mary could only nod wordlessly and let the tears fall; but that night in the dormitory she made a vow to herself that never, never, whatever happened, would she desert him as Flora had. She also decided that since she was now thirteen, and was going to have to look after him, she was not a child any more, so she would stop calling him Daddy. It must have been about this time that his new name of Colly came into use.

One of the first changes he made at Gatt's Rise when the war was over was to get rid of Flora's piano. Mary watched forlornly as four men loaded it into a van and drove it away to be sold in Tellermann's auction rooms in Swinester. 'Why is the piano going away?' she asked. But his only explanation was: 'All that interminable jazz. . . .' He was systematically clearing the house of all Flora's belongings.

As time passed he dropped little bits of poisoned information into Mary's ears. 'Flora was a flirt,' he said. 'I made the mistake of thinking it was just youthful high spirits in her, but she didn't grow out of it. She was always frivolous. *Flora was a light woman.*'

Was that such a terrible crime? In her imagination Mary saw a ball of thistledown torn from its flowerhead and scattered by a rough wind, so prettily floating, a thing of beauty, but a wrecker when seeded. Flora was like thistles: she had spoiled a good pasture. There was so much anger and contempt for her in Colly's voice that Mary thought there could be no hope for her anywhere on earth. 'And that man Sandy What's-his-name, he's just a jumped-up jack-in-office – nothing but a clerk in some insurance company who's suddenly found he's got a voice. A *crooner*, if you please! In some band or other. He's a bounder really.' Colly explained that he would undoubtedly grab and squander all Flora's own money, but not one penny of his, Colly's, would he get his hands on.

The past, in Colly's telling of it, was bad and bitter. 'Flora was a Bright Young Thing in the Twenties, you know. And a thing of beauty too. But not a joy for long – not in my eyes. So you needn't worry about not being pretty like her.' Then seeming to realise it might be hurtful to tell a girl, however young she was, that she was no beauty, he added: 'You needn't worry about that, because I'll always love you.'

Did that mean other people wouldn't? Mary wondered. As time passed, beauty, the idea of it, became somehow dangerous.

'Brittle . . . and a bit silly too, Flora was,' he said. 'And predictable. That's when love ends: when you know exactly what the loved one's going to say.'

After Mary left school Flora stopped sending her postcards, but for some years more she used to send a card at Christmas with her love scrawled in her own handwriting and kisses added. There was never any address. The envelope was always typewritten and the postmark somewhere near London, Putney, or Potters Bar; and once a covering letter from a solicitor was enclosed, simply saying she had asked him to send it. These missives revealed very little about her life, but they were precious to Mary. She hid them in a biscuit tin under her bed, and kept them secret from Colly, as Flora obviously intended her to do. Then for many years Mary heard nothing from her. Gradually the painful feelings surrounding her memory receded and were submerged in the muffled and shadowy, the subaqueous movements of past things wishfully forgotten. Flora became part of history. Like some twentieth-century mutation of Bruno the Bold, Sandy Boston had carried her off in his Humber. That they had once been happy together during the war Mary remembered; but what had happened to them since she did not know.

SEVEN

Mary hoped, as she went to the garage for her car that
Thursday before Christmas, that the petty session wouldn't
take all day. The accused would all be juveniles she knew,
and as she started up the engine and backed out into the
yard she thought about them: sad, frightened little boys,
not criminals at all, mostly rather unintelligent, many from
disorderly homes in which it was difficult for them to discern any consistent pattern of behaviour to imitate, or even
a daily routine to follow. Apart from one or two exceptions
they were certainly not rebellious in court. It was a good
thing, she considered, that they were frightened. There was
nothing like a good fright to deter them from committing
another offence. And it was, she reminded herself, an
encouraging fact that the great majority of juvenile
offenders brought before the courts for the first time did
not appear again. Gregory Barton would argue that the
little devils had simply learned how to evade being caught;
but Mary thought he credited them with greater cleverness
than they possessed.

She considered the value of the short, sharp shock. This
of course was what a first appearance in court was, provided it was administered fairly soon after the boy was
caught, so that he was not given time to forget what wicked
action of his had brought him there. In all the arguments

being bandied about as to the value of the short, sharp shock, people seemed to be unaware of the importance of the timing of it. What good was there in sending to a detention centre for his shock a teenager who was already a hardened criminal? The shock should be administered before he had settled to the habit of crime. Unfortunately it was usually meted out too late and boys left detention centres so often no better than when they went in.

Just such a youth was Wayne Williams, a truculent teenager who now stood before the bench, refusing to take the oath because he didn't believe in God or the Bible. Gregory Barton, greatly irritated, had to present him with an alternative form of words before he could be questioned about the burning down of a barn and the destruction of a farmer's hay.

The defendant flicked his lank, greasy hair out of his eyes as he took the printed card and read falteringly: 'I promise to tell the truth, the whole truth, and nothing but it – the truth, I mean.' Mary watched his eyes shifting wildly about the room, his thin, too mobile features and jerky gestures as he replaced the card on the shelf of the dock, and asked herself: how could he fulfil that promise? How could he, or indeed anybody, know the whole truth of any deed, even if, and perhaps especially if, he had done it himself? And how, through his own turbulent feelings and with his limited vocabulary, tell it? How could he filter out the factual grit from the turbid waters (greed, rage, desire for the solace of love or pleasures long denied, the conflict between his will to power and the necessity to bow his head in order to survive) in which it was dissolved? The best he could produce would be something like a tabloid headline: the fact distorted by a cracked mirror into a freak image of the truth.

Wayne Williams was guilty of the offence. He had a past record of thieving and acts of destructive vandalism. He had been given warnings, hours of Saturday attendance at an attendance centre, probation, and now all that was left to the magistrates was to sentence him to a detention centre. It was too late, Mary knew, and probably the other magistrates did too. Nobody believed he would be rehabilitated. All they were doing was rendering him harmless to the public for a few months. Mary sighed. She supposed he would progress to the adult court in future years to receive longer and longer prison sentences as he settled down into the hard core of recidivists who cause most of the trouble to keepers of the law.

A last-minute case was added to the list, not a juvenile but an old man, a tramp in tattered clothing with long, matted hair and beard and a bloodstained bruise on his forehead, one Cornelius Jones. Last night, when he had been in a state unfit even to tramp, he was locked up in the police station. Now he stood before the magistrates accused of drunk and disorderly behaviour in a public place, of causing damage to a window of the police station by throwing a brick through it, of resisting arrest, and of inflicting assault and bodily harm on a police constable while resisting arrest. However aggressive he might have been last night his head was bloody now, but certainly not unbowed, as he cringed before them. Mary couldn't help wondering if that lump on his forehead was due to his hitting a hard object in a drunken staggering or from encountering a hard truncheon in the struggle. A young policeman brought as evidence to the court a large purple bloomer over one eye; and the defendant agreed that he had inflicted it.

The chairman turned to Mary. 'We don't need to retire over this one, do we? We all know Cornelius.' Then he raised his voice to pronounce sentence: 'Cornelius Jones, you will be sent to prison for one month.'

To Mary's surprise the man bowed low and ceremoniously. 'Thank you, your Honour, thank you. I am deeply grateful,' he said. And as he strode jauntily from the courtroom in the company of the policeman he had injured he called out cheerfully: 'And a Merry Christmas to one and all!'

As the courtroom emptied Gregory Barton turned towards the bench, and laughing a little said, 'Well, I'm glad we were able to do poor old Cornelius a good turn. We've given him food and shelter for the worst weeks of the winter.' Seeing Mary's astonished expression he explained: 'He does the same thing every year at about this time, you know. It's his way of coming in out of the cold for the festive season.'

Turner and Dunster laughed. 'We have to temper justice with mercy, especially at this season of goodwill,' Dunster said.

They separated, wishing each other Happy Christmases. Mary found her car, and picking a pot of home-made marmalade out of her shopping bag, she placed it in the glove compartment before driving off to Colm's Walk in Upper Coldacre.

Mrs Wetherley was surprised but pleased to see her. She accepted the pot of marmalade with due thanks, and invited Mary to come inside. With proper dignity she also accepted Mary's rather tardy condolences on the death of her husband, along with her good wishes for a happy retirement in her new home.

'I see you've settled in very comfortably,' Mary said. 'It's nice and warm inside.'

'I just had to have central heating installed,' said Mrs Wetherley. 'Seeing as how Upper Coldacre is famous for its temperature.' She ushered her guest into the front room. 'It's years since we met. Seems funny somehow – but it's really nice seeing you.' She smiled; and through her pale and crinkled face her former beauty suddenly shone.

Near the fire a majestic feline eunuch, inscrutable as an antique Egyptian deity, sat on the small tea table Mary remembered.

'Get down, you bad cat,' said Mrs Wetherley. The cat took absolutely no notice of this command, but bestowed on Mary a very haughty stare before shutting his eyes as if he didn't like the look of her.

'That cat's a snob,' said Mary.

'Do you hear that, Nemo?' Mrs Wetherley gave Nemo a sharp shove off the table. A silence fell. 'And how's that dog of yours with the big tail?'

'Alas, poor Buzzby! He's dead of course. We buried him under the elms at home. No, I haven't got another dog. Tom keeps the Welsh collie in the cottage. He's very much a farm worker, that dog.'

'You'll have a cup of tea, Miss Chicon? I'll put the kettle on.'

While she was out of the room Mary examined the small silver cups on the mantelpiece, and read the inscriptions: David Sibelius Wetherley High Jump 1949, David Sibelius Wetherley 100 yards Sprint 1950. On a side table covered with a lace runner were framed photographs of David in school uniform, David a young man as she remembered him, another young man very like, but not exactly him, and another which she stared at a long time of David with a young woman in a white dress and bridal veil. Of course she'd heard years ago that David was married, so why did this photo chill her with dismay? She scrutinised too greedily the bride's face. Pretty, yes, she had to admit. It was an old black-and-white photo so it was impossible to be sure how dark her hair was under the white lace, but it seemed curly. Mary was caught holding the frame when Mrs Wetherley entered with a tray.

'You knew David was married?'

'Yes, I did hear that.'

'That's David's son.' Mrs Wetherley jerked her head backwards at the photographs as she placed the tray on the table by the fire. 'William's eighteen now. He's taking his A levels and hopes to go to Oxford next year.'

'Like his father?'

'David didn't go to Oxford. He went to Birmingham. He studied law.'

128

Mary nodded. 'So he's a solicitor now?'

'Yes. He's done well. It's a good thing he didn't go into the tailoring business, though his father wanted him to. There's no future in it these days.' There was a short silence as she poured tea. 'William's going to study maths and physics at university. They say he's very clever – though where he got all that science from beats me.' She paused and glanced up at Mary. 'Milk? Must be his mother, I suppose. She's a science teacher.' Another short silence. 'Did you know this cottage once belonged to my great-grandfather?'

'No. But that's very interesting. And rather romantic too.'

'Yes. He was a skilled weaver in the days when a lot of weaving round here was done on looms in the front rooms of cottages. So I dare say his loom was in here then, where I'm sitting now.'

'Is that why you bought the cottage?'

'In a way, yes. He was a Chartist, you know. People nowadays don't seem to have heard of Chartists. They've been forgotten, along with all they did for workers' rights – and for getting the vote too, of course. He was for rights, but not, he always said, for machine breaking. But when the trouble came over the new, more productive machines, and weavers were laid off work, a lot of hungry men got angry. And after that he couldn't get work round here at all. So he moved to Somerset, which is where I was living when my mother died, and my aunt – who was housekeeper to Lady Abersyllt up at the Grange – took me on and trained me, first as tweeny, then as parlour maid.'

She stopped her flow of history to lift the teapot.

'More tea, Miss Chicon?'

Old age and widowhood seem to have made her talkative, Mary thought as she proffered her cup.

'Lady Abersyllt gave me this tea-set as a wedding present. I was but twelve when I first went there.'

Mary looked closely at her cup. It was the same china that Buzzby's tail had swept to the floor, but fortunately did not break, that afternoon in the tailor's bow-windowed parlour in Frenester High Street twenty-five years ago. 'Were you happy up there?' she asked.

'I suppose it was a happy time. . . . But you forget things, don't you? I used to do a lot of reading aloud to my aunt in the housekeeper's room in the evenings after work. Mad on books I was – and my aunt too. We loved reading. We did look forward to those evenings, I remember.' She raised her eyes and gazed over Mary's head towards another place and another time. 'When Lady Abersyllt discovered that I liked reading she used to let me borrow books from the library there. She was very kind to me, Lady Abersyllt.'

Nemo pushed his noble head between her knees, and she stooped to tickle his ears.

'She had a funny way of talking too. "Rachel," she used to say. "You have a devouring mental curiosity; and if we don't feed it we'll come to grief." ' A bubble of laughter broke through and spread across Rachel's wrinkles. 'That's why she lent me books: to stop me from coming to grief. Though of course even books can't always save you from that.' A faint shadow of sadness passed over her face.

Nemo jumped up into his mistress's lap, spilling her tea.

'Bad cat!' She spoke indulgently, and did not remove him. 'You wouldn't believe it, but there were ten servants up at the Grange then. They've gone the way of all flesh, and Lady Abersyllt too. And the house sold to a banker from London I hear. "The old order changeth, yielding place to new. And God fulfils himself in many ways," as Tennyson wrote.'

'Has your grandson seen your new home?' asked Mary.

'I don't see much of them,' she replied. Again that faint shadow of mourning passed briefly over Rachel's calm features. 'I shall be alone for Christmas. But perhaps when the lad's at college I shall see more of him.' Mary didn't ask if by 'him' she meant her son or her grandson.

When Mary rose and began wishing her hostess a happy Christmas Mrs Wetherley accompanied her to the door; but she kept her hand on the latch for some time as if unwilling to let her visitor go.

'I've often wished,' she said hesitantly, 'that you and David . . . that things might have gone differently. But then, of course, I knew it could never be.' Mary said nothing. 'Will you come again, Miss Chicon? It's been so nice seeing you.'

'I will if you call me Mary.'

'Call me Rachel then, Miss Chicon. And please convey my seasonal felicitations to the Colonel.'

Seasonal felicitations? Mary couldn't help smiling as she stepped down the garden path towards her Mini. Lady Abersyllt's musty old library books up at the Grange had undoubtedly shaped Rachel's turn of phrase.

'Brigadier Flower has invited us both up to the Manor for Christmas dinner,' Colly announced, and seeing Mary's expression of dismay quickly added: 'The food's quite good now, you know – now that the Brig has taken over control of the kitchen himself.'

'Well, that's something. It couldn't have been worse.'

'No more of Fading's execrable messes now,' he assured her. 'By a judicious sprinkling of herbs, a careful skimming off of fat, and the dolloping in of good red wine he has lifted those dishes from the subordinate class of stew into the exalted status of casserole. And it will save you work,' he added as an afterthought.

'OK,' agreed Mary, remembering that Hannah had been invited by Marjorie and Tom to eat with them at the cottage on Christmas Day, and calculating quickly that the turkey she'd ordered could be put in the deep freeze, and the Christmas pudding she'd made would keep indefinitely. 'But how do you think poor Fading's taken his invasion of her kitchen?'

'I'm sure she's delighted to be relieved of a dreary chore. She lives only for her jungle, you know.'

It was Hannah who that year cut branches of red-berried holly to decorate the hall, and pulled streamers of ivy off the trunks of elms to twine over the banisters. It was Hannah who collected all the Christmas cards and balanced them over loops of string attached to curtain rails. All this activity made her bubble with an excited, a happy expectation of the great day to come. Among the Christmas cards was one which Mary did not give Hannah to hang on her lines. It had been addressed in a typewritten envelope; it was signed 'Flora' in a rather shaky hand, and it was enclosed in a formal letter from a solicitor. Mary read this quickly, then folding it carefully with her mother's card she placed it inside the wallet in her handbag with her keys.

For Christmas Colly had bought Mary a colour television; to Hannah he gave a cheque to be paid into her Post Office savings account. Hannah was already putting her earnings for farm work into the Post Office, though some she'd spent on Christmas presents: a tie for Tom, a bottle of perfume for Marge, a box of high-quality writing paper for Mary, and a box of chocolates for Colly. She wasn't too sure about the last. She had given it a lot of thought, but in the end decided he might eat the chocolates during their games of chess, in which case he'd have to offer her one or two, which would be nice. Mary gave Hannah a guitar. The gift took Hannah completely by surprise. She stroked the strings several times, producing a harsh discordant sound; and her beautiful eyes filled with tears. She let the instrument fall to the floor, ran suddenly to Mary, and threw her arms round her neck. Mary was moved by this display of affection, and had to blow her nose; and Colly was so acutely embarrassed he had to raise his copy of yesterday's *Times* to block the scene from view.

'I can't read music, you know,' said Hannah.

'No? But you have a good ear. There's a booklet there, too, to help you play the right accompanying chords. I'm sure you'll be able to pick out the melodies by ear.'

Hannah took the guitar to the cottage to show it off to Marge and Tom.

'They won't believe it,' she said happily. 'They'll be that

surprised!' She stuffed the parcels containing the tie and perfume into the pockets of her school mac, and carrying the guitar in its case as if it had been some holy relic she hurried away down the drive. Mary watched her go. If she had been a religious person she would have prayed then; she would have uttered a hymn of thanksgiving, her heart was so full of gratitude. The child's going to be all right, she thought. And what's more she feels for me a little of that love I have for her. For Mary it was already a happy Christmas, and a day of triumph too, because in spite of everybody's misgivings her experiment in fostering was going to be a success.

The creaking heavy hobnailed door of the old manor was opened by Fading Flower, so nicknamed by Colly years ago on account of her pepper-and-salt hair, her clothes to match, her skin the colour of ancient manuscripts, and her scarcely audible voice. Mary accepted a gin and tonic. She was thankful that booze was one thing Fading wasn't timorous about. They sat down in the vast drawing-room heated only by a small electric fire and wondered what to say to each other. The place was obviously very seldom used. Mary glanced around at pallid chintz covers on an ancient three-piece suite, and noted at one end of the room sliding glass doors leading to a conservatory. A small smooth black-and-tan dachshund sidled up to her and raised pleading eyes to her face. Absentmindedly Mary stroked his nose.

'Don't take any notice of him,' advised Fading. 'He wants food. That's all he ever thinks about. He has no soul at all!'

Mary laughed and enquired what his name was.

'He's called Mister,' said Fading. 'Though why he should be dignified with that title I can't imagine.'

In the dining-room, which was considerably warmer, Mary complimented the chef on the food and wine and her hostess on the pretty table decorations. Ten scarlet-skinned apples had been transformed into ten rotund Santa

Claus figures with the aid of walnuts as faces and cotton-wool for hair and whiskers. They stood in a ring around a glass bowl in which floated the star-pointed leaves and white flowers of Christmas roses, which in spite of their name Mary had never before seen blooming at this time of year. Mrs Brig's green fingers had achieved this small triumph. She added very little to the conversation. Her voice was in any case so soft it would have been difficult to hear it above the small sounds of forks scraping on plates and crackle of red recycled paper napkins, let alone the almost continuous booming monologue produced by the Brig and interrupted by Colly's sharp barking comments. Mary observed that the little dog was wedged between his mistress's feet, and that she surreptitiously dropped him titbits from her plate throughout the meal.

'To absent friends!' boomed the Brig, raising his glass of burgundy.

'To absent friends!' the others murmured, standing up and sipping. The Flowers thought of their son in Military Intelligence, far away in the Middle East. Mary thought of Hannah, of the letter in her handbag and her mother, and wondered what absent ghost Colly was drinking to.

The ladies left Colly and the Brig to their port and army nostalgia, and took their coffee into Fading's jungle. It was wonderfully warm. More heat must have been expended in the conservatory for the sake of her exotic plants than in the whole of the rest of the house. This was Fading's own special world. Palms and purple bougainvillaea covered the walls, tropical creepers with brilliant orange flowers cascaded from the roof, and beautiful rare orchids stood proudly on the shaded shelves below.

'Oh I say!' cried Mary. 'Orchids! How wonderful!'

Fading Brig put down her cup on a metal table, and picked up a pot out of which grew a white-faced flower with a purple centre. 'Paphiopedilum,' she said softly.

'It has a baby-face,' said Mary.

' "With purple-stainèd mouth",' whispered Fading. She

smiled as she replaced it. 'I'm quite proud of growing that. But the others, the big cymbidiums, they're much easier to grow than people think. Not difficult at all, you know. Rather provocative beauties, don't you think?'

They sat down on comfortable cane chairs.

'You heard we're going to have to fell all our elms?' asked Mary. 'It'll be a sad loss. We won't have a rookery any more either. I shall miss the rooks, though people say they're ugly birds, harbingers of death and all the rest. . . .' She thought of their reproductive clamour, the way they asserted their territorial rights to certain branch-forks for nesting, claiming partners, warning off rivals or whatever other messages their loud strident cawing broadcast.

'The elms don't suffer when they're cut down,' said Fading. 'They don't feel it. Perhaps they know deep down inside their roots that whatever else we do to nature we can't stop the spring.'

Mary looked at her in surprise. She had never heard Fading say so much.

'It's a miracle, don't you think? The spring, Keats's green felicity . . . and not so far away now that the shortest day is over.'

'Well, I don't know,' said Mary. 'I always think January and February are horrible months to get through.'

'But they'll pass. They'll pass. And then we'll see the annual miracle of green fire.'

On the drive home Mary told Colly how Fading had surprised her. 'She lives in that jungle of hers quite happily, you know. That's how she gets by. I do believe she's a poet. She has some sort of inner life.'

'I'm glad to hear it. She shows few outward signs of living.'

'I think her assumption of fading is some sort of protective camouflage.'

'You mean the Brig beats her?'

'Good heavens no!'

135

'I wouldn't put it past him. And in view of her cooking it wouldn't be surprising.'

'Don't be absurd, Colly. Poor Mrs Brig! She must be old now. And the old do fade – as you will one day.'

He shot her a baleful glance. 'I'm not old yet,' he declared. 'Not by any means. As for Fading – she looked just the same thirty years ago.' But excess of after-dinner port had reduced his firepower. He laid his head back on the neck-rest and closed his eyes.

'It's a good thing you have me to chauffeur you home,' said Mary; but she was glad he was sleepy. She would let him snooze before the fire in his study while she retired to the kitchen. She would sit down and open her bag; she would take out of her wallet that strange letter, and read it over again slowly.

EIGHT

Mary waited till Hannah had gone back to school and the felling of the elms had begun before driving down southwest to Grovesend-on-Sea. Colly had proved less difficult than she feared when she told him what she was going to do.

'Do you have to go?' he asked.

'She's very ill, Colly. She may be dying. She's asked to see me.'

'Why should you obey her summons after all these years of silence?'

'She is my mother, Colly.'

'No longer. She sacrificed that position when she deserted you.'

'It's not a matter of position. It's a blood tie.'

He walked about the study in agitation, backwards and forwards across the carpet, backwards and forwards. He stopped at the fireplace and resting his elbows on the edge of the mantelpiece he stared into the fire.

'I warn you to be careful, Mary,' he said gloomily without looking up. 'She was always selfish and manipulative. She almost certainly wants something out of you. Money, probably.'

'We don't know what she's suffered, Colly. She may have had a very sad life,' Mary argued on her mother's behalf.

'I dare say she has. That wouldn't surprise me at all; but she took her own course, and she's responsible for it. No one else.'

'She may have changed, you know,' Mary suggested. 'Time may have changed her a lot.'

'People don't change – certainly not for the better. Usually for the worse. . . .'

She went over to him and put a hand on his shoulder. 'I don't think we should regard her as dangerous,' she said. 'She's old and sick now. For all we know she may be on her deathbed. Perhaps she feels guilty, knowing her time is up. Perhaps she wants me to forgive her.'

He turned and took her in his arms, and for a few seconds held her in a powerful embrace. 'Well, just be careful my dear,' he begged her. 'And do guard against your over-tender heart.'

It was a still cold January day when Mary backed her car out of the garage and drove away. She felt no qualms of anxiety as she left the house. The tree-fellers would be busy till sunset; Colly would be occupied helping them to slash side shoots off the fallen trunks and pile the trash together with the diseased bark on to a great bonfire, while Tom worked the circular saw powered by the tractor's motor. They would cut the wood into metre-length logs and stack them neatly to dry out during the summer months. There was going to be plenty of fuel for log fires for a long time to come. When Hannah came home from school she would warm up and serve Colly the supper already cooked for them. Afterwards perhaps they would play chess.

The sight of Somerset brilliantly green even in winter lifted her spirits. She glanced at her handbag on the passenger seat to make sure the letter with the addresses she needed was still there. The letter itself was a short one, and by now she knew its contents by heart. It had an official heading: *Saddleir Beeby and Box. Solicitors*. Below this was a typed paragraph:

138

Re: Mrs Flora Boston (formerly Chicon) at present living at Meadowsweet Nursing Home, The Esplanade, Grovesend-on-Sea.

Dear Mary,

Your mother, who is a resident at the above address, is very anxious to see you. She has been very ill, and I think should be visited soon. When you have seen her will you telephone me as there are one or two matters it will be necessary to discuss? It may come as a surprise to you to learn that I am looking after her affairs. I trust that you yourself are well. I would like to add my own Christmas greetings to hers on the card enclosed.

Yours, David Wetherley.

Mary had not told Colly the name of Flora's solicitor. He had not asked for it.

Grovesend-on-Sea was a town built in the late nineteenth century to provide holidays for middle-class families from the industrial Midlands and the North. She drove through the streets of Victorian terraced houses no longer providing holidays even in summer to families which nowadays were all flying further afield to Spain and Tenerife. The apartments were occupied now by respectable elderly retired couples, and no doubt many widows too, who, remembering carefree summers in what to them must have been the warm south, decided to end their days here, hoping perhaps to recapture something of the happiness of youth. She wondered if they were disappointed. The streets in January seemed empty and desolate, the rows of look-alike houses had a forbidding aspect, their windows draped with lace or nylon net as if in an attempt to screen unseemly secrets from the inquisitive.

The esplanade was a wide front overlooking an expanse of water across which a steady wind blew in from the south-west. In all honesty you couldn't call it the sea, this great brown outlet of the Bristol Channel through which one of the highest tides in the world surged, churning the mud into the funnel of the Severn and then scouring it out twice daily.

She located a big gaunt double-fronted building with a billboard claiming to be Meadowsweet. The façade was softened by glazed verandas on either side of the door. Peering in as she cruised past she could see no occupants, but palms, doubtless in tubs, pressed themselves against the glass. She didn't stop till she'd found a suitable lodging for the night in a guesthouse advertising vacancies.

'You'll have to park your car round the back of the block,' said the landlady, Mrs Rowan, a plump rosy-cheeked woman with hair dyed a sinister unwavering black.

Mary threw her overnight bag on the bed of a first-floor room whose window faced the Channel. It was double-glazed, and the room was quiet.

'It'll soon warm up,' said Mrs Rowan, stooping to turn on a radiator. 'You can make your own hot drinks here.' She indicated a side table loaded with crockery and tiny packets of tea and instant coffee: 'I'll bring you up some fresh milk.'

'Thank you,' said Mary. She sat down at the window and unwrapped her sandwiches. She had to admit that the skyscape, though uniformly grey, was impressive. It was filled with huge clouds advancing landwards like some ominous armada with dark, tattered sails. Winds from the Atlantic had scooped up bucketfuls of water vapour which they were about to drop as rain all over the West Country. Into her mind crept the words of a sad and lovely poem written heaven knows how long ago by the ever popular Anon, but still speaking with a fresh voice across intervening centuries:

> Western wind when wilt thou blow
> The small rain down can rain?
> Christ, if my love were in my arms
> And I in my bed again!

The words had always moved her compassionate heart, and now she thought of the unknown poet. Was he a Crusader lying in the shade of a tent pitched on hostile desert sands who, sickening, dreamed of home? Or was he some sailor idling in the doldrums, sweating as he swung gently in his hammock and longed for a breeze? That poem had always called to her, though she herself had never lain in bed with a lover, and perhaps now never would. It was Flora who must have had more than her fair share of such experiences, if Colly was to be believed, and he after all had known her well.

Mary tried to picture Flora, but couldn't remember her face at all. By an effort of memory reaching out into the past she could catch pieces of flickering images: the turn of a shoulder, the flick of a wrist, a hand spilling cigarette ash. That was all. She couldn't remember the face. She examined her own mixed feelings about her mother. She couldn't truthfully admit to any feeling of love for her; but she felt no anger either, perhaps because Flora had never been cruel or angry towards her. She had simply been absent. It was the absence for which Mary cried in the school dormitory after lights out, searching the darkness above her pillow for answers which never came. Why had Flora done this to her, making her different from other girls who had proper families? Why had she run away from Colly, who was so good and kind and brave? Flora was lost to them; in a sense she had died. And now here she was unexpectedly undergoing resurrection in this dreary seaside town, in a nursing home with the unsuitable name of Meadowsweet.

No. She felt no love for Flora, nor even any pleasure in the prospect of seeing her again. All she felt was dread compounded of a complicated mixture of uncertainties: would they recognise each other? What on earth would they talk about? What would Flora expect of her? Would she be disappointed in her daughter, regard her as an unattractive awkward country bumpkin? Mary remembered

Colly saying of Flora: 'She was essentially an urban person. She hated everything to do with farming – wouldn't soil her hands. She used to have her hands manicured by a beautician, you know.'

Mary looked at her own hands, at the slightly chapped skin, and the short unvarnished nails. She stood up. She couldn't put off any longer the meeting, confrontation, revelation or whatever it was going to be. She braced herself; she was a soldier's daughter.

'Is there a phone I can use?' she asked the landlady.

There was one in the hall, where Mrs Rowan stood near enough to overhear every word Mary uttered. She turned her back on the woman, trying to exclude her, trying to control her own apprehensions as she dialled the number and heard the bell ring in his office. She wondered how much he'd changed in the intervening years, what he felt, how he looked now. She scolded herself that it was silly to feel like this, as excited as a schoolgirl over her first date; but she couldn't help it. 'Is that Saddleir, Beeby and Box? David Wetherley? Yes. It's Mary. I'm just going to see my mother now. Shall I come to your office afterwards?' She spoke in a rush, but he replied quite calmly: 'Is it really Mary? I can hardly believe it's really you.'

She was being foolish, she told herself, probably imagining things, but she thought she detected in David's young, cheerful voice an echo of her own feelings. Happiness surged through her; she couldn't stop it. 'I don't know what to say, David,' she almost sang. 'It seems so strange bumping into you again like this. It's so long since we met.'

'I think we're going to be able to pick up things as easily as if it was yesterday,' he said. 'I've thought of you so often.' He asked where she was staying. He said he would pick her up at six and take her out to dinner, where they could talk in a more relaxed atmosphere than the office could provide.

'Till 6 p.m. then.' His voice changed suddenly to one

dealing with strictly business matters, and she guessed that somebody else must have entered the room.

'Till then,' she said severely, though her mood was swinging crazily between joy at knowing they would meet and fear that she would disappoint him. At least she would have time for a bath and to change out of her travelling clothes, just as she'd hoped when she packed her elegant little for-special-occasions black dress, and the pearl necklace and earrings Aunt Dot had once given her. She put down the receiver, and walked past Mrs Rowan in the corridor without even seeing her.

Stale overheated air met her in the hall of Meadowsweet. A grey-haired nurse in a uniform of royal blue advanced towards her.

'Miss Chicon? Oh yes. We've told her you're coming; but I'd better take you to her room – just to remind her. She forgets a lot of things.'

The nurse slid aside the lift door to allow the exit of a white-haired figure pushing a Zimmer frame.

As soon as the nurse opened Flora's door a dense blast of tobacco smoke hit Mary, making her cough.

'She's not allowed to smoke in the lounge,' said the nurse, with a certain weariness, 'but we can't stop it up here.'

Mary could see hunched beside the window a little frail creature with stiffly permed hair the colour of brass, who turned and asked: 'Who is it?' The voice grated like the rusty hinges of a gate.

'It's your daughter, Flora. It's Miss Chicon.'

Mary took the proffered hand with its thin nicotine-stained fingers and nails like claws, which had certainly not been manicured professionally or otherwise for a very long time.

'Is it Mary?' Flora uttered a bright, brittle laugh like the sound of a baby's rattle. 'You've grown so much I didn't know you!'

'I'll leave you two alone then,' said the nurse. 'But please will you call at the office on your way out, Miss Chicon? I think Matron would like to see you.'

Flora made a face at the departing nurse. 'She's going to sneak on me,' she said. 'Going to tell you how naughty I am.'

Mary took a seat opposite Flora, and as she bent she caught a faint whiff of what might have been whisky on her mother's breath. 'You have a nice view of the sea here,' she said.

'I always liked the sea,' said Flora.

Mary remembered all those postcards from seaside towns. There was a short silence. Mary looked at her mother, seeing her fall into the same category as Hannah's fag-end blondes. Best to be straightforward, she thought. It would be silly to beat about the bush uttering polite nothings.

'Are you happy here?' she asked.

'Oh yes!' Flora smiled. 'All equal here in the sight of God and Matron. No special distinctions here. The communism of decay, you know. . . . Food's awful, of course; but the nurses are kind. And the other – people – nice. . . .'

Mary hesitated before her next question. 'And Sandy? I remember Sandy Boston.'

There was a pause. Flora flicked ash on the floor. 'He died. I don't know when exactly. . . . We retired to Grovesend when he stopped singing.'

'Oh I'm sorry, Flora! I am sorry.' Flora's eyes were blank as Mary stumbled on: 'I remember dancing the foxtrot with Sandy at Vi's house. You played the piano. "Smoke gets in your eyes", it was. . . .'

Flora laughed then. This time it seemed a more human sound, and her eyes came to life. 'Fancy you remembering that! Vi's dead,' she added.

'Oh, is she? I'm sorry. She was always good to me.'

Recalling the incident had somehow broken the ice

between them. They looked at each other, and smiled slowly, almost with affection.

'How's that father of yours?'

'Well. Busy cutting down trees at present.'

'That should suit him – cutting down anything that was flourishing.'

'Well, these are diseased elms, as a matter of fact,' Mary defended him.

'Are you married?'

'No.'

'I expect he wouldn't let you marry.'

Mary was silent.

'Francis was always good at discouraging. Generous with criticism but parsimonious with praise, that was his way.' She sucked on her cigarette and inhaled deeply. 'Given you Gatt's Rise instead, has he?' Her expression focused into shrewd attention.

'As a matter of fact, yes, he has.' Mary was surprised that Flora was not quite as senile as she had first appeared. There must be parts of her brain, pieces of high ground sticking out like islands in her memory, words, phrases, events which had not yet been washed away by the general flooding caused by the ageing process.

'Have you been very ill, Mother?' she asked.

'On and off,' said Flora. She paused. 'And are you happy, Mary?' For the first time Flora's voice seemed to express some feeling.

'Yes, I am. I'm perfectly all right, Mother. You don't need to worry about me. Marriage isn't everything, you know. Very lucky I am, in lots of ways.'

'That's good.' Flora nodded. Their momentary contact disappeared. Silence fell. There seemed nothing else to say. At last Flora sighed. 'Come again, will you? That would be nice.' She rose and tottered towards the door, gracefully waving her cigarette. Mary was being dismissed; but in her mother's quick, jerky movements she suddenly caught a glimpse of Flora's younger self. She thought of Colly's removal of her piano, of his words: ' . . . All that interminable jazz!' And tears filled her eyes.

'And when you next come, bring a bottle of sherry,' said Flora. 'Food's terrible here. So I can do with a drop of sherry sometimes.'

On the stairs a mixture of smells assailed Mary. The faint odour of old bodies and disinfectant hung in the air, with overtones from kitchen and lavatories filtering through the powerful perfume emitted by stephanotis flowers in a pot donated by a Christmas visitor and now resting on a table on the landing. She could see through the open door of the first-floor lounge a row of old people slumped in armchairs like effigies of their former selves. She could hear but not see the television. Jolly comedian voices and waves of happy audience reaction filled the room; but the watchers here were paying no attention to the entertainment. They sat with bowed heads, asleep or staring at their own hands folded in their laps. Mary noticed an upright piano against one wall, and between it and the window overlooking the sea two palms in pots. Palm Court Hotel, Last Stop Before the Other Side, would have been a more suitable name for this place, she thought.

As Mary entered the office Matron's majestic bosom, firmly battened down under the hatch of her navy blue uniform, rose from behind a majestic mahogany desk. She extended a soft plump hand.

'Do sit down, Miss Chicon.'

Mary meekly did as she was told. She felt nervous, like a child expecting a reprimand. She stared at the carpet at her feet; but the nightmarish intertwinings of its garish flowers only added to her anxiety. 'I thought we should have a little talk about your mother.'

Mary raised her eyes to Matron's disapproving stare. 'She has been with us now for four years,' her voice said; but her eyes added: 'And this is the first time you have been near her.'

'I had no idea where she was till quite recently,' Mary

explained. 'My parents were separated more than thirty years ago.'

'I see.' There was a pause before Matron spoke again. 'I think she's happy here with us.'

'Oh! I'm sure she is,' Mary hastened to assure her. 'She said so. She told me she was.'

'Did she? I'm glad.' Matron looked at her again more kindly, then seemed to hesitate. 'We don't want to have to move her, of course. Mr Wetherley looks after her affairs. He's been very good to her, you know. I expect he'll explain things to you.'

Mary wanted to know just how ill Flora was. What was the medical diagnosis? Was she just suffering from old age, or was there some serious illness added? Cancer?

Matron quickly reassured her about that.

'I wonder – ' Mary began. 'I don't want to . . . I mean . . . but she did ask me to bring her a bottle of sherry. Is that allowed?'

Matron frowned. 'It was strictly forbidden by the hospital, but I'm afraid it seems very difficult to stop her getting it. I think she persuades visitors, who perhaps feel sorry for her. She's been admitted here twice after being dried out. Once she fell downstairs and fractured her skull. It wasn't really safe for her to live alone any more. That's why she came here.'

'Thank you for telling me, Matron. Is there anything else I could bring her?'

Fruit was suggested. And fruit drinks.

'Cigarettes?'

'We can't stop that either; but she does keep to her own room in winter in order to smoke. In summer she spends all day smoking on the veranda.'

'Thank you,' Mary said again. 'I'll try to come again soon.'

The Stag and Antlers was an old country pub on the edge of Exmoor. It had a reputation locally for good food. David had booked a corner table near, but not too near the great open chimney with its iron basket full of logs which burned with a fierce heat. As they entered he could see that Mary was even more tense than he was himself. What she needed was a good dollop of muscle relaxant as quickly as possible. He would have to limit his own alcohol intake, since he was driving; but he hoped he'd be able to drink a little and dilute its effects by stretching them out over a long leisurely evening.

'Sherry, she said. 'Dry, please.' She raised her glass and smiled at him over the brim. 'This is what my mother wants me to supply her with at the nursing home.'

'Shall we drink to our reunion?' he suggested, smiling. He felt extraordinarily elated. As they clinked glasses and sipped they were both furtively measuring each other under cover of conversation.

'Was it a shock seeing her after all these years?'

'We didn't recognise each other at all; but yes, it was a shock. The place was a shock – all those half-dead old people. . . .'

Mary thought he had changed very little, and that little was for the better. That soft indecision of youth about the mouth had vanished, all his features were firmer. He had put on a bit of weight, but in her eyes that made him handsomer than ever. He looked what he had not at eighteen, strong.

He pushed the menu towards her, but she ignored it. He thought: her years have blessed her. All that hard physical work she has been doing, lifting bales of hay, carrying heavy buckets, tramping over muddy fields in big boots, all that hasn't coarsened her at all. It's given her some sort of inner power and resilience. He had never before thought of her as athletic, but he did now. She seemed alert and springy. Peeling off her close-fitting black dress with his imagination he could see the body underneath: slim, taut, shapely and absolutely undefiled. She was some sort of goddess, a vestal virgin, trailing like Wordsworth's childhood a cloud of glorious pastoral innocence.

'How bad is it, David? I mean, does it really matter if she drinks a little if it makes her happy? If I were there, you know, I think I'd take to drink too.'

'It's more than a little she needs to make her happy, Mary. I believe she was drinking a bottle of whisky a day before she landed up in hospital. Her liver's damaged, and I suppose there's always the danger of DTs. You'd have to talk over that side of things with her doctor next time you come. I hope there's going to be a next time?' He positively beamed at her over his glass. 'What are you going to eat? Best to stick to English cooking. We're rather far from France here on the western edge of Britain.'

'Nothing better than good English lamb,' said Mary stoutly, 'unless it's Welsh. I ought to know about lamb, since we produce it.'

He was still smiling, twisting the stem of his empty glass. 'You look wonderful, Mary. So young. Glowing really. You don't seem to have altered at all.'

She blushed. 'I expect it's the pearls,' she said modestly. 'People say pearls make the skin glow, don't they?'

'Pearls . . .' he said speculatively. 'Pearls are very romantic jewels if you consider their history. A Renaissance prince might drop a pearl into wine and let it dissolve before he offered it to a loved one or an honoured friend. And just think of the hardship and danger pearl-fishers endure when they dive deep down into tropical seas to cut the oysters from rocks on the seabed! In some places they have to carry spears to fight off sharks, you know.'

'I think mine were made by clever Mr Mikimoto's method of tickling oysters,' she said. He was tempted to say he envied Mr Mikimoto's pearls their ability to lie so comfortably on her neck, but decided it would be ill advised so early in their re-acquaintance.

The waitress stood beside the table, pad and pencil at the

ready. They ordered roast lamb with redcurrant jelly and roast potatoes and parsnips to go with it.

'And what about a little claret at the right temperature?' he suggested.

'Have you become a gourmet over the years?' Mary asked.

'I had to find my consolations.' He was still smiling as he watched her.

'I saw your son's photo,' she said. 'I thought he looked just like you.'

'William's still living with me – during the vacations, when he can't find anything more interesting to do. The young,' he added, meeting Mary's questioning gaze, 'are great roamers nowadays, always gadding about the globe.'

'Isn't it dangerous sometimes, this back-packing to the ends of the earth? There are dangerous places still, aren't there?'

'I suppose the young like danger. But the main dangers are diseases. He does get all the right jabs before travelling.'

She didn't ask about David's wife, but instead pronounced the lamb to be excellent. 'Quite as good as lamb from Gatt's Rise, I do believe.'

'Good.'

They fell silent as they enjoyed it, till Mary asked: 'How did you get mixed up with my mother in the first place?'

'It happened soon after I came to work here with Saddleir Beeby and Box.' He twisted the stem of his glass between his fingers. 'She was never divorced, as you must know. She was still Mrs Chicon when she and Sandy Boston retired here in Grovesend. They found it a very respectable place and decided it would be best if she changed her name by deed poll to Boston. That's where I came in. I managed the legal side of things for them. Of course I knew immediately she was your mother. And I've looked after her affairs ever since.'

'I thought Flora might be dying when I received your

letter, but she obviously isn't. So was there some other reason she had for wanting to see me?'

'I expect she's lonely. And maybe she has a lot of time to think about the past; but what's worrying her now is: she needs money. It's costing her £600 a month at Meadowsweet. She's used up the remains of her capital, and nearly all of what Sandy Boston left her. He composed songs as well as singing them, you know. I suppose they spent most of it living it up. There's still a trickle of cash coming in from copyrights, but not enough.'

Mary dropped her fork on her plate. 'Good heavens! What will happen? Will Matron turn her out on the streets?'

'Not Matron, but the consortium which runs this chain of homes might do so if she can't pay the fees. What happens is this: when Flora's capital drops to a minimum the DHSS picks up the bill and pays the difference between her income – in her case it will be only her old age pension by that time – and the cost of the home. Unfortunately Flora was put in rather an expensive home, too expensive for the DHSS. So she would have to move into a cheaper one. She doesn't want to move because she's familiar with the staff, knows the routine there, and so on. . . . As a matter of fact she really does seem to be happy there.'

'So she wants us to pay her fees?'

'Not yet, but quite soon. Her capital will run out in about six months' time.'

'But this is terrible!' gasped Mary, making calculations in her head. 'Where can we find £7,200 a year for her? And that's after tax! And she may live for ages yet!'

'It is a dilemma,' he conceded.

'I'm quite sure Colly will refuse,' she said. 'He will argue, quite rightly I think, that she left him more than thirty years ago, is no longer his wife, and has no claim on him at all.'

'The awful truth is, Mary, that since they are not divorced she is still legally his wife. They could, by the way, get a

151

divorce now under the new divorce laws within two years, if both agreed.'

'Colly would hate going through all that.'

'And even at the end of it she might still have a claim.'

'What claim? She was only married to him for ten years before she ran off. She deserted me too, you know.'

He leaned across the table and held her hand.

'It's a very hard thing for me to be your adversary in all this,' he said, 'but you see, Mary, Flora is my client, and I have to fight for her rights.'

'Rights? What rights?' Mary's voice was angry and agitated.

'Yes, she has rights in all this, and I'll tell you why.' He then explained that when Flora married the Colonel she had a personal fortune of £6,000 which in 1931 was a substantial sum. She put £4,000 into Gatt's Rise for various projects: to repair the roof of the house, to erect better outbuildings, to buy a ten-acre field beyond the canal, and so on. Two thousand pounds she kept in her own bank account. She was now claiming that she had a right to the capital she had put into Gatt's Rise. Moreover the value of it, owing to inflation and the rise in land and property prices since the Thirties, had increased.

'But David, this is terrible news! I had no idea – ' Her normally rosy cheeks were drained of colour, and her hand shook as she drank what remained in her glass. 'I suppose I ought to tell you,' she said, putting down the empty glass on the white cloth, 'that Colly made over the farm to me when I was forty in order to escape death duties. I am now legally the owner of Gatt's Rise.'

'So all this trouble will fall directly on you?'

'Not entirely, David. Of course Colly still has most of the say in important matters.'

'Because you let him,' said David sharply. He didn't at all mind being adversarial towards the Colonel, whom he regarded in his own mind as 'that monumental egoist', a man who had exploited his daughter, using up her life and happiness for his own purposes.

'Farmers aren't rich, David,' she said. 'Not farmers like us. We don't make enough profit to pay out nine or ten thousand a year indefinitely. It would mean selling more and more land, which would of course reduce our profits. And this process might go on for heaven knows how many years.' The situation was frightening. 'With everybody living so long nowadays this must be a problem all over the country, isn't it?'

He nodded. 'I don't think people have woken up to what is happening,' he said. He refilled her glass. 'What about a pudding, Mary?'

She shook her head, but accepted coffee, which they sipped in silence.

'Coffee's not too good,' he commented. 'Too far from France here.'

'Very soon,' said Mary, 'longevity will no longer be something to be proud of but something to be dreaded.' She stirred more sugar into her cup and spoke thoughtfully.

'This has been a nasty shock for you, Mary, but there may be some way out. Take your time thinking about it. And come and see Flora again.' He smiled. 'I like Flora, you know.'

'Do you see her often?'

'Fairly regularly. She likes my company. She's not really lonely though; she's so popular with the other patients – plays the piano and sings for them, makes them laugh. She's so light-hearted.'

Mary found it strange, remembering Colly's dictum: 'She is a light woman', that in David's estimation it was only her heart that was light.

The expected rain was falling as they drove back to her guesthouse, not in a western drizzle but in heavy slanting lines like rods of steel, which exaggerated in her the feeling that she was trapped in a cage with no way out. He stopped the car by the billboard advertising vacancies.

'I hope you'll forgive me for bringing this trouble on you,' he said.

'Of course, David. It's not your fault. I know that.'

'I think you'd better bring her chocolates, not sherry,' he said as she opened the door on the passenger side.

'Thank you, David, for the nice dinner. It was lovely seeing you again. I've got a lot to think over. But I'll be in touch.'

'I hope what I've said won't give you sleepless nights. And let me give you dinner again next time you come.' He put a hand on her shoulder.

'Yes. All right. That would be wonderful.'

He couldn't keep her in the car any longer. She ran through the rain up the steps to the door, and after a few seconds of fumbling with a key she called over her shoulder: '*Au revoir* then David!' before disappearing into the house.

Au revoir meant I'll see you again, she was thinking as she ran upstairs to her room. She began to hum Noël Coward's old song, remembering that Christmas in London with Aunt Dot, that New Year's Eve in the night-club when the song had made her cry, and Uncle Bertie had handed her his enormous white silk handkerchief. This time it didn't make her cry. This time in spite of the seemingly intractable problems she had to face she was singing with joy as she seized the pillow from the bed and using it as a partner she waltzed round the room.

Mary drove home at a leisurely pace. She knew that as soon as she got back to Gatt's Rise she would be called upon to do so many tasks that she would have no time to think, which was what she needed to do. She stopped once or twice on the way in places where she could enjoy distant views, the contemplation of which she always found put problems in perspective. Worries never seemed so large when seen against sky spaces blown clear of any human feeling and landscapes patterned by centuries of human

154

toil, continually changing but continuing, long after the toilers had vanished, still to be our earth.

She decided to present Colly with an edited version of events. She would not tell him about all the financial problems until she understood them more fully herself. She determined to make enquiries about the whole subject at the local Citizens' Advice Bureau, from Hannah's social worker, and perhaps from her doctor. She smiled to think how surprised he would be by a visit, since neither she nor Colly had been ill for years. Colly, she knew, would never willingly go through a divorce, but Flora might do so in order to help her claims. Mary had no experience of divorce cases. Divorce was not dealt with by the magistrates' courts; but separation and maintenance matters were. She shuddered remembering cases brought before the Frenester bench when she'd had to arbitrate between contestants in marital disputes, when men had claimed as part of their essential living expenses money for their beer and cigarettes, and women had fought tooth and nail with a sort of mad desperation for the extra pound per week for their children's maintenance. She remembered all too well the recriminations hurled by husbands and wives across the courtroom, the rage and hatred, the desire for revenge displayed in the squabble over the last shards of a broken marriage in language nasty and brutish but not short. The vituperation was often so fulsome that it had to be checked by Barton, who intervened, treating the protagonists as a nanny might her troublesome charges, with: 'That will do now. That will do.' After a day in court spent listening to marital disputes Mary always felt dirty.

She hoped David would persuade Flora against this course. It would be horrible if old unhealed wounds were dug up and uncovered to the gaze of lawyers and a curious public. Colly certainly hadn't forgiven Flora, and it was probable she hadn't forgotten her own injuries. It was just possible that she wanted, even after thirty years, her pound of flesh as well as her nursing-home fees. She probably

knew that Colly had some investments which added a small
annual income to his army pension, and she had quite
likely imagined she might bring him down a little by claiming from his personal income rather than from the farm,
which she now knew, since Mary had in all innocence
revealed it to her in conversation, no longer belonged to
him. Yes. Everything should be settled out of court if possible. What it meant in the end, she realised, was that it was
something her own conscience would have to decide. What
moral obligation did she then have to Flora? Colly had
a moral obligation because he used her money all those
years ago for the improvement of his farm. And was that,
Mary asked herself in the sudden bleak illumination of
that winter's day, why Colly had found it convenient not
to divorce Flora? If he had, her loan (or gift?) to him would
have come to light, and he would in all probability have
had to repay it. And now he had in a sense passed on his
guilt to Mary when he made her the legal owner of the
farm.

She sat at the roadside in her car and looked out over a
hill at Somerset below, beautiful even in her winter dress.
The wide, slightly undulating plain of chequered fields,
pastures and ploughed earth, some showing the faint
bluish-green luminescence of just sprouting winter wheat
stretched away to distant rounded hills, soft and grey as
the breasts of doves, with dove-grey, bosomy clouds brush-
ing over them. She began to feel her problems were not
insuperable. Perhaps time and events as much as her own
actions would solve them. Flora after all was not going to
live for ever. Mary blushed then to have to admit that in
reality what she was hoping for was her mother's death.

She started the engine and moved off. She thought with a
grimace of disgust of Meadowsweet, of all those old people
huddled under one roof, kept warm and fed but isolated
from their families, their dead friends, and their own past
selves. Their bodies were still ticking like ancient rusty

clocks, but where had their minds gone? Meadowsweet was a house full of shadows, of ghosts not yet dead.

She supposed it would be better for Flora to be at home. But in whose home? The prospect of installing her at Gatt's Rise to suffer a continual psychological bombardment from Colly's hatred and hostility was unthinkable. And where else could she go? Mary reflected that this was not only her personal problem; it must be one shared by thousands of women. In previous generations daughters took on the care of elderly parents. That was when they were primarily housewives and their husbands were wage-earners. Now daughters were often wage-earners themselves, sometimes the only wage-earner in a family unit whose man was unemployed, or absent, when looking after an old mother would mean sacrificing her own and perhaps a family's livelihood. And because of the longer life expectancy we were all said to be enjoying, by the time daughters did take on the care of mothers in their eighties they themselves were often old age pensioners. As always, the rich were all right Jack, because they could afford to pay someone to look after their aged without eroding their capital. The poor would have no choice but to bundle their elderly sick into whatever accommodation their locality offered; but the not-so-rich, the middle-income group, those people who in Mary's opinion were the backbone and heart of England, they would have to dig up and sell the hard-earned, accumulated wealth of generations invested in land and property, even their homes, for cash to be poured into the hands of nursing-home owners.

Her indignation melted away when with the soft inward glow of happy reminiscence she thought of David. She couldn't stop herself recalling the details of those few precious hours spent with him last evening: how he looked at her tenderly, almost hungrily she thought, how he grasped her hand across the table to give her courage, how he talked about pearls so lightly and cheerfully, when she could hear in his voice an echo of many other things he wanted to but dared not say. There was more in his heart, she believed, than mere courtesy or simple friendship. All the time he was trying warily to come closer to her. He didn't know – how could he? – what after all these years she felt about him. Abruptly she reined in her imagination, tried to discipline her thoughts. I must be realistic, she scolded herself, I must be sensible. He is married. He has been married for twenty years and has a son. He didn't talk about his wife. Nor had his mother that time Mary visited her in Upper Coldacre. She had presumed then that the old lady had been making an effort to save her guest's feelings, and perhaps to save herself a little social embarrassment. Perhaps those were David's motives too. He probably enjoyed a perfectly contented marriage from which Mary was of necessity excluded. Probably her own wishes were making her read into the exchange of ordinary polite conversation romantic overtones which were not there. I must go home, she told herself, back to Gatt's Rise, to Hannah, Colly, and hard work. It was better and safer to subdue, even if she couldn't entirely abandon, foolish fantasies.

NINE

As soon as she parked the car in the yard Mary could hear the whine of the circular saw. When she got out she felt at once the air was colder than at Grovesend. She could smell the sharp delicious scent of wood smoke rising not far off, and she saw the bonfire when she approached the men. The two professional tree-fellers were measuring out lines and areas and calculating the position of the next fall. Tom nodded a greeting, but she couldn't hear what he said above the noise of the saw, so she waited, standing at a safe distance from it till he paused in his work.

'Wind changed this morning,' he said. 'There's a high on the way, coming from Russia with love, and probably bringing snow, if we can believe the forecast.' He looked harassed. Mary knew he wanted to get the work finished before lambing began in a couple of weeks. 'If there's a lot of snow we'll have to stop felling.'

Mary nodded. He had to be free for the lambing. The ewes were always his first priority. She moved on, stepping carefully over cut logs. Colly looked up when she stood near him, but he did not interrupt his work. A giant elm lay prostrate; its branches holding bundles of twigs woven into nests by rooks last year were entwined with brambles and elm suckers on the ground. Colly was busy freeing the great trunk by slashing off side shoots and ivy with his billhook. He knew as soon as he saw her that she had been dragged into some trouble by that mother of hers; but it could wait for an hour or two, when work on the felling would finish for the day.

Mary walked towards the bonfire and stood there for a moment enjoying its warmth and watching the smoke billowing gently upwards, blue and translucent as an opal, and like an opal holding glints of fire from the embers rising in it. Then she went indoors to make herself a cup of tea and to prepare Hannah's meal.

Colly heard the forecast of snow after the six o'clock news. He scowled moodily. He knew tree-felling would have to be postponed. He hated being idle, and he had enjoyed slashing with his billhook. Hannah seemed moody too. She refused to play chess with him, or even to watch television. Instead she took her guitar up to her attic bedroom, and in spite of its near freezing temperature she remained there strumming chords and plucking notes repeatedly. Luckily the sounds were muffled somewhat by closed doors and distance, or they would have driven Mary mad.

She had noticed some change in the psychological atmosphere at Gatt's Rise, a new electrical alertness, a wariness between Colly and Hannah, who seemed to be avoiding each other. She wondered if they had quarrelled while she was away, but she was too preoccupied with her own worries to think much about it.

'I thought so,' said Colly when Mary gave him a brief and edited account of her visit to Grovesend. She did not allow his contempt access to Flora's drinking habits, nor did she mention David's name. 'So she wants you to pay her bills? What about that no-good crooner of hers? Can't he look after her?'

'He's dead, Colly. And anyway all the money he left her has been used up. She's been in the nursing home for four years already, and it's costing her £600 a month.'

'Good God! And why can't she look after herself?'

160

'She's been ill. She's losing her wits a bit, and she's had some falls – the last one bad enough to fracture her skull.' She didn't explain that Flora had fallen downstairs in an alcoholic stupor. 'I think we'll have to help her out, Colly.'

'I don't see why. She's no longer one of us. All this is no affair of mine, as you well know. Nor of yours, my dear.'

'Do you think the Trotters still want the ten-acre field on our north boundary?' she asked. She saw him stiffen, his eyes glinting like spear points.

'Over my dead body!' he declared.

Snow fell in the night. Mary could see from her bed the big soft flakes twisting as they dropped slowly outside her window. It was very quiet. Falling snow always made her feel uneasy. She remembered the great blizzard of '63 when cattle were walled up in drifts and sheep buried in cold white graves within a few hours. She couldn't sleep, so she got up, and slipping on her dressing-gown she stood at the window and looked out. A light was moving across the paddock, cutting a wavering path through the darkness. It must be Tom, she thought, going on his night round, checking the ewes. He would go over the canal bridge into the ten-acre field where they were gathered in the lee of a shed of straw bales. It must be nearly midnight.

She got back into bed and tried to sleep, but images of old, white-haired creatures flitted one after another across the blackness beyond her eyelids, and voices murmured to her, mingling with her own thoughts. *We don't want to move her ... You'll come again? ... Her loss of memory is due to booze, not senility. That's why it's patchy. She can't remember what happened during her drinking bouts. That's why she can't remember Sandy Boston gasping out his last. She was out for the count while he was dying ... I like Flora, you know ... light-hearted ... Au revoir David, my darling, my beloved. ...*

She was suddenly woken by a noise from the real world, which frightened her because she thought at first there might be a burglar in the house. It couldn't be Tom. He never came inside at night. She listened, pulling the bedclothes up to her chin. A door opened somewhere; she could hear the creak of floorboards; there was certainly someone moving about. Then there was a thud immediately above her head, and voices, two voices. Good heavens! There was somebody in Hannah's room. She slid out of bed again, and shivering with cold as well as fear, she seized her dressing-gown once more before emerging on the landing. Above there was a skylight through which enough moonlight filtered to warn any intruder of her presence, so she hid behind the bulk of a big Victorian wardrobe which occupied most of the space between her and the stairs, and holding her breath she listened intently. She could hear voices again. There was an angry exclamation from Hannah, followed by a very familiar male voice with its own peculiar Edwardian intonation and ambiguities:

'You're not a very sentimental gel, are you?'

'No! Not at all!' Hannah's reply was sharp, staccato and uncompromising.

Then there was some scuffling which muffled more of Hannah's words till suddenly she cried out in clear, loud angry tones:

'Get off me! You hairy dirty old man!'

Mary shrank behind the wardrobe as if she had been hit.

There was a thud, and a few seconds later the attic door burst open and Colly stumbled out. Through the skylight cold bright moonlight suddenly shone down the staircase and on to his dishevelled figure. His dressing-gown was undone, and its hem and sash trailed behind him; his iron-grey hair which was normally so neatly combed now fell distractedly about his eyes. Mary stood absolutely still while he descended, his head hanging while he fumbled with the cords of his pyjama trousers. No longer every inch a soldier, he looked like a mongrel stray that had been kicked. At the landing he turned away from Mary and went into his own room on the other side. A moment later Hannah must have shut her door, for Mary heard the latch click. Neither of them had seen her. She closed her own door very quietly, and sat down on her bed.

By this time her legs felt weak and her hands were trembling. She felt sick. She was beginning to believe what she had seen. Was Colly, the brave warrior of El Alamein, the hero of her schooldays, Agamemnon the victor of Troy, the upright judge and one of the elect reduced to this? *Oh my beloved father....* She put her hands over her ears but could not make them deaf. 'Get off me! You hairy dirty old man!' That was what Hannah had called him. It was horrible, horrible.

After a little while she crept downstairs into the kitchen and sat by the comforting warmth of the Aga. She could hear the small sound of clinker falling out of the furnace inside the thick steel box. She made a cup of tea and drank it slowly as the cold, muffled, snow-laden dawn broke on her crumbling world.

Although her inner world was utterly changed Mary moved through her daily work routines as if nothing had happened; nor did she notice any difference in the way Colly and Hannah behaved at breakfast. In any case it was usually a rather silent meal. Mary was enthralled and horrified, like a spectator at the theatre watching a drama being enacted between the other two, who were unaware of what she'd seen the night before. It was her habits and long-practised disciplines which drove her mechanically through that day.

'Wear your wellies, Hannah,' she said. 'Take dry shoes in a plastic carrier.' At the back door she looked out at the unmarked snow. 'It's not very deep. I think the bus will make it.' She kissed Hannah on the cheek, and spoke to her with more tenderness than usual. 'Take care, my little love,' she said. And for a moment Hannah clung to her without a word before stumbling out, head bent against the wind.

Mary came back into the kitchen and sat down at the

table opposite Colly. He didn't look at her; he was busy reading *The Times*. Every time she looked at him she saw him in a clearer, more cruel light. Throughout that day her eyes were stripping him of the protective layers of his assumed virtues and prerogatives. *Droit de seigneur* I suppose is what he thought he had, she told herself. It was a total disregard not only of Hannah's well-being but of hers as well. How could she continue fostering the girl in an atmosphere of deceit? Hannah had been entrusted to her care and protection at Gatt's Rise, but how could she be protected from moral danger now? Yet if Mary resigned her position as foster mother and sent the girl away Hannah would be blamed again; she would be marked as impossible to handle, out of control, a disruptive adolescent, and might even be sent to a high-security home where she would be in contact with dreadfully delinquent girls, and made utterly wretched for years to come. It would of course be out of the question to tell Miss Harris the truth of the matter. The scandal would be too great, too terrible for Colly to bear. She didn't think she could have borne it herself either. She was already in her mind telling lies by deciding to omit the truth.

She examined Colly coolly across the table. She saw him as somehow much older than he'd been yesterday; but no pity entered her heart as yet. Instead she was filled with such a whirlwind of rage that her hands shook. She hid them in her lap under the table, and tried to control her voice, breathing deeply and then speaking as if she were calming a runaway horse.

'I have been thinking about Flora's problem,' she said. He looked up and met her eyes at last. He saw there anger and hostility that he never expected in her, and blamed Flora for the change. 'I have been thinking that we might be able to leave Flora undisturbed at Meadowsweet for the rest of her days by getting the DHSS to top up her payments.'

'But I understand what they're willing to pay won't be enough?' he queried.

'If you and I both subscribed something from our incomes every month I think it might be possible to bridge the deficit.' She spoke carefully and firmly. 'And in that way we wouldn't have to sell off any land.'

'You sound as if you've read up all the jargon,' he said crossly.

'Only some of it.'

'Well, you can dismiss that solution right away. Not one penny of mine will I pay out for Flora's benefit. You of course can do as you like.' He raised his paper and pretended to read on.

Mary took a deep breath; she braced her shoulders. 'In that case,' she said, 'it rather looks as if the Trotters will get the ten-acre field they've always coveted.'

Colly was shocked. He could hardly believe his ears. He knew Flora was an evil woman, but that she could persuade Mary to such lengths of foolishness, of rebellion against his own better judgement after so many years of sweet docile acceptance of all the right ways he'd taught her was truly appalling. He put down *The Times* slowly. He spoke with a deadly slow malice: 'So you will be Goneril to my Lear after all? How I have been mistaken in my trust.'

There was a silence in the kitchen then so deep Mary could hear a clinker fall into the ash inside the heavily insulated shell of the Aga.

'That is absurd, Colly,' she said. 'I am not turning you out of house and home to wander about in the snow. I'm simply trying to raise a bit of money to keep my mother comfortable in her last days. Did you hand over the farm to me expecting to tie up my will and conscience as well as avoid death duties?'

He glared at her. 'I expect a little gratitude,' he said.

'And when have I not shown gratitude? she asked.

He made no reply; but they both knew that at Gatt's Rise the balance of power had shifted slightly.

The wordless warfare in the house continued between the three of them; they kept apart and only met at meals which were eaten in silence. Mary was unnaturally watchful of Hannah, who was spending most of her time at home in her bedroom. Mary took an electric fire up there, as she knew how cold it must be just under the roof. She examined the lock on Hannah's door, and was pleased to find it moved easily when turned, and the key was in place on the inner side of the door, though she felt pretty sure Colly would not risk another humiliation there.

She ventured out in her Mini. The snow had been swept from the main road, which had been gritted, and the way was cleared to Swinester, where she entered the Citizens' Advice Bureau and made enquiries about what allowances could be obtained from the DHSS for old age pensioners in nursing homes. She attended court in Frenester as usual on Thursday. After three days the snow melted as a warmer, mist-laden wind blew in over Gatt's Rise. On the fourth morning Hannah was late for breakfast. Colly, who was always irritated by unpunctuality, glanced up from his paper several times enquiringly at Mary, who was anxious that she might miss the school bus. She left the room at last and went upstairs to look for Hannah.

Her room was empty, the bed unmade, Hannah's working jeans and jersey lay in a heap on the floor. Her school clothes were still hanging in her cupboard, but her best clothes were gone, and her guitar was nowhere to be seen. Mary hunted feverishly through the drawers of the little dressing-table and found that Hannah's Post Office savings book which she usually kept there was missing. She had also taken with her a photo of herself riding Rollo, which Mary had taken last summer. On the dressing-table was a piece of ruled paper torn from an exercise book, and to it was pinned a single withered cowslip. Across the paper was scrawled in large rather childish handwriting: 'it's not your fault. It's Me. I shall never forget you.'

Mary sat down on Hannah's bed, and holding the paper with its dried flower she wept.

After a while Colly came to the foot of the stairs.

'What's up, Mary?' he shouted. 'Why don't you come down to breakfast?' And as there was no answer he climbed the last flight to the attic and saw his daughter weeping.

'She's gone,' said Mary.

He touched her shoulder. 'It's not your fault,' he said. 'You did your best. You mustn't blame yourself.'

She stared at him through her tears in disbelief. At least he hadn't said 'I told you so!' We are all imprisoned inside our own limitations, she thought. It is difficult to escape.

TEN

The baby calves had not yet been brought in for rearing so Mary still had a little time to herself. She took to wandering across the fields, over the lock-gate bridge and along the canal towpath, reconstructing in her imagination the way Hannah might have taken in her flight. Mary wondered if she had begged a lift on the early barge and jumped off at Stanton where the canal dived under the main road to the north. Here she might have hitched a lift in a lorry to Gloucester or Birmingham, and perhaps later to London. But the bargees denied having seen her at all that morning.

Mary was slightly comforted by the thought of the small sum accumulated in Hannah's Post Office savings account. That would ensure her safe keeping for a couple of weeks at least; but the thought of her tramping the streets of a big city, wet, cold, lonely and hungry, and worst of all homeless in January, made Mary shudder. What would become of her? The thought of all the dreadful possibilities filled her with anguish.

In spite of Colly's admonition: 'It's not your fault. You did your best. You mustn't blame yourself' she did blame herself. Of course it was Colly who had in the end pushed Hannah out of the warm nest at Gatt's Rise by his behaviour that night; but Mary couldn't help asking herself if she wasn't in the long run to blame for the way things had turned out. Perhaps it had after all been folly on her part to offer Hannah shelter and a home against what was now shown to be the better judgement of others more experienced than herself; certainly it was folly to allow herself to love the child as she had.

'She'll be back one day. You'll see,' said Marge in an effort to console her.

'She left her guitar with us on her way to school the day before she did a bunk,' said Tom; but neither of them had had any inkling of her intentions, nor any idea which way she went. Nobody had seen her go. The police were informed, and Hannah's name was placed on a Missing Persons register, a number of people were questioned, including some of her classmates at school; but no clues emerged. Miss Harris interviewed both Mary and Colly. She expressed sympathy with Mary's distress; she agreed with Colly that with such a girl as Hannah this outcome might have been expected. She was deceived because neither Colly nor Mary told her the full story. Lies of omission Mary confessed to herself, lies, lies. . . .

On Thursday when Mary attended court she was greeted with a smirking condescension by Gregory Barton, and a kindly but slightly complacent satisfaction by the other magistrates. It was hard to bear.

'I'm ever so sorry, Mary,' said Beryl, switching off the Hoover in order to enjoy a gossip, 'ever so sorry. I know how fond you were of her. But then, that's the sort she was, wasn't she?' Beryl was disappointed in her hopes of hearing more because Mary was obstinately silent.

In Frenester at the paper shop on the corner where people often lingered to exchange the time of day, customers stopped talking when they saw her enter. In the High Street one or two strangers cast covert but curious glances at her as she passed. It was really humiliating to know that everybody was talking about what had happened at Gatt's Rise, that everybody thought she was a fool.

But Fading Brig arrived one morning carrying a pot containing an orchid. 'Cymbidium,' she said. 'Keep it in a cool place and it will flower for a month.' Fourteen buds drooped from the long stem, six of them in flower, pale green and lemon with brown velvet blotches on their lips. 'It's a green thought in a green shade,' she said, smiling mysteriously. She made no reference whatever to Mary's grief. Mary kissed her when she left. Fading understood. It would take tender green shoots springing up during the coming year, during other seasons and years to come, new events and perhaps new friends, to grow over and obliterate her pain.

Each day that passed, every breakfast time when she surveyed her father across the table added a delicate layer of the varnish of cynicism to her raw feelings. Over and over again she asked herself as she watched him eat, was he just an old-fashioned hypocrite knowing he had done evil and trying to hide it from her, or could he possibly have persuaded himself that Hannah's running away was nothing to do with him but simply due to her own instability? It shocked Mary profoundly to suspect after all these years of blind faith in him that he was a clever, thoughtful man with no understanding of himself at all. It was difficult to believe that a man of intelligence could have so little insight. Know Thyself, that first commandment of the ancient Greeks, engraved in stone on the temple of Apollo at Delphi, he had often paid homage to in words; but how deeply had he ever probed himself in order to fulfil it?

She was slowly acquiring an encrustation of disbelief, protective and permanent. She was beginning to see him as old, a creature belonging entirely to the past, and Gatt's Rise itself as in a way an anachronism. Why had she never before seen him as he was: a selfish, arrogant, and sometimes rather cruel old man?

Colly, alarmed at her lack of response to his talk, and at the sight of her pale stricken face, which even he began at last to notice opposite him at mealtimes, tried to cheer her up by reading out titbits of news from *The Times*. He had no idea she'd seen him on the stairs that night, and presumed her grief was entirely due to the loss of Hannah's company. He found it hard to understand why she took it so badly, but explained her depression on the grounds that she was female after all. And women did go broody over the young. And perhaps she was nearing her change of life too. Every evening when at an unusually early hour she said, 'I'll go to bed now Colly. I'm tired,' he would follow her to the foot of the stairs and repeat anxiously, helplessly: 'Yes. Yes. Goodnight. God bless you my dear.' And she, wearily climbing to her bed would think: does he still believe in God?

In the little hours of the night when sleep did not bring down the longed-for obliterating curtain on the previous day, when the appalling truth about the final act of her existence still to be played out was revealed to her, she was dismayed. Was the rest of her life to be spent caring for two old and increasingly dependent parents whom she no longer loved, with nobody to talk to except eccentric old ladies like Fading Brig and Rachel Wetherley, with no bright humming-bird like Hannah to streak through a dull day? It was indeed a desolate grey future she saw before her. I must get a dog, she thought. Would that be reason enough for living? Fading had her jungle of green felicity, Rachel Wetherley her books to ward off grief; but Mary could see no escape route available to herself.

She did not pay her second visit to Grovesend-on-Sea till February. She took the opportunity to go then although it was a cold windy Saturday, because she knew that as soon as the calves arrived she would have very little time to spare. She couldn't help thinking of Hannah as she drove away: Hannah's delight in the calves, that little song and dance of pleasure she'd performed on the straw in the byre, and her obvious love for the creatures as she fed them.

Where, oh where was Hannah now? May God protect her, Mary prayed.

'Mrs Boston's in the lounge,' said Nurse. 'I think she's entertaining the other patients.'

Mary could hear the tinkling of a piano as, armed with a large box of chocolates, she stood in the doorway. Flora was seated at the piano strumming and singing in her husky voice: ' "Happy feet! I've got those happy feet!" ' Suddenly she jumped up, and grabbing the cushion from the nearest armchair, tipping its occupant forward (mercifully to be saved from a fall by the Zimmer frame that fenced her in) Flora tottered round the room performing a quick foxtrot with her imaginary partner and uttering croaks of: ' "Happy feet! I've got those hap-hap-happy feet!" '

She was like a puppet being jerked by the strings of her past memories. In the semicircle of sitters some were asleep, some smiling, but two laughed aloud, and one clapped enthusiastically and cried out: 'Do it again Flora!' Obligingly Flora made another circuit of the lounge till the sight of Mary standing in the doorway brought this revelry of the aged to an abrupt halt. She staggered and would have fallen if Mary hadn't caught her in her arms.

'Oh!' Flora cried. 'I didn't see you!' A blast of whisky hit Mary as her mother gasped for breath.

'You'd better see your visitor in your room,' said Nurse. She too had smelt the whisky, and her tone of voice was severe.

In the enclosed atmosphere of the lift the smell became overpowering. Mary wondered if it was the alcohol which had propelled her mother's dancing. Flora seemed a good deal more lively than she'd been before.

As soon as the nurse left them Flora lit a cigarette. They sat down by the window.

'How's that pretty cousin of yours – Vicky?' asked Flora.

'She's married,' replied Mary. 'Someone in business. I don't see anything of her nowadays.'

Flora inhaled deeply. 'You're not going to see me turned out of this place are you?' she asked.

'Not if I can help it. But I shall probably have to sell a field to meet the costs.'

Flora looked at her steadily through the tobacco fog.

'I suppose you haven't forgiven me for deserting you,' she said.

'Well, it wasn't all hap-hap-happy feet for me when I was little,' said Mary tartly.

Flora turned away to gaze out of the window. After a minute she said, 'I did try to get some access to you after the war, you know, but Francis absolutely refused to let me see you. And I couldn't get a divorce then, which might have made some legal access possible.' She tapped ash to dislodge it into an ashtray on the windowsill.

Flora was certainly far from senile this morning. Mary wondered if the whisky had actually cleared her brain. 'Thanks for the chocs,' she said. 'I suppose you thought sherry wasn't good for me. Or did Matron tell you not to bring it?'

'How do you manage to get it?'

'Oh! One of the cleaners sometimes helps. She pays less than I give her for it, you know. But don't tell, will you, or she'll get the sack. I'm sorry it's you who's having to do the selling off,' she rattled on. 'I'd have liked to take the farm from Francis, bit by bit, to bring him down as he did me.'

'Do you still hate him, Flora? It all happened an awful long time ago.'

'Like yesterday to me.' And then in a sudden burst of rage she cried: 'Did you know he once called me a bore? *Me* boring? – with my zest for living – my gift for fun? – when I was always the life and soul of the party in the days of the Bright Young Things!'

Mary watched her coolly. She could just imagine how tiresome that indefatigable brightness might become. Flora with an angry gesture stubbed out the end of her cigarette on the ashtray, and immediately lit another. Her mood changed, and she relaxed as she inhaled the nicotine-laden smoke; she became reflective, almost melancholy.

'Fairies at the bottom of the garden was very much the Twenties thing,' she said. 'Only pretty little romantic creatures hiding in the shrubbery then. Never any sex. Sex was a No-Go area. So I was ignorant about it, and horrified too, when it came to the test. Your father never forgave me my ignorance. I suppose, to be fair to him, he had his hang-ups too. He needed encouragement perhaps; but I didn't know how to give it to him.'

'I'm sorry,' said Mary. She had no wish to hear her mother pour out all these confidences, hurtful and rather shocking for her. She was afraid they might prove to be more than she could bear, but her sense of fairness made her say: 'I suppose marriage was a disappointment to you both. Was that it? But he must have loved you once, Flora.'

'He admired my beauty, and he admired my bit of money too. He wanted to possess them both; but he didn't like me much in bed. As a matter of fact I believe he thought of sex as a dirty but necessary act. Something that had to be got through as quickly as possible. Not like Sandy, who loved every minute of it. Sandy was never in a hurry. He never made me feel an inferior animal as Francis did. What your father liked was very young, common, easy-to-rumple girls. He was always running after the maids, you know. I was so bloody innocent I didn't know what was going on at first. I couldn't understand why so many of them gave notice after a month or two. They used to stand with eyes cast down and say they were sorry to go. In the end I asked a leaver: "Why do you all give notice? What's wrong with the house? Smell of drains in the scullery or something?" And this one, who'd always been a bit outspoken and had to be reprimanded more than once for not holding her tongue, looked me straight in the eye and said: "It's the Master, Mum. Can't keep 'is 'ands off me bum, Mum!" I suppose I must have changed colour. I know my hand flew to my mouth. It was such a shock – more of a shock because I realised what a fool I was not to have noticed. But this girl saw what she'd done: thrown a hand grenade into my life, really. She burst out: "Oh Mum! I'm sorry, Mum!" and fled from the room – up to her bedroom, picked up her little cardboard suitcase, and ran out of the house there and then, without collecting her wages. I had to post them on to her. Sexual harassment I suppose you'd call it nowadays, but I dare say he regarded it as *droit de seigneur*. Yes. I was shocked. Truth is shocking – stranger than fiction, and more shocking too. I was very fond of your father once; but after that I began to watch him. And then I began to dislike him.'

'I'm sorry,' sighed Mary. She felt too weary to weep. 'I'm so sorry. So sorry, Flora. . . .'

'Marriage isn't easy at the best of times, but when you actually dislike your husband it can come to be a pretty good hell.' Her mood changed again. She waved her cigarette in the air, making a serpentine silhouette of smoke against the window. 'But then the war came, and he went away. And everything was easier. And then I met Sandy.' She puffed several times, her mind resting happily on Sandy. 'We used to go to the races a lot after the war. Sandy loved gambling more than horses; but we both loved the atmosphere of the racecourse. The Grand National was my favourite race. I usually backed an outsider, and sometimes I won. My heart was always in my mouth when my horse came up to Becher's Brook. And now I'm coming to my own deepest ditch. It won't be long before I fall into it.' She waved her cigarette in the air again. 'Well, you can see for yourself I'm half-dead already. It was Sandy who kept me alive.' She laughed. There was little self-pity in the sound. 'And now he's gone all I've got is the old dears to amuse.'

In spite of everything there was something courageous about her. Mary thought: she is a gallant old woman, like

Marie Antoinette, silly and frivolous in life, but gallant in the face of death.

'About the fees,' said Mary as she rose to go, 'we'll manage somehow. You don't have to worry about that.'

'You'll come again?' asked Flora, looking up out of eyelids slitted against the stinging smoke.

'Yes of course.' Mary leaned down and kissed her cheek. 'And bring a bottle next time!' called Flora as Mary reached the door.

David picked her up at Meadowsweet and took her off in his Volvo to the Holly Bush for a pub lunch. As it was a Saturday the place was full of locals, and noisy. They had to push their way to the bar.

'I'll have a gin and tonic – with ice and lemon,' she said. 'And a beef sandwich. Yes. A streak of horseradish would be nice. Thank you.'

Happily David looked at her. He was very glad to see her; but something about her appearance made him pause, made him subdue his bubbling excitement at having her all to himself again. Something bad must have happened to her. Her face no longer seemed so young and carefree as it had only three weeks ago; there were dark shadows round her eyes, which were inattentive, withdrawn from his, as if she was brooding on some nasty secret.

'We've got the whole afternoon,' he said expansively. 'Isn't that wonderful? What shall we do with it?'

'What about going for a walk along the shore?' she suggested. 'I'd like that. And I've got the right shoes on,' she added, noticing that he was wearing a suitable windproof anorak over his pullover.

The wind had dropped a little, and a thin wintry sunshine stroked the flat brownish expanse that was Grovesend's beach at low tide. The water seemed very far away. They walked along the firm, dried-out edge of muddy sand quickly to keep warm. The place was deserted. This time the prospect of the immense sky full of wispy white clouds scudding over the estuary, and the feeling that she herself was but another grain of sand on the fringe of the Atlantic, did not dispel her misery. At the end of the long beach they turned inland up a slope and into an area of dunes which gave some protection from the wind.

David took her hand and asked: 'Has something happened, Mary? You look so unhappy – not at all like last time.'

She nodded, and tears welled up into her eyes, but she couldn't speak.

'You can tell me, dearest girl,' he said. 'I shall understand.'

Then and there between sand dunes and under the lee of stiff marram grasses bent by the winds above their heads she began to tell him in disjointed sentences, between gasps and sobs, all the wretchedness of the past few weeks, first of all Flora's revelations which were uppermost, being most recent in her mind, the story of Colly's attempted seduction of Hannah and how Hannah had disappeared leaving no trace nor clue as to her destination, and finally stammering out something about her own feelings at the loss of Hannah, and her shock and disillusionment at what Colly had done. All sorts of things she'd locked up inside her for years came tumbling out of the Pandora's Box of her memory. He was alarmed at the passion of her grief, but he held her shaking body in his arms and let her cry. 'My poor Mary!' he murmured. 'My darling girl!'

'And Gregory Barton and the magistrates, and everybody in Frenester now knows about Hannah. They'll all be saying it was my fault – which in a way it was.'

He knew only too well what all the town wiseacres would be saying behind her back, nodding with pleasure and clacking because a woman with more love in her heart to give than the whole pack of them put together possessed had been made to look a fool, and what's more, had to bear having that love thrown back in her face. Not knowing the full story, of course – how could they? His face reddened with anger and his pulse quickened at the thought of that crowd of her detractors, and he longed to defend her against them all, till it struck him that the person she most needed defending against was herself.

'There, there!' he said, as if trying to soothe a child. 'There now. It's not your fault. I know. I know.'

He saw her as like a moth emerging from the prison of its pupating sac, where it had been slowly growing to maturity, and was now shuddering off this carapace. It was a kind of metamorphosis she was undergoing. She was in travail, shedding her old assumptions and certainties. Giving birth to a new self was bound to be painful, just as the great muscular effort of childbirth was. Perhaps this was what it was like when a true believer loses his religious faith, he thought. From his own experience of growing up he knew it was a necessary process in any advance towards a new understanding of truth, or even the acquisition of a new learning, when old beliefs and old habits had seemed safe and pleasant. It was an unmasking of false gods, which most of us go through in adolescence. And Mary's adolescence had been unnaturally prolonged.

She checked her tears at last. She looked round as if surprised to find herself where she was. A sudden gust of wind blew up the little gulley where they stood and whirled dry sand around their knees. She shivered.

'I must go to Mrs Rowan's to book in for the night,' she said.

'Certainly not!' he objected. 'You're not in a fit state to stay alone in any dreary B and B. You're going to come home with me and let me look after you.'

'But I can't!' cried Mary, aghast. 'I really can't meet your wife with my face like this, all red and swollen up!'

'My wife? I haven't got a wife. Didn't my mother tell you?'

'She told me you'd married a science teacher.'

'So she was – is – but Helen's not teaching at Grovesend any more. She's living with her boyfriend in the Midlands, where he's head of business studies in a tech. I've been on my own now for more than a year. I thought you knew.'

'Oh!' said Mary, sniffing. 'I'm sorry,' though she wasn't sorry at all.

'William decided to stay with me,' said David as they got into the car. 'But he's away with friends for the weekend – birdwatching in Brecon. So you've only got me to worry about.'

They drove to Meadowsweet to pick up her car before driving on in convoy to his house. It was a modern house on the edge of the town, with big windows and a view over open fields. As soon as they were inside he lit a fire in the sitting-room, and when the flames were spurting through the logs he took her coat.

'No. You sit down and relax, Mary. I'm going to get the tea. It's you who needs looking after for once.'

Mary was grateful for the hot tea and the warmth of the fire. She felt stunned, as if her mind had been emptied and wiped clean. 'Lovely cuppa, David,' she sighed. After sipping in silence for a while she said, 'I think I've been unfair to Colly. I suppose it's a wonder really that he's endured all these years of celibacy without taking a mistress. Perhaps it was only when he was young that he was such an old goat.'

'He was a bit of an old goat with Hannah, wasn't he?' David saw the Colonel in a different light, not as a goat but as a powerful old ape keeping his females in subservience and waiting for the chance to pop his seed into the youngest, most physically fit and promisingly fertile of them. He saw the Colonel's reputation for Roman honour and uprightness as a façade, but a weapon too, a sort of remote-control laser beam through which he kept the males of the tribe in order. His greatest need was to keep control; and the reason he was still bitter against Flora and her paramour was because they had escaped from it. He even wondered if the old devil hadn't planned that attempted seduction in order to drive Hannah away from Mary. He

179

was, he believed, quite capable of such a thing. 'He's a monumental egoist!' he blurted out.

She stared at him for a second, making him think that perhaps he had gone too far, till she asked: 'Doesn't biology tell us that all living creatures are fundamentally selfish? Survival is our first instinct.'

'Of course,' he agreed. 'But there are ways of survival, aren't there? Social and collective care to aid survival. . . . Personal survival need not be destructive of others – at least not within the tribe.'

'That's just it, David. You were not within the tribe – not his tribe anyway.'

'His tribe consisted of one man: himself. His individualism is positively fanatical.'

She nodded thoughtfully. 'My survival kit has always been in keeping a low profile. A soldier keeps his head down when the bullets fly.' It was a confession; and it gave him another glimpse into her life as years of submission to a more dominant will. Indignation made him put out his hand to grasp hers.

'But there are times of peace, aren't there?' he insisted. 'Bullets don't fly all the time.'

'Oh but they do, they do. Mostly the air is full of bullets.'

She has lived in a state of spiritual siege, he thought; and now she has been badly wounded.

'I'm surprised my mother didn't tell you that Helen had left me. I suppose she was ashamed to think any woman could discard her precious son!' He laughed, but there was some bitterness in his voice. 'She was a good mother, and a good wife really. Perhaps I'm the sort of man who always wants what he hasn't got – Shelley's divinely discontented man who in practice can be a bit of a pig.'

'She didn't make you happy then?'

'I don't think she was very happy either. There were other reasons. Helen's a brainy woman. It's quite possible she just got bored with me. But to be fair to her I think she

180

always knew I still hankered after you. I think she always felt that for me she was second best.'

Mary took her hand away from his. 'That must have been awful for her,' she said. 'You make me feel so guilty.'

He felt snubbed. He didn't know what to say to her then, how to proceed. He wanted to make love; but he wasn't quite sure yet what she felt about him. In any case she was probably too exhausted by all the emotional turmoil she'd been through to be able to cope with his love just yet, with his problems, and with all the fresh choices they would heap on her. He knew he must wait and bide his time. He reminded himself wryly that his life had inured him to waiting.

There was a Sony music centre by the fireplace, and a stack of boxed tapes and classical LPs in their decorative sleeves. He found the one he wanted, then slipped it on and let it run. The orchestral overture to Verdi's *La Traviata* began to fill the room, and soon the soaring magical voice of Maria Callas rose in the air. He linked his hands behind his neck and leaning back in his chair he shut his eyes. 'Love, the heartbeat of the Universe, mysterious, exalted, torments and delights my heart,' she sang; but the words were only a faint shadow of the glory of her singing.

'Divine Callas!' he sighed. Tomorrow he would tell Mary how, even in the days when his marriage was still salvage-able, he sometimes dreamed of sending her tapes of music through the post, coded messages of love, how once he indulged a fantasy about sending her for a Valentine an aria by Puccini. Puccini's arias would melt a heart of mill-stone grit, he'd thought then. But he never sent it because on second thoughts he realised that it was the Colonel's heart that needed melting, not Mary's. Tomorrow he would tell her all this. But Mary had fallen asleep in her chair.

Then David went to his son's room to put a clean sheet and duvet cover on the bed before taking Mary up the stairs. She didn't even undress, but fell into the bed in her pants and bra, and thus she slept for a full twelve hours.

She woke to find a tray of tea and toast and marmalade beside her, and was for a few seconds bewildered that Mrs Rowan had served her breakfast in her room, till she remembered she was in David's house, and he was looking after her.

She got up to go to the bathroom, where she took off her clothes and slipped on a dressing-gown. She washed the nasty taste of yesterday out of her mouth with a toothbrush, and then went back to bed to have her breakfast. David heard her moving about, and soon came upstairs to join her. He came in carrying his own cup of tea. He was looking tousled, his copious, still blond hair unbrushed, his dressing-gown cord untied and its tassels trailing on the floor. He sat down on the side of her bed.

'Slept well?'

'Like a top. I feel marvellous – thanks to you.'

'I think you're remarkably resilient.' He drank his tea.

'This must be William's room,' she said, noticing a cricket bat in one corner and a poster of David Bowie with his Spiders from Mars stuck up on the wall.

'Past loves and past enthusiasms of the young: sudden and brief,' said David dismissively. 'Although my own youthful passions seem to have persisted somehow. I've always dreamed of you, you know.'

Mary put her cup down. She stretched out her hand and stroked his cheek. 'You're not all that old yourself, are you?' she asked.

He slipped the dressing-gown off her shoulders and sat staring at her for a moment. He was amazed at the whiteness of her skin. She had not been one for basking flat on her back on the Costa del Sol. 'Oh my lily-white girl!' he sighed. 'You're almost too beautiful to touch!'

'But I want you to touch me,' she said.

He touched her breast lightly, he stroked the skin over her shoulders, her back, her hips, her thighs. She leaned forward and kissed him softly and lingeringly on the lips.

'I feel like Anon,' she said.

'Anon?' For a moment a horrid fear seized him that she was trying to put him off. She told him about the poet Anon, the lonely exile longing for his home in the west. 'Christ, if my love were in my arms/And I in my bed again!' She knew now how the homesick sailor felt when he at last dropped anchor in a safe haven. She put her hand round the back of his neck to touch those wispy curls, the thought of which had always made her feel weak at the knees, and pulled him down into the bed.

'Lucky, lucky Anon!' she whispered.

She trailed her fingers along his spine, making him shiver with excitement. Having schooled himself to think he must be gentle, even cautious in their first love-making, he was surprised to find how eager she was.

'We've got something to celebrate,' he said when they arrived at the Stag and Antlers rather late for their Sunday lunch. 'It'll have to be champagne today. We're going to drink to a new era.'

Undoubtedly there was a note of triumph in his voice. He glanced up at the pub sign as they passed under it, at the noble head of the old stag with branched antlers. He smiled grimly, imagining two stags fighting, knowing himself to be locked in combat with the Colonel now. Colly had won the first round all those years ago when he had trampled coarsely on delicate young love; but it looked as if he was going to lose the second. David knew he could wait for what he wanted. Time was on his side now, not on the Colonel's.

PART TWO

The Priest's Tale

ELEVEN

I was surprised when Mary Chicon called on me at the vicarage without warning on that January afternoon. The road downhill to Mudcott had been gritted and the dirty melting snow thrown aside by passing traffic was still piled up under hedges, and it was very cold. I supposed that the weather must have put a stop to the tree-felling which I knew was going on at Gatt's Rise, so perhaps she was at a loose end. Of course I'd heard on the grapevine about Hannah's moonlight flit, so I expected Mary to be distressed about that, distracted even, with worry about what might happen to the girl. But all the time she sat with me in my study with her eyes on the floor, her hands twisting and untwisting on her lap, I felt that there was something more on her mind she wanted but couldn't bring herself to tell me. When I asked her what was the matter she replied: 'Guilt and remorse.' I remember wondering what on earth such a virtuous lady could be suffering guilt and remorse for.

'I'm sure you're not to blame about Hannah,' I said. 'The girl would have run away eventually from any home, however good. She's so wild.'

She didn't seem convinced.

'Perhaps she'll come back,' I suggested. She looked at me

uncertainly, and I could see her thinking: Perhaps. Perhaps not.

'I've thought of that,' she said. 'But it won't be till after she's eighteen. Then she'll be free of care and protection. The order will cease to operate then.'

I nodded. She opened her handbag and took out an envelope, and out of this she took a faded pressed flower and handed it to me.

'Cowslip?' I asked. 'It no longer has any scent.'

'It's nearly a year old, you see,' she explained. 'What d'you think of this?'

The flower had been pinned to a brief letter from Hannah which I read.

'There you are!' I said happily. 'Just what I said. She loves you. And I bet she'll turn up again at Gatt's Rise one day.'

'You think so?' Poor Mary seemed to think we were clutching at straws. 'I only hope she doesn't catch pneumonia meanwhile. She'll probably be homeless.' She folded the flower inside its letter and replaced it in her handbag. 'She did take her overcoat,' she added. 'And a pair of stout shoes.'

'Well, that shows some sense, doesn't it?'

When she left the house she turned at the gate to thank me. I promised I would pray for her. 'And if you don't believe in prayer,' I said, 'I'll sing for you instead next Sunday.'

'Oh yes, I do believe in that. Music is a form of prayer, really. It isn't only the food of love, is it? It's the balm for our remorse. Just think of that Ukrainian hymn-singing! Russians do seem to understand remorse. And thank you Theodore. Thank you.'

Again I wondered what she could have done. She carried that look of the walking wounded which I recognised. I thought then: She is a nice woman, a person of real goodness, a rare soul in fact. Sooner or later she would be bound to get hurt; she was the caring kind. I was sure she'd welcome Hannah back, though I very much doubted if the Colonel would be so forgiving.

It was not till several weeks later that Colonel Chicon was struck down. Felling of the elms had been resumed as soon as the snow disappeared. He was, I heard, in the act of cutting away the ivy clinging to a fallen tree, and slashing off the suckers sprouting from its roots, and being the sort of man he was no doubt he slashed with fury, perhaps imagining himself besieged by the barbarian hordes he'd battled with all his life. In the end it was not they but the enemy within that got him: rupture of a brain artery. He bent suddenly over the prostrate elm and fell limply on its bark, his legs astride the trunk. He lived another six months. Mary looked after him at home. He couldn't speak, and he was paralysed on the right side of his body. She used to read to him in the afternoons, and in the evenings the barbarian hordes of television entertained them. I often thought of her during that time. The old warhorse would certainly not have gone gentle into that good night. I dare say he did his fair share of raging. Whatever burden of guilt and remorse she carried must have been expiated then.

Mine was not the only life Hannah played havoc with; she must have put poor Mary Chicon through the shredder when she disappeared two winters ago. Hannah does seem to be the sort of person who trails disaster in her wake. But I hasten to add that it's not really Hannah's fault that I have ended up in this place. The fault, dear Brutus, is not in our stars, nor even in other people, as we all know.

Everybody is very kind here; but in my hospital aquarium I feel, if not a fish out of water at least a fish immured inside its green walls, floating in its thermostatically controlled temperature, fed by a continuous supply of unappetising NHS food, and encouraged by the steadily permissive voices of the staff. The people here seem to regard my grief as a form of sickness; but I know I have come face to face with the truth. I can't blame Hannah for that. It was simply the circumstances that surrounded the poor child's life and what followed from my friendship with her which revealed to me that the world is a black hole unlit by the eye of God.

I first met Hannah when she was a child in her grandmother's house, a crumbling old place with peeling walls, full of the smell of dampness from the water that flowed under the adjoining mill and of dust and chaff from the warehouse. I remember walking in the garden with her after her gran's death, and trying to comfort her. It was a wet and neglected garden. So much bramble and burdock grew across the paths I had to pick burrs out of my cassock for days afterwards, and each time I pulled at those hooks I was haunted by the recollection of Hannah's stricken face, beautiful even in its tear-stained state, and those large eyes which I can only call begging eyes, begging, that is, for love, as she asked me: 'What will happen to me?' She was eleven years old.

The psychiatrists don't of course tell me what to do, but I have been given to understand that I am expected to delve into my past memories to try to understand what has happened to me. So I am dutifully trying to remember and record anything which may prove to be of importance. I find it difficult to concentrate at times, and my mind wanders off to more recent memories; but I believe they think childhood is what matters, so I shall have to force my attention back to that. I must try to remember and pigeon-hole its events into an orderly pattern.

I am nearly fifty-nine years of age. I was the younger of two children. I don't remember my father; he was just someone who had somehow failed my mother. He left her when she was thirty-three, for no reason that she could tell me. She used to say he was not really cut out to be a father; but she forgave him. She had to, of course, being a practising as well as a believing Christian. He also left her with my sister Angela and myself and the house we lived in, but very little money. My mother gave music lessons to help make ends meet. She was a gifted pianist. She taught me to read music and to play the piano, sitting beside me while my small fingers stumbled over the keys.

'Black and white men all living together on the keyboard,' she told me. 'If you hit them carelessly they jingle jangle in a jungle, but if you play them thoughtfully and tenderly – why, hear what a lovely harmony they make!' Music and brotherly love all bound together in a neat propaganda package suitable for a six-year-old. . . .

I think she must have fallen in love with a certain young curate after my father disappeared. She used to give him chocolate biscuits with China tea, which I shared with them.

'How is young-fellow-me-lad today?' he always asked me; and before I had time to answer he was patting my head and telling me I was fine, just fine, which statement he followed with a high, whinnying laugh. Sometimes to add insult to injury he added: 'Everything's just hunky-dory then?'

I wonder why I never kicked his shins. It was probably because I couldn't locate them exactly under his long black cassock. After he'd left the house she used to sit down at the piano and play Chopin, endlessly it seemed to me: yearning *études*, tender *berceuses* and furious *appassionatas*.

It was music which drew her to religion, and it was certainly the music of the liturgy combined with the noble concept of man's love for man which attracted me to the Church, and which held me so long enthralled by Christian orthodoxy. It was terrible for me when I began to suspect it was slavery, for indeed, like the Prisoner of Chillon, I learned to love my chains. I think when I first met Hannah and her grandmother I still had faith. My mother of course always wanted me to go into the Church; but it was some time before she persuaded me.

I read English at university, where I was blissfully happy because suddenly free, free to lounge about with new friends discussing the life none of us had yet lived, free to be as untidy and unwashed as I wished in my own bed-sit, free from my mother. I came down with a second-class honours degree, after which for a time my life seemed aimless. I longed to be a great writer. 'Poetry has got her bodkin in our back,' wrote Turgenev to Flaubert; literature had hers in mine. I didn't aspire to poetry. I knew even then that poetry was beyond me. That muse requires such a fine distillation of thought and language that even her most gifted and dedicated acolytes sometimes trip over their own feet as they try to climb her altar steps. I was pretty sure I'd make a complete ass of myself in her service; but I thought I might write a novel. I had enough sense to understand that my literary talents were not the sort to earn me a living, especially as the way my mother had brought me up, without a father, with very few friends, and over-protected from coarse realities, had made me pedantic, too fastidious, and certainly out of tune with the current vogue for novels about macho young men who stagger from bar to bar and bed to bed recording their thirsts, belchings, retchings and excretions, and kicking up the occasional verbal felicity on the way to the dustbin. In these urban fields I am obviously as dead as the dodo. It did occur to me later, when I took to roaming alone round London, that I belonged to an extinct species, and finally that I was in fact extinct. I suppose that's what the doctors are trying to rescue me from: extinction.

To write I needed a small income, not to mention a subject to write about. Dropping out of work and drifting on the dole into squats didn't appeal to me at all. For one thing the clean habits implanted in me by my mother could not tolerate the dirt and smells which are all part of the squatting scene. I owe my mother everything. She was a single parent and gave her life to bringing up me and my sister, but she suffered from a dirt phobia, and sometimes (after I had friends to tea) she added disinfectant to the washing-up bowl. So I had to work. I took a job as a junior master in a prep school, and found to my surprise that I loved it. I was learning to live independently, if not in a man's at least in a boy's world in which I had some influence and acquired some respect. I enjoyed the burbling cheerfulness of small boys, their liveliness, inquisitiveness, and charming animal grace. Helping to shape their emerging individualities soon became for me a fascinating occupation. Of course there were the usual number of bullies; but I no longer feared them as I had in childhood. It is surprising how much more attractive bullies appear when regarded, hierarchically speaking, from above instead of below. Our public schools could not be run without them. They are as necessary to education as sergeant-majors in the army. We recognise them as group leaders and call them prefects. I believe, although a certain part of my soul (my mother's?) repudiates this, that democratic notions of equal justice and equal rights to free speech among schoolboys are absurdly illusory. The child is a primitive. He understands tribal rules; he may love or hate, but he accepts the tribal chieftain, whether paternalistic or despotic. Liberalism comes late to man, to some men not at all.

There was among the boys one whom I shall call Absalom after that biblical character. Perhaps I should explain since in some quarters the Bible is not so often read as Freud, that Absalom was the son of David, the third son, famed for his beauty and his luxuriant hair. It was this hair which was the cause of his downfall. In my own case it was not Absalom who fell but I. He was a beautiful child of twelve of the Nordic type with soft flaxen hair and a tender skin, which flushed easily, showing his quick feelings, and slim limbs already beginning to grow long. His pale blue eyes met mine with friendly frankness and his whole character seemed disarmingly honest and affectionate. He used to come to me on certain evenings in the summer term for coaching in English. He was due to take his Common Entrance and hoped to leave us for one of England's famous public schools.

On this particular June evening I stood at the window

193

of my second-floor study overlooking the cricket pitch. The window was wide open for it was very hot and still, but the click of the bat, the murmur of approval following a successful shot and the sudden triumphant shout announcing the batsman's downfall seemed muffled by heat and humidity. Or perhaps these had induced in me a trance-like state, for I didn't hear the boy enter nor was I aware of his presence in the room till he was suddenly beside me. He startled me so I spoke abruptly.

'You're late, Absalom!'

'Yes, sir. Sorry, sir.'

'You're late,' I repeated lamely.

'Yes, sir! Sorry, sir! It was all because of the Painted Lady.' He drew from his pocket a grubby handkerchief in which a frail creature limply fluttered and I recoiled involuntarily.

'It's all right,' he reassured me. 'She won't hurt you. She's nearly dead. They don't live long, you know.'

'That's not true, Absalom. Mine sometimes lived for days under a jar.'

'Really, sir? Were you interested in lepidoptera?'

'Rather! Still am – '

'I'll get some ether from the lab. That kills them quick.' I thought how much more efficient he was in the matter of killing butterflies than I had been when, as a child, I guiltily watched their death flickerings under the glass.

'I say, sir, you haven't got a box or anything I could put her in temporarily?'

I moved hastily to my desk and emptied a small white cardboard box of paper-clips. We transferred the powdered beauty carefully to her white coffin and bound the lid down with a rubber band. Our heads were very close together during this transaction, and once when his soft hair suddenly flopped across my face I was filled with such a confusing flood of emotions that I felt weak in the legs. I sat down and opened my copy of Keats's poems. I waited while he sat down opposite me, fumbled among his books and fumbled again in finding the page.

'Well, Absalom,' I said patiently. 'Have you read the poem?'

'You mean "The Eve of St Agnes", sir?'

'Yes.'

'It's rather long, sir.' He sighed.

'Very well, then. I take it you've read the first page. We'll begin on the second. Take "Soon, up aloft, the silver, snarling trumpets 'gan to chide". That's good, isn't it? – "silver, snarling trumpets"?'

I made him read it aloud. Then I read it. I explained the meaning of 'argent revelry, with plume, tiara, and all rich array', I tried to interpret the romantic heraldic scene into simple schoolboy English, I questioned him to test his comprehension. He kept sighing, and I knew he was bored. However much I liked the boy I had to admit that his soul was certainly not transfigured by Keats's poetic fire. A vague feeling of disappointment and defeat was beginning to settle on me when he remarked, 'But I like that one about Chapman's Homer, sir.' And suddenly he stood up beside me, and in a loud, bold and joyful voice that might have been Chapman's own recited:

' "Then felt I like some watcher of the skies
     When a new planet swims into his ken;
Or like stout Cortez when with eagle eyes
     He stared at the Pacific – and all his men
Looked at each other with a wild surmise –
     Silent, upon a peak in Darien!" '

He didn't even look at me. He was winged by words which transported him to an unknown continent. He was an explorer, a fearless navigator, a conqueror looking down upon new dominions and centuries of history yet to come. I was filled with joy and uplifted with gratitude. It was moments such as this that made my job worth while. I could not trust myself to speak.

'It's good, sir – isn't it?' Uncertainty was creeping into

his brief vision. It seemed to me at that moment vitally important to reassure him so that he might keep if possible for ever this golden glimpse of man's destiny bright in his imagination. I drew him towards me and hugged him. I let him sit on my knee and rumpled his soft hair. Thus far my actions were still perhaps within the confines of culturally acceptable behaviour. Unfortunately I then kissed him. When he dabbed his cheek with his handkerchief I knew I had betrayed myself. This was no spiritual joy. Such a surge of love swept through me that I experienced a powerful erection, and in sudden confusion I was afraid he might be aware of it. I pushed him away, stood up, and walked to the window. The game was finished and the last batsman was taking off his gloves.

'All the same, Absalom,' I heard myself say, 'you'll have to learn "St Agnes". You'd better memorise the first fifty lines before next Monday.' I didn't look at him.

'Yes, sir,' he said behind my back, and left the room.

During the night I woke in a sweat seeing the face of Absalom floating above me. He was a large fish. His round cruel eyes stared unwinking past me, and in his downward-curving grin he gripped a white cloth in which dangled the small, naked body of myself.

O my prophetic soul!

Surely, surely I told myself, I should have recognised this state of affairs long ago. The fear had, of course, occasionally crossed my mind before; but I was always able to rub it out. I had often flirted with girls I met at parties, and even kissed one or two. The fact that I'd never had a love affair with a woman I explained to myself with some resentment as due to the habit my mother taught me of distancing myself from others. Moreover my shy, sensitive soul cringed before all those bouncing, hoydenish females with loud laughs and clumsy high spirits. I had always hoped that one day I would meet some rare, gentle girl who could guess my feelings, who would look at me with wordless tenderness, and then I would clasp her slender boyish body in a passionate embrace. I spent a horrible week.

On Sunday the Head found an opportunity to talk to me. He was a large, hairy man of great vigour and jollity who fumbled with words. The boys used to call him Bumfluff. His study was of course much larger than mine, and on the first floor. The tall sash windows were shut against the rain which had been falling steadily since morning. No white cricketers stood around the soft green pitch (they were all writing letters home), no joyful young voices broke the silence as I faced him across the heavy oak table he used as a desk, a pseudo-Jacobean horror with bulbous legs. I found my knees jutting uncomfortably against one of these, and fidgeted several times trying to avoid the contact.

'A rather tricky – er – situation . . .' he began. 'The fact is – well how shall I put it?' He was obviously acutely embarrassed. 'Young Absalom – um! ah! – He has lodged a complaint.' He stopped and stared miserably down at the table with its burden of white papers. Then he laughed shortly and, as if spurred by his own jollity, stumbled on: 'I don't know – I can't believe – What *do* you think? He says you . . . um! ah! – fondled him!'

I made absolutely no comment. I wondered if he had ever forced himself through such an interview before. He looked up at me with desperate entreaty.

'I was pleased with his work,' I said slowly. 'I put my arm round his shoulder and told him so.'

'Quite! Quite!' he nodded, and paused, leaving me to wonder what Absalom had really told him. Had he vaguely hinted, told the exact truth, or had he invented more? Frantic images flickered through my mind like some medieval painting done on video, some Garden of Delights by Hieronymus Bosch with young Absalom himself kneeling naked on the lawn with a daffodil stuck up his arse.

'Nothing of this sort has ever happened before?'

'I don't know what you mean by *this sort*. Certainly neither my actions nor my intentions have ever been in any way abnormal towards boys – if that's what you mean.' I was excessively calm.

Poor Bumfluff must have been greatly relieved, for after this he burst into unrestricted speech.

'Good! Good! Of course that is exactly what I believed myself. Some boys nowadays have odd ideas. Naivety and sophistication are often crudely mixed in them. I've never liked Absalom much myself. There is a vein of cynicism in him, I think. This must have been distressing for you. I'm sorry. But of course you understand if the boy spreads rumours it could have a bad effect on discipline . . . and further – ' an unimaginable Nemesis quite bowled out his sentences – 'The long-term effects – dreadful – devastating, yes, devastating – Not to be imagined!'

'I quite understand. I suggest that in the circumstances Mallory takes over Absalom's English tutorials.'

It was a psychological error. If I had had the courage to continue coaching Absalom, had attacked him and demanded an apology, had laughed at his fantasies, perhaps I might not be here now. The fact is my own feelings of guilt made me afraid of the child.

'It was a simple impulse of affection,' I said, working up a show of indignation. 'I was pleased with his work. It certainly won't happen again. I had no idea Absalom had such a nasty mind.'

'Yes indeed. I must say it's been rather a shock to me too.'

The big jolly man was sweating. He took out his handkerchief and wiped his neck. 'I'm very sorry about it all. Embarrassing in the extreme, I must say.'

I began to laugh.

'It's rather funny, really. All so surprising when you come to think of it, isn't it?'

My laughter convinced him. He stood up and offered me a glass of sherry.

'Basically cruel – boys . . .' I remarked as I sipped it.

'Well, they're nearly all hunters really,' he said. 'Clever little savages baiting traps for all unwary schoolmasters, don't you think?'

We agreed over a second glass.

Hell opened for me as I left that room. I could no longer look into the pale, frank eyes of young Absalom. At every corner of each corridor I was expecting to catch whispered scandal about myself. What shocking suggestions were being relayed from ear to ear about me? What under-blanket sniggering of my indecencies tinkled through the dormitories after lights out? How did they speak of me? Did they call me pervert, pansy, homo, pouf or fairy? I knew what taboos of horror and contempt were still attached to these words, and as the next week dragged by I became in my own conscience an outcast, although I had done nothing wrong. I no longer belonged to my protecting mother; no other woman loved me, and perhaps no woman could. I didn't get on well with men, and now even innocent children recoiled from me. I was a filthy thing. Guilt like a fog began to hang about my imagination, obscuring the safe landmarks of reason and experience.

I no longer felt any joy in my work; I taught badly and dully; my classes became noisy and unruly. At the end of each day I was tired and dispirited. I felt ill and often left my food untasted. How I lived through the remainder of that term I don't know, but it came to an end at last. Bumfluff, in spite of his broad hairy chest and his jollity, which I thought of as outward signs of inner bravery, did not have the moral courage to sack me face to face. He wrote me a letter, after term ended, saying he thought it would be in my own interest to seek employment in another school. He advised this more for the sake of my own happiness and peace of mind than his, and offered to stand as referee. He assured me of his support in any application I made for another job, and vowed my work had always been satisfactory, indeed extremely promising, that I had the gift of inspiring enthusiasm, lighting a beacon

in the youthful imagination etc., etc. His style florid, protesting too much. . . .

I did not go home for the holidays. I bought a BR ticket
to London. Single. InterCity. I began to drift towards those
very squats I had so much dreaded. I began to see the
world as a nasty dirty place full of hostile faces. There was
a madman who slept on the floor beside me in our boarded-
up basement who thought the world was a gigantic pellet
of shit extruded in prehistoric times by a mammoth from
outer space, and that he was, that we were all rolled up
inside this excrement. The night after he confided to me
his private philosophy I stole from the pocket of his jacket,
while he slept, a bottle of capsules. I had seen him swallow
one of these with water from time to time. I swallowed the
whole lot of them with milk from a carton.

I don't know what happened after that. When I woke
up I was in a white hospital bed looking into the big white
beautiful smile of a black nurse, who in a sundrenched
Jamaican voice was trying to persuade me to drink a cup
of tea. And that was when I met Dr Gootfahrt for the first
time. His name brought instantly to mind Absalom and all
my other prep-school boys. I thought of them not with
tenderness exactly but with a happy tolerance. I could just
imagine what hay and havoc they would make of the good
doctor's name: Banger, or Jet-Bang he would be called, or
possibly Bean Bag, or perhaps more airily Farty-Pops. I
couldn't help smiling. He is a large kindly man, heavily
bearded, and I believe is quite famous in his own world for
abstruse papers published chiefly on the continent of
Europe on such subjects as 'The Aesthetics of Coprophilia',
and 'Narcissistic Regression and Hypochondriasis'. My own
illness does not fit neatly into any of the defined categories.
I was grief-stricken: bereaved by the loss of my own youth
and innocence, and horror-stricken at the recognition of
the monster in myself. A nervous breakdown is what my
mother called it. I believe it has other names: alienation,
identity crisis, midlife crisis if you happen to be the right

age for that, which I was not. What I was really suffering from was sadness; and at what depth does sadness become a sickness? I believe I had every reason to be sad. At birth I had been endowed by chance if not by God with a nature not exactly run of the mill. Through this misfortune I would be denied the ordinarily expected joys of love and family life. I was alone in a strange unfriendly world; I didn't know what to do with myself; I didn't know what decisions to take, let alone how to decide them. It was all too difficult. I threw in the sponge.

Throwing in the sponge was the proper diagnosis. No doubt it should be given a learned Greek or Latin name: *Ejecta spongia*, or more correctly *Ejectandum spongiae*, or would it be *Ejiciens spongiam*? Here I am floundering about among the flotsam and jetsam of forgotten Latin grammar when it strikes me that any twentieth-century psychiatrist must be better equipped than I to define the world he has to live in and its ills, and would probably dub my disease tersely as Fall-out.

My mother of course was delighted to have me home. She fussed over my meals, washed my clothes, tutting with very loud tuts over the state of my underwear. She folded me up inside her unselfish, overpowering, devouring care. It was summertime. I sat in the garden listening to birdsong and smelling the scent of roses intertwined with jasmine in the arbour in which I sat. The curtains billowed out, carrying with them the sounds my mother's fingers were producing on her piano. It was all reminiscent of a scene described by a thousand aspiring young writers of romantic fiction. What they don't mention, and I do, is the greedy, positively devouring desire for love that shuddered towards me over the grass.

Well, I couldn't sit the rest of my life out in her garden, could I? She wanted me to go into the Church. I thought of it as a safe haven where I would be protected, a place of peace where there would be fewer temptations, fewer Absaloms. I decided I'd better try to develop a vocation for the priesthood. I always doubted parts of the Creed; but I liked the noble concept of man's love for man; and I understood (rather too well perhaps) the idea that the child holds the key to the Kingdom of Heaven.

I will pass over my training to be a parson, and curtail my curacies. A curate is a sort of clerical dogsbody, and I was several times that animal. My life was dull till I was promoted to be vicar in my present parish of Mudcott. It is where the River Frene dives over a natural stone weir to gouge out a deep basin before meandering away through low-lying fields rank with reeds and buttercups, and slides over muddy fords where cattle drink. Once, before men dug rhines and drainage ditches here, these were marshlands, badlands too wet to cultivate, infested with horsetail, that plant surviving from a period long, long before the appearance of man upon the planet, a time so ancient that it is recorded only in the compressed vegetations of deeply buried coal. Mudcott is a sleepy village innocent of crime where nothing ever seems to happen. But I don't let that deceive me. It is in just such places forgotten by history, and perhaps by God too, that terrible things are done.

My influence was small. I was lucky if my congregation swelled to twenty through the influx of visitors at Christmas and Easter. Perhaps I didn't have the gifts required by the job; but I do believe that even an Augustine or an Ignatius Loyola couldn't have done much in Mudcott. As I made the acquaintance of my parishioners I began to feel like that nineteenth-century bishop who was warned that all his clerics could be divided into three categories: those who had lost their wits, those who were about to lose them, and those who had none to lose. My parishioners belonged entirely to the last group. Very few of them came to church at all. My services were attended by a handful of old women who were loyal and devoted servants of the Church as they saw it. They managed all the activities; they sang loudly and obstinately in cracked voices, often out of tune, and usually dragging at the tempo of the liveliest hymn. They told me what to do. Of course I needed their help. I couldn't get rid of them; but I was determined to make changes. I began by refusing to wear vestments of any kind, apart from my cassock, and by completely reorganising the Sunday School teaching. These two measures alone were enough to set my church cats caterwauling. I then opened a youth club in the village hall. Nearly all the young people lived on the council estate. They were regarded by my hard core of workers as city-overspill: a form of sewage. I was warned that the youth club premises would be smashed up, and that if I allowed the sexes to mix some sort of unspecified but disgusting orgy would develop. I wanted to preach to them one day the wonderful message of Christ to all men, the great simple truths washed clean of ancient dogma and academic dust. I believed the young, in spite of their apparent anarchy, were seeking for God, while the rest of us, corrupted by cynicism, sneered at their confused endeavour.

I let the members organise the club themselves. Three of the boys began a pop group, which immediately increased membership. I soon discovered who could sing, and mentally marked them for my future choir, which was later enriched by several young voices. I was happier; things were moving slowly in my direction, although apart from my choir singers the young never came inside the church at all, until only last year I had the bright idea of producing a Nativity Play in modern dress accompanied by the singing of Negro spirituals. It was a great success. It was attended by the parents and friends of my actors and singers, and the church was full to overflowing. I was complimented and thanked by many parishioners who for years before had ignored me. That day I was truly happy.

Over the years there remained, however, one thorn in my flesh. With the vicarage I had inherited a housekeeper. She had looked after a bachelor vicar before me, and considered she knew more about how to run church affairs than I ever would. Naturally she disliked changes of any sort. My predecessor had been High, liking embroidered vestments, incense-swinging and that kind of thing, which I did not. She missed these rituals.

'It was different in the old days.' She made her feelings known when she served my meals.

'Yes Sarah?'

'The Reverend Crossley was local, of course. He knew our ways.'

I was a foreigner from Birmingham, which was to her, who had lived her whole life in this West Country village, as remote as the Faroe Islands. Foreigners were enemies. She didn't really live in the modern world but in some ancient tribal settlement of her own imagining. She was given to sudden outbursts of temper when she had to face things beyond her understanding, or which she couldn't manipulate to suit herself. I always knew when she was in a rage because that was when she sang hymns over the washing-up. The hymn-singing, far from soothing her, seemed to lash her fury. Pans were bashed about and crockery hustled on to shelves with such vigour that I feared for its survival. I used to sit rigid in my study awaiting the final crash. The Nativity Play in jazz and jeans proved more than she could bear.

'I shall not be here tomorrow, sir.'

'You'll spend Christmas with your sister then?'

'Yes sir.' She thumped down a dish of potatoes on the table.

'I quite understand, Sarah,' I said, speaking as quietly as possible. 'I can manage for myself perfectly well. Anyway you should take the day off. And I hope you have a very happy Christmas.'

'I never used to have Christmas Day off, sir. Never did – not in the old days. But blasphemy, sir – well, it's too much!' She scurried out with my soup plate, and I heard her clashing it with other wretched china in the sink.

So that was how I came to be alone after my morning

204

service on Christmas Day when Hannah arrived with her baby.

'Good heavens!' I exclaimed as I opened the front door in answer to her loud knocking. 'It's Hannah!' It was indeed, and her yelling infant as well.

'Well, fancy!' she said cheerfully. 'You remember me, then?'

'Of course I do. I was very fond of your gran too. We both were, weren't we? Come in. It's much too cold for that baby outside. Baby looks very young,' I added dubiously.

'Born three weeks ago,' she said. 'Came out of hospital ten days ago. Had to leave my friend's bed-sit. Crying babies not allowed.'

I ushered her into my study where a coal fire was burning.

'I didn't know where to go,' she continued, lifting the baby and patting its back. 'And suddenly I thought of you. I knew you were kind, and I knew I'd be safe with you. You were just what I needed. That's why I've come.'

She never did beat about the bush. But the Lord be praised! I was needed. Perhaps I was created for this very moment?

She sat down and pulling a swollen breast from under her jumper shoved the nipple into her baby's wide-open mouth. I didn't know where to look! I stood above her awkwardly, thinking how like fledgling birds with their wide-open, red, squawking beaks the human young are.

'Don't be shy,' she said in the ensuing silence. 'It's only natural. I don't suppose you've seen a baby suck before? Neither had I till I saw Emily at it. You don't have to teach them, you know. They just know how to do it. You have to put it in their mouth of course. They can't crawl for it – though some daft mothers in the hospital expected them to!' She burst into a peal of laughter. It was her special kind of laughter: innocent, joyful and, yes, aggressive. It's what must have protected her like a shield from the outrageous fortune which had been hers, and now would protect her child. It was heart-warming to hear it, as it was to watch all that young mother-love overflowing into the baby's mouth. During the feeding she told me her troubles, all predictable if you knew, as I did, her childhood and adolescent history, her running away from Gatt's Rise, which must have been an excellent foster home, and her disappearance two years ago in London.

We had a lot of fun that Christmas Day. We found things, including an old cot, among the jumble sale items, to furnish a room for her. And then we ate Christmas dinner together. Sarah had left a cold chicken for me, and Hannah made some apple fritters.

'My gran used to make apple fritters,' she said. 'Lovely they were, all brown and crunchy and sprinkled with sugar.' Hannah's were not, I guess, as good as Gran's. They were rather over-frittered; but I was so elated at what was happening to my life that I ate them, finding even the charred bits palatable. To say that Hannah wolfed them down would be an understatement.

'You can scrape and scrounge and earn a bit here and there doing odd jobs, waitressing and cleaning, maybe begging a bit,' she said, 'when you're on your own, if you've got a friend who has a squat to keep the rain off you at night; but all that's not on when you've got a little 'un hanging on to your tits. It's a different scenario entirely then.'

'Well, you must stay here, Hannah. With Emily. It is Emily?'

'Emily,' she cooed. 'Or just Em, or little old Emily. What you fancy. I called her Emily after this girl, see?'

I didn't; but I waited.

'Her name was Emmeline, this girl in the caff who helped me when I was near down and out. "You need a bath," she says to me. "Well, I can't get that off the streets, can I?" I said. "You're too young to be running around like this," she says.'

It seems this girl was a waitress in a cheap café where

Hannah took refuge and a cup of tea on a cold wet morning not long after she arrived in London. It was still early in the day, and there was no one else in the shop. Hannah had no money left after paying for her cup of tea, so this Emmeline passed her a ham sandwich over the counter when the proprietor was out in the kitchen. And then she sat down opposite Hannah and they began to talk.

'The next thing she was offering me a put-you-up bed in her bed-sit. Her idea was I should work at the caff weekends, when they were busy and needed the casual, extra like. And I could pay her something towards her rent. We told the boss I was eighteen, and he asked no questions.'

'So at least you had a roof over your head,' I commented with some relief.

'She was great, Emmeline. Saved me from falling into the pits. So that's why I called my baby after her. I wonder what my baby will call herself? Milly, most likely. I had an aunt once called Milly. Millicent Batherswick. Nuts she was.'

'Who's Emily's father, Hannah?' I asked, putting down my spoon on an empty plate.

'I don't rightly know,' she replied. She scraped some sugar up and put it in her mouth before she explained. 'We used to go disco-dancing at a club sometimes, Emmeline and me, on Saturday nights after work when we weren't too knackered. I liked the music and the dancing and all the swirling scattered lights. It gives you a high, you know.' She looked up at me doubtfully. 'Well, it did me, any road. So I didn't need any of those drugs to make you feel good. But one night a boy I was with gave me some sweets. "*Special*, for you," he said. And before I knew it he'd popped one in my mouth. I must have swallowed a few more later. I can't remember much what happened after that; but I know we went outside and climbed into the back of a car that wasn't locked up. It must have been then that I got pregnant. I wasn't on the pill, see? Didn't

207

think I needed it because I didn't intend any hanky-panky with strange men. Can't even remember what he looked like now. Gary, that was his name.'

She rose from the table, collected our plates, and took them to the sink. She knew I was shocked; and I think she was ashamed and wanted to hide her face from me. She leaned over the sink talking with her back to me. 'I went on working almost to the month Emily was born. I wore a big loose kaftan at work to hide what was happening to my belly. I was scared to go to a doctor. I did think of giving a false name and all that at the doctor's surgery, but I was scared they'd track me down and the law would catch up with me, and I'd be locked up for absconding. So I got no dole of course, and no money out of maternity benefit or anything. At the end I was living off my friend.'

I didn't interrupt her. She came back to the table, and sitting down she put her elbows on it and her chin in her hands and stared out into the past beyond my head.

'When my time came she called the ambulance, and I was taken to hospital. My, was I glad to be in that safe warm place! – even though I did do a bit of yelling and swearing when the head was coming down. Gave a false name, and my friend's address, and added on a few years to my date of birth when they asked me. D'you know, a nurse with a pen and clipboard asked me what was my religion when I was in the middle of a labour pain? "God knows," I shouted at her. "God knows! I don't." I was gasping. "Write down holy roller or something. Roll on! Roll on, and let's get this over!" '

She began to laugh, which brought her back to the present. She looked straight at me then. 'But afterwards,' she said, 'when they sent me home, well, I couldn't stay on with Emmeline paying her no rent, could I? So that's when I thought of you.'

'You did quite right, Hannah. I'm glad you've come.' I accepted her story. It was probably more or less the truth.

She was completely infatuated with her child. This emotion was overcoming any anxieties she might have felt for the future; her whole being was concentrated on the present. And I was learning that though I'd often preached about maternal love I had never before understood it. It was not something calm and spiritual; it was a powerful animal passion that had taken possession of her. I was amazed and shaken when I watched them together. The sight made me feel uncertain of myself. I felt puny before this tidal wave of emotion which was sweeping away the signposts of my usual behaviour.

Sarah did not return for several days. She was definitely punishing me. My heart sank as I realised I would have to give her some explanation for my latest blasphemy – sheltering the orphan and the outcast – so when she did return I invited her into my study for a glass of sherry.

'I hope you had a happy Christmas, Sarah. Shall we drink to the New Year together?'

'Happy New Year, sir and many of them!' she said, and sipped.

Encouraged by her good humour I described Hannah's arrival on the very birthday of Jesus.

'I couldn't turn away the young mother with a newborn babe like the innkeeper in the old story, could I? Although they were not attended by hosts of angels, nor visited by kings and shepherds their need for shelter and kindness was as great as Mary's was.'

'There's other places for the likes of her to go to,' she objected.

'Well, it won't be for long, Sarah. We'll have to find somewhere suitable for her to live as soon as she's strong enough. Meanwhile perhaps she could help in the kitchen?'

'That she won't. Not in my kitchen.'

'Well perhaps, cleaning the house . . .?'

'Maybe upstairs,' Sarah allowed. 'She'll have to do that baby's washing in the bath upstairs. And there's an old electric cooker in the scullery where she can do her cooking.'

I was not well enough armed or armoured for the domestic battle which ensued. I could never tell whether I was winning or losing; but Hannah simply accepted Sarah's hostility and remained within her own boundaries on the first floor. It was almost as if the two women, like rival robins, claimed and guarded their territorial rights. Hannah only visited me when I invited her to, which was always when Sarah was out, and then we dropped our voices like conspirators. It was a week later, when Emily's nappies were hanging out to dry over the vicarage lawn, waving shamelessly in the breeze, that Sarah commented suddenly: 'What will people say? I mean, a young unmarried mother and a bachelor vicar living together!'

'Why, Sarah, I'm old enough to be her father!' I protested. I could not explain that my sexual appetites were not aroused by Hannah, nor could be by any woman; but Sarah pursed her lips. 'And as you well know we are not living together, but only under the same roof, and only till such time as a suitable home can be found for her. So you'll have to tell the village gossips the truth, won't you?'

'I never gossip about vicarage affairs!' she declared indignantly.

'Well, perhaps just this once, it might be diplomatic to do so,' I suggested.

It occurred to me that perhaps the best thing for Hannah would be to go back to Gatt's Rise. I was pretty sure that Mary Chicon would forgive her desertion and welcome her back with open arms. But Hannah objected when I put the proposition to her.

'Oh no! She'll never forgive me. And what about her father – the old dinosaur?'

'You've no need to worry on that score,' I said. 'The Colonel is no longer with us. He has moved on to whatever Valhalla is reserved for old dinosaurs.'

'Is he dead?'

'He died of a stroke – the second, it was – the summer after you ran away.' But even this news wouldn't persuade her to return to Gatt's Rise.

'Maybe after I'm eighteen,' she said. 'When they can't put me in care no more. Is Mikey still alive, d'you know?'

I knew nothing of Mikey. News of him had not filtered down to Mudcott.

'What about Tom and Marge? Are they still there?'

'Was Tom the farm worker? I did hear he'd gone – taken a job on a big farm in Northamptonshire, I believe.'

'That'll be nothing but cereals over there,' she said. 'He'll miss his sheep.' She added: 'I left my guitar with them.'

TWELVE

Hannah made no demands on my time and attention at the vicarage. It was I who broke in on her thoughts. She was preoccupied exclusively with her baby's needs. Once I heard her singing a snatch of some old West Country song as she washed nappies.

> ' "An' there vor me the apple tree
> Do lean down low in Linden Lea." '

'What a lovely song!' I exclaimed.

'Yes,' she agreed. 'Gran used to sing it often. I like all them Ls.'

'It's called alliteration,' I said. 'Using the same first letter for a string of words to make a sort of ringing in the mind.' She looked at me attentively. 'It's a very old poetic form,' I went on, 'not only in English, but in other languages as well.'

'Yes?' She didn't regard me as some old fuddy-duddy reeking of library shelves. She thought of me as a source of knowledge. I was surprised by her curiosity and also, as time went on, by the depths of her ignorance.

'I missed a lot of schooling,' she explained, 'that year I ran away and was took to court. Pity, really!'

I gave her poems to read. Soon she was asking for other

books ('to keep me busy while Emily's gorging herself'), and sometimes when she came across a word she didn't know we looked it up in the dictionary together. I began to wonder if her natural talents wouldn't flower with further education.

'Would you like to take some GCSEs?' I asked her. She was hanging out nappies.

'Exams?' she queried, a peg between her teeth. 'I don't think I'm that clever.'

'What nonsense!' I declared. 'You would certainly have been clever enough if you'd stayed at school.'

'Well, it's done now, en' it? Can't be undone, as Gran used to say. So I must lump it.'

'You might stay here, and when Baby's a bit older go part-time to college.'

What were my motives in this scheme? No doubt they were partly selfish. I was trying to keep her with me for a little longer. We were both solitary souls stranded on our separate islands. Events had thrown us together, and we were able to assuage each other's loneliness. Was that such a bad thing? Moreover I did truly believe that study, by its discipline, would anchor her in more regular habits than she had yet learned, and would also open her active mind and fertile imagination to new worlds more rewarding and healthier than the denizens of her old London haunts could show her. Hannah was more practical than I.

'And who'd look after Emmy then?' she demanded.

'We might persuade Sarah to do it,' I suggested. 'It would only be for part of the day after all.'

'She wouldn't like that, Rev. Emmy's a bastard to her, if you'll excuse my language, and too dirty for her to touch. Emmy's little backside would foul her pure hands in more ways than one!' She made a joke of it although her words were bitter. 'Anyway, I'd never leave my baby to be looked after by anyone. I'm going to give Emmy all the love I missed.' So I said no more; but she must have repeated some of our conversation to Sarah, because a few days later as Sarah was serving my lunch she fired an opening salvo.

'Some folks have more luck than others.'

I waited in silence for further elucidation of her train of thought.

'Virtue doesn't always get its right reward, does it, sir?'

'That's very true, Sarah. But that's what heaven's for: to right the wrongs done on earth.'

'That may be so, sir. But it's not fair, is it, that some that's done wrong should get all the help that's going here?'

'What are you trying to say, Sarah?' I helped myself to potatoes.

'I never got no one to look after me, let alone my baby – which I never had! – so's I could go on to higher study!' Her voice rose in indignation.

So that's it, I thought.

'Well of course, Sarah,' I agreed, struggling to be diplomatic, 'it was often very hard, and unfair as well in your young days. I know that. But you see we have better educational opportunities for the young now. Better education for boys and girls means more enlightened men and women, and they in turn can teach their children more. Education is the future, Sarah, for all of us.'

She made no reply, but banged down a dish of Brussels sprouts on the table in front of me. Conversation recommenced with the appearance of apple pie.

'She should never have been allowed into the vicarage. People are talking.'

'But Sarah, I couldn't have turned her out into the street – on Christmas Day too. It was my Christian duty to give her shelter.'

'She should never 'ave come back to places where she's known,' argued Sarah. 'People don't dirty their own doorsteps, do they? Not decent people.' She had grown very red in the face, always a sign of worse to come.

'The baby is blameless,' I reminded her. She stood silenced by this, so I went on: 'It will only be for a short

214

time now. The health visitor will advise her, and the social worker, as to housing. She'll have to find work, I suppose. But it's a pity,' I added. 'Hannah is an intelligent girl and could benefit from more education.'

'Well, *I* never ran away from home to London and picked up with all sorts of men! *I* never brought back a bastard with such a brazen face! *I* was never took in off the street to read poetry with the vicar!'

'No of course not, Sarah. You were well brought up by good parents – '

It was too late. She had flounced out of the room, loudly banging the door. She did not come back, and I was forced to fetch the coffee from the kitchen myself. I think this episode finally established siege lines within the vicarage. On one side was Sarah doing her work grimly, unwillingly and in silence, on the other myself attempting to communicate and trying to maintain politeness. Hannah flitted about upstairs, took Emily out in the old pram she'd managed to buy with the help of her social worker, fed herself in the kitchen when Sarah went out, and spoke to me when we passed each other on the stairs. It was a state of affairs which I found unnerving.

'Hannah,' I said one afternoon when Sarah had gone to visit her sister, 'come into my study, will you, please?' She carried Emily in her arms and stood waiting. 'She's beautiful,' I said. 'Is she gaining weight well?'

'Of course she is,' replied Hannah, and continued without any change of tone, 'Jealous. That's what she is. Jealous because you've been good to me. People are like that.'

'You mean Sarah?'

'Who else?' She paused for a moment before adding: 'I think I'll have to be moving on.'

'But Hannah, where will you go?'

'I've been talking to the health visitor. There's a place in town where you can leave the baby while you go out to work. And anyway I can get the dole for a while. I shall manage somehow.'

I looked at her sadly and in silence. It seemed to me such a pity, such a waste that this charming child with much natural intelligence and goodness of heart should be thrown out into a voracious world at a time when she was most in need of care and protection.

'You've been good to me,' she said. 'Sarah thinks it's because of me big boobs and me big brown peepers; but I know better. I know you don't want nothing from me. You're just good, like Gran was.'

'Am I, Hannah?' I murmured, quite overcome by her praise.

'Yes,' she said, and blushed suddenly. 'Gran used to call you Reverend Disability. Only among ourselves, of course. "What's his disability, Gran?" I asked. But she wouldn't tell me, so I began to think it must be a wooden leg you kept hidden under your cassock. It was only when I grew up I guessed you were not like other men.'

So she had always known. Was that what made me safe for her to come to in her hour of need? Her knowing made me feel guilty, though my conscience was absolutely clear. The trouble is I have become a split person with two consciences: my own, and that which has been foisted on me by others. The law now allows homosexual love between consenting adults; the Church does not. Nobody allows pederasty. I have not committed that crime, but I desire it. I know I have it in me to do it. The guilt marks my soul although I am not guilty.

'We all have some weakness,' I said. 'You and I are more easily wounded than most. Perhaps that's why we understand each other.' She said nothing. 'How old's Emily? Three months? Well, stay a little longer – till the milk dries up. Then you'll feel stronger and better able to cope with the world.'

'I shall cope all right. If Emmy needs anything she shall have it. She's more important than my own life, you see. But yes, I'll stay on a few months, then. I wish I could do something for you Rev – to show I'm grateful.'

'Well, I've been thinking, Hannah, that it would be nice to have you in my choir. You've got a good, strong, steady voice, and I'd be glad of it for the Easter services.'

'OK,' she agreed. 'That 'ud be nice.'

At first she brought Emily in a carrycot and laid her on a pew. I believe the baby enjoyed the singing. At any rate she never cried; but after a few weeks Hannah decided to leave her in the bedroom, as she was always fast asleep by 8 p.m., the hour of the choir practice. Afterwards Hannah got back in time to cook herself a snack (Sarah had gone to bed) before giving Emily her night feed. By now I was learning quite a lot about baby care. Sometimes I held Emily in my arms and made encouraging noises, to which she responded in a most delightful way with gurgling sounds and many kicks and jerks of her little legs and arms. 'It's what the health visitor calls socialising,' Hannah explained. Emily was a beautiful, normal child, and her glowing health and high spirits were ample proof of her mother's loving care.

I suppose I must have been too involved with my parish duties and the pleasures of my adopted family to wonder if Sarah's grim silences might be pathological. Looking back I can see that her work had been slipping into a certain uncharacteristic slovenliness, and that sometimes when I entered her kitchen I caught her sitting absolutely still, hunched up over the table. Once I did ask her: 'Are you all right, Sarah? Not ill or anything?'

'Nothing wrong with me, sir.' She rose clumsily and stumped across the rough flagstones to pick up the kettle.

'Sarah,' I ventured, 'these old houses with their stone floors – aren't they very cold? I mean, for your feet? Are you warm enough in here?'

'Nothing wrong with me, sir,' she repeated. 'Nor with the floor neither.' So I left her and said no more.

She was out visiting her sister that Wednesday evening when we returned from choir practice, a little later than usual as it happened. I didn't mind how long the rehearsing lasted because I loved my choir. It was Mr Pollock the organist who made us late. He's a good man, a cobbler, a careful honest craftsman, and a member of the ancient Guild of St Crispin, patron of shoemakers. I'm glad he enjoys playing the organ; but on this occasion the volume of sound issuing from it completely drowned the voices I was trying to train in the nave below. I was hoping to teach Hannah to sing Handel's lovely aria 'I know that my Redeemer liveth', but every time her sweet young voice began to rise through the cold air of that March evening Mr Pollock blasted some overwhelming chords above our heads. Afterwards I drew him aside to plead for a little more abstinence in his accompaniment.

'I want the pure line of the recitative to come through by itself.'

'Not the right place for recitative,' was his judgement. 'All very well with massed choirs in Cardiff. But not here. Not in our village church.'

'I don't see why not, Mr Pollock, when Hannah has such a good strong soprano. We should make the best of it, don't you think?'

'Oh Hannah!' he exclaimed in such a sarcastic tone that I was alarmed. He shot me a quick, hard glance as he wound his long woollen scarf round his neck. I had frequently been irritated by this scarf, which was so ludicrously long that I went in constant fear of his tripping over it and strangling himself accidentally. 'The congregation always gets restless with recitative,' he said. 'What they really like, Theo, is a big polyphonic sound. People don't like music that wanders about. They like a firm shape and strong rules, like in life. That way they feel safer.'

'You're probably right there,' I admitted. He was altogether too familiar, calling me by my Christian name, far too young to be permitted such familiarities; but of course I permitted them. 'But you can't accuse Handel of wandering about. A bit of hopping up and down in the *Messiah* I grant

218

you, but all in good order. His musical behaviour is never irregular.'

'Handel's OK,' he allowed. 'It's Hannah who won't keep time.'

'That's exactly why I'd like to try it through again next week, Mr Pollock, if you don't mind.'

I knew he did mind; but we parted on that to-be-continued note little knowing that our difference was over something which had already come to an end.

As Sarah was still out, Hannah and I made ourselves a drink of cocoa and sat down for a few minutes at the kitchen table munching biscuits and warming our fingers round the hot mugs. We didn't speak. We had no need to. We were both happily tired.

'Em's calling,' she announced at last.

'I didn't hear her.'

'No, Silly. Neither did I. I felt it, here.' She pointed to her chest. 'In me boobs. They leak a bit when they're too full.'

She whisked herself off and I heard her running upstairs. I took the mugs to the sink and ran the tap over them, when suddenly the house was filled with a horrible noise, an inhuman soul-chilling howl. Could it possibly be Hannah, so recently singing in serene and holy phrases of her Redeemer, who uttered that dreadful cry like a fox caught in a trap?

I ran to the bottom of the stairs.

'What's the matter?' I shouted, my voice pitched unnaturally high by fear. 'Hannah, what is it?'

She made no reply, but I heard her coming down with slow, hopeless steps. The hall light fell on her and the baby in her arms. She pushed past me into the kitchen, and laid Emily on the table.

'The kiss of life,' she hissed. 'How do you do it?' But Emily had long passed the possibility of revival by any kiss. She was dead. Her little hands, and her cheeks, too, were cold.

219

'What's happened? How?' I asked.

'I dunno,' said Hannah. She did not weep, but rocked the baby to and fro as if she were still alive and crying desperately.

I ran to the phone and called up the doctor, who as luck would have it was at home, and came at once.

'Was she quite well, earlier today?' he asked.

'Never better,' said Hannah.

'No snuffles, nor cough?'

'No.'

'Taking her feeds well?'

'Yes.'

'And she had her first immunisation four weeks ago you say?'

'Yes, doctor. She's nearly four months now.'

He was sitting on a chair opposite her. He touched the baby's cold cheek. He looked searchingly at Hannah. Then he got up and walked round the table to face me.

'It's what we used to call cot death. Sudden Infant Death Syndrome is what the pundits call it now. We don't quite understand how it happens. Sometimes it comes out of the blue, like this. Always very distressing.'

He went back to Hannah.

'You're going to need a sedative tonight, young lady,' he said. He pulled a small bottle out of his black bag and put six capsules on the table.

'Give her one tonight,' he said to me. 'I'll leave the others to your discretion. I shall have to inform the coroner – sudden unexpected death, you know, has to be reported. He'll send the police.'

'Police?' I echoed. 'What on earth for?'

'I'm sorry', said Dr Marten. 'Has to be done. But it's a mere formality in this case. I shall be here when they come; and I shall tell them what I think.'

When he left the kitchen to phone the coroner's officer Hannah stood up, the dead baby in her arms.

'Seems as if I'm cursed,' she said.

'We are both cursed, Hannah,' I said. I put my arms round her, and we stood together weeping.

After a while she moved away from me.

'Let's lay her out in her little cot,' I suggested. 'Shall I bring it down for you?'

'No!' she cried fiercely. 'I shall keep her by me, here in my arms, as long as ever I can – till they come and take her away.'

'They' were soon flitting in and out of the house like the Fates whose forms they had assumed in Hannah's mind. They were the visible embodiments of organised society. First came an Inspector in plain clothes accompanied by a policewoman in uniform. They arrived at the front door at the same moment as Sarah arrived at the back. They noted her absence and her arrival. Dr Marten tried to explain the circumstances of the child's death.

'How do you know she wasn't suffocated?' the Inspector asked.

I put my hand on Hannah's shoulder to steady myself as much as her.

'Well,' said Dr Marten, 'she's not blue, and there are no marks of pressure round her mouth. Nor, of course, any marks of violence.'

'But you would agree it doesn't take much to snuff out a baby's life?' the Inspector pursued.

I thought it horrible.

'That is so,' said Dr Marten calmly. 'The post-mortem will show any more evidence there might be of the cause of death.'

'Just so, just so,' said the Inspector. But Hannah covered Emily's head with one arm and shouted: 'Nobody's going to cut my baby up in pieces!'

We all fell silent, and at last the doctor intervened in a soft voice: 'In cases of sudden unexplained death it's the law, Hannah. It's inevitable, I'm afraid. Let me take Emily now. I'll see she's not harmed.'

Reluctantly, Hannah released her hold and let the doctor

take her baby from her; but as soon as she felt her arms empty she began to howl. I hugged her tightly for a few moments. Her body was shaken by such violent sobs that I thought: nothing, nothing will ever heal her pain.

During the next few days, in between visits from funeral directors, social workers, her health visitor and from Dr Marten, Hannah drifted up and down stairs, in and out of rooms like a restless ghost. In the background stood Sarah, an image of vengeance, silent but ever present.

I must say the coroner acted very quickly, and Dr Marten phoned us immediately he'd received the report: no evidence of unnatural death. He came to see Hannah later that day. He seemed able to make her talk a little, which I could not. I believe they talked about her future. Afterwards I offered him sherry, which we both drank thoughtfully.

'What was the cause of death?' I asked.

'I don't know,' he replied. 'Nobody knows for sure, as yet, what these cot deaths are due to. It's one of the medical phenomena not yet understood. It's probably a mixed bag of causes. Some are due to a sudden overwhelming virus pneumonia; in some cases the infant simply stops breathing: spontaneous apnoea ... They think the respiratory centre in the brain is sometimes immature, its rhythmic pulses not absolutely established. In some there may be an absence of immunity to infection, or a profound anaemia.'

I could see he was talking to himself as much as to me.

'It must be very distressing to see as much death and sorrow as you do, Dr Marten. I often wonder how doctors survive.'

'If doctors had hearts as tender as yours, my dear fellow, we'd all jump in the nearest river. No, we have to learn to distance our feelings a bit from the case in hand, so that our judgement is not impaired. That is not to say,' he hastened to add, 'that I think your action in taking Hannah into the vicarage was misguided. It was a Christian act; but unfortunately she seems to be a girl ... well, disasters do

222

seem to flock round her. . . .' He puffed his pipe energetically. 'I am very glad the post-mortem has cleared all suspicions away. I must say it did cross my mind that Hannah – '

'You don't mean?' I interrupted. I was shocked.

'Well you see,' he said at last, 'the balance of their minds – women's minds – is often disturbed by childbirth. They are often quite irrational, not only in the immediate puerperal period but also while they are breast-feeding. They have been through exhausting physical effort and great hormonal and psychological changes, during which they need support and affection. In the case of a young inexperienced, unmarried mother, with no home, no job, and no husband, the anxieties are very great indeed.'

'Hannah showed no sign whatever of mental disturbance,' I objected. 'In fact she was very happy here.'

'Nevertheless she carried a heavy burden on her childish shoulders,' he suggested.

'She loved the baby!' I cried. 'She revelled in her motherhood. She never found it a burden!' I was indignant.

'Quite so, quite so.' He paused, sipping his sherry.

'It is a catastrophic event – sudden unexplained infant death. Just because it is unexplained, suspicions and hostilities are stirred up, and everybody near the case gets involved in violent, sometimes uncontrollable emotions.'

'Yes,' I agreed. 'I fear that is so already at the vicarage.'

'The elderly woman,' he pursued, 'your housekeeper, I believe?'

'Sarah.'

'Yes. She is very silent. I have an uncomfortable feeling all is not well with her. She's not a patient of mine, so I can't interfere.'

'She hates me.' I stated it baldly. 'Her hostility showed itself gradually when I took over, and has, I believe, increased with time. She has been here so much longer than I; and she resented the changes I made in the parish and in church ritual. Latterly she has made it plain that she objected very much to Hannah's presence here.'

'Not the baby's?'

'Not, I think, the baby's. It was chiefly Hannah she disliked.'

'Do you think she feared for her job? – that Hannah might replace her?'

'I never thought of that. It simply never entered my mind.'

'It might have entered hers.'

'I suppose it's possible,' I admitted. 'She is certainly jealous of Hannah. She even suggested that my feelings towards Hannah are impure – sexually.'

'And are they?'

A long silence fell between us. How could I explain that my desires lay on the other side of the ultimate taboo?

'Her gran used to call me the Reverend Disability,' I said at last.

After an even longer silence, during which he smoked quietly, and I presume pigeon-holed my disability among medical phenomena not as yet understood, he remarked: 'A wonderful old woman, her gran, healthy and humorous, strong as a rock. Let's hope Hannah has inherited more genes from her than from her flighty father.'

'The years she spent with her gran were happy ones,' I said.

'A charming old place, the mill. I remember the house-martins nesting under the eaves of the warehouse.' Dr Marten sucked his pipe-stem. 'I can see them now, flitting in and out. I remember telling the old lady that Shakespeare said the air smelt wooingly where house-martins nested. And she replied with her rich, old-fashioned country courtesy, and – yes – a hint of flirting too: "The air do indeed smell wooingly Dr Marten when you do come to visit us." And then she gave me a sidelong quizzical look, and a little smile at her own flattery that took all the bombast out of me at once.'

I thought of the garden at the mill full of the scent of self-sown candytuft. I remembered walking with the old lady along the banks of what she used to call her Blissy Brook, and chiding her for her absence from church. Her reply was that Easter and Christmas supplied her with enough hymn-singing for the whole year, and then she added unexpectedly: 'When I do walk through my buttercup meadows alongside the millstream in May, with the wet grass coming up to my knees and two blackbirds singing like crazy angels in the old elms, I do believe I'm nearer to God there than in any church.'

'She was some sort of pagan really,' I said. 'She had a flowering bush beside the porch, I remember, bright orange it was, like flames bursting out of the wood in early spring, about this time of year when it's still cold outside. Some sort of japonica I believe it was. Gran called it her Burning Bush. "And it speaks to me with the voice of God," she said, "like what Moses heard. But of course – " and here she laughed a little – "I dare say it says what I want to hear." '

Dr Marten then asked me if there were any relative, however distant, who might give Hannah a home temporarily – till she got over her tragedy, was how he put it. When he saw I was unwilling to reply he said: 'We'll see, we'll see. No hurry as yet. Meanwhile look after yourself as well as other people. This must have been a great strain on you too.'

I led him to the door. I walked with him to the gate and stood for a moment gazing across the graveyard to the blackthorn hedge marking its boundary. The frail white flowers shone on their black threatening branches like stars in winter. They were like Hannah, delicate and lovely but vigorous enough to emerge into a hostile environment, and survive through frost and bleak winds to blossom on the black thorns. That was where I wanted Emily to be buried, under the blackthorn hedge. But Hannah had other ideas. 'I want her to lie beside Gran,' she said. 'Gran's arms will keep her warm in the dark same as they did me. That way they'll both turn back into the earth together.'

I didn't argue with her. I thought it best to allow her fanciful notions full play if they comforted her a little.

The funeral party consisted of myself and Dr Marten, Sarah and her sister Vi, and Hannah with a cousin the doctor and the social worker had between them somehow managed to track down. She wore a black leather jacket armed with metal buttons and buckles and hung with chains, and her hair, which was purple, stuck up from her scalp in spikes. Her name, as alarming as her appearance, was Marleen Batherswick. I did not take to her.

It had rained heavily all that week, but the rain stopped as our small procession trailed down the path from the church to the freshly dug plot. For this funeral I had donned a white surplice over my cassock. The wind played havoc with all these skirts, blowing them about in a flurry of black and white folds, and I felt a fool, my legs revealed up to the knees by the gale as I stood above the grave. I read aloud Psalm 91 in a loud firm voice hoping that the great and wonderful words of the Psalmist would strengthen Hannah's soul: ' "For he shall deliver thee from the snare of the fowler, and from the noisome pestilence. . . . Thou shalt not be afraid for the terror by night; nor for the arrow that flieth by day. . . . For he shall give his angels charge over thee, to keep thee in all thy ways. They shall bear thee up in their hands, lest thou dash thy foot against a stone." ' It was my personal message to Hannah before she lost her child's body for ever.

' "Man that is born of woman hath but a short time to live . . ." ' I chanted the burial service. ' "He cometh up, and is cut down like a flower . . ." ' I glanced at Hannah's white face. I remembered Emily with her cheeks like rose petals. Ah! like a flower indeed. . . .

As the small coffin was being lowered Hannah turned away, but when it came to rest she fell on her knees in the mud and peered into the hole.

' "We therefore commit her body to the ground; earth to earth, ashes to ashes, dust to dust . . ." ' Hannah picked up a handful of wet soil and tried to crumble it above the coffin, scattering the morsels as if she were feeding birds. While I was watching this I heard the thud of a stone hitting the little box, and looking up I saw Vi put an arm round Sarah and pull her away. It made me angry to witness this demonstration of Sarah's implacable hatred, and also of Vi's concern for her, as if she were the victim on this day instead of the unfortunate infant and her mother.

After the funeral we all felt relieved, the terrible events of last week hidden, as Emily was, in the earth. While we drank sherry in my study Dr Marten pushed Hannah up to her bedroom to tell her what to do about her breasts. The poor child was suffering from the engorgement caused by the untapped milk. The cousin must have gone with them. I don't know where Vi was – in the kitchen, I suppose. I picked up the newspaper while Sarah collected the glasses. She turned, holding the tray, at the half-open door.

'She did it, didn't she?'

I glanced up.

'There was never any pillow in the cot, so she must have done it with her hands,' she said.

'Good God, Sarah!' I cried. 'What are you saying?'

'Stands to reason, don't it? Nothing to keep her from higher education now!'

'Sarah!' I shouted. 'If you don't check this wicked talk we won't be able to continue working together!' But she had left the room, letting the door swing to, not with her usual slam of rage but with a slow, determined click.

By the time the trio came downstairs again Hannah had struck up a remarkably warm friendship on such short acquaintance with Marleen, whose arm was twined about her waist.

'Marleen has invited Hannah to stay with her for Easter,' said Dr Marten, smoothly ignoring the venomous look I shot him.

So they left me. Why did he do this to me? Was I a bad influence on her? She had been happy at the vicarage, happy enough to sing. Now she would not on Easter Day, in her sweet clear voice without tremolo reassure us both that our Redeemer had survived torture and death. I could make no objection. I was not her guardian. I had been but a temporary refuge for her, that was all. She promised to come back; but I could foresee that she would drop out of my life. She had already 'moved on'. I was left alone in the house with Sarah, linked only by habit and mutual hatred.

I did not sleep that night. My body tossed and turned in my distress, and my mind twisted restlessly around that day's events, asking their meaning. Somehow I crawled through Good Friday. I was thankful for once for my small congregation and for the short and simple service. Sarah gave me a poached egg for tea. We did not exchange a word. She didn't appear again, which I thought odd; but as I was not at all hungry I simply went into the kitchen and made myself a pot of tea, which I carried back to my armchair beside a fire which had gone out. And there I sat, unable to control my thoughts. It was like walking on a treadmill which was moving faster than my step. I could see no way off it, and no reprieve from the endless, wearisome, meaningless climb. I must have fallen asleep for I woke suddenly. My watch said 4 a.m. What had shaken me awake? Call it a nightmare if you like, but I believed it was the truth thrusting itself into my consciousness at that horrid hour when the soul is dragged naked before the Bar of Justice. I believed that it was Sarah who had done the deed, placing her hand gently over the baby's mouth, leaving no mark. It was all suddenly clear to me. Sarah told the policeman she had been with Vi at the time; but she hadn't gone to Vi's house till after we left for choir practice. There was a time – who knows how long? – when she was alone in the vicarage with Emily. I remembered the plain-clothes officer's words: 'It doesn't take much to snuff out a baby's life,' and Sarah saying 'She must have done it with her hands.' Sarah knew there was no pillow; she knew exactly how it was done.

And it was all my fault. Through my lack of wisdom and my selfish desire for Hannah's affection I had allowed this thing to happen. My lack of understanding and charity towards Sarah had fuelled her malevolence. I had slighted her, preferring Hannah's company, favouring the new-comer and rejecting the old and faithful servant. I should have known that the emotions being aroused by this new situation in a simple soul of limited intelligence would be too difficult for her to comprehend and too violent for her to control. My warped nature and my insatiable desire for love had created catastrophe. I saw my own guilt; I felt the black hood descend over my head.

Dr Marten had assured me that there was no question of infanticide, that the post-mortem made that absolutely clear; but I was not so sure. I didn't sleep again; but I lost count of time passing. It must have been Easter Sunday when a distracted Mr Pollock burst in on me.

'What's the matter?' he shrieked. 'Why aren't you in the church? Everybody's waiting. And I've been playing the Introit over and over again. It's my Bach Chorale. And you know I can only play one,' he added on a calmer note, reproachfully, as if that were my fault too. His voice trailed off. 'What's the matter, Rev?'

He must have read my answer in my appearance, for I made no reply.

'You're ill, very ill. I can see that. Whatever shall we do?'

I'm afraid I laughed. It was what the psychiatrists call inappropriate laughter; but it seemed to me entirely proper at the time.

'Make a great, big polyphonic noise, Mr Pollock,' I suggested. 'Lots of thumping chords. Stun them with poly-phony! That will make them feel safe from all adversity.'

He bent down and peered into my face.

'I'll send for the doctor,' he said, and fled from the room.

229

It was a terrible dereliction of my duty to my flock on this the most important festival of the Christian calendar. What happened in the church I never learned. Nor do I care.

That Easter I attended Verdi's Requiem Mass by myself inside my head. I could hear the great orchestra and the choirs singing: *Dies Irae*, Day of Wrath, Day of Judgment, the terror felt, the menace recognised. . . . Weeping and wailing and wringing of hands of no avail now before the seat of ultimate truth. . . . Rhythmic blows on the drums punctuated by shrill soprano cries for mercy, followed by the long lament of falling notes till the soul is ground down into the dust by the sentence of a vengeful God. *Lachrymosa . . . Dies Irae . . .* I have been judged and have been found wanting. Theodore Brown is dropping down into oblivion; he is a lost soul.

I had these absurd visions, you see, of my little church filled with glorious sound rising up all for the greater glory of God, such music as might perhaps be heard after months of disciplined rehearsal by dedicated musicians in Gloucester cathedral at the time of the Three Choirs festival. I was ever one to imagine I could make a silk purse out of a sow's ear. That was all the material I ever had; and I myself was no exceptionally gifted choirmaster. Pigs indeed – and pearls before swine. . . . And that of course shows what's wrong with me. I am guilty of pride. I don't think much of my parishioners; I don't really love my neighbours at all. I once read somewhere that when Verdi died, and his coffin was carried through the streets of Milan, the watching thousands began to sing. They sang the song of the Jewish slaves from *Nabucco*, which he composed while Italy was still under the heel of Austria. I doubt if even for Verdi Mudcott would look out for a moment above its sty.

A young doctor came to visit me later. It seems Dr Marten had taken a few days' leave that Easter, and this young locum took his place. He prescribed pills for me, small white ones for the daytime and yellow capsules for the night. I think perhaps he was not as cautious with his drugs as Dr Marten would have been. Since I longed for sleep as a man lost in the Sahara must long for water I took two of the night capsules immediately, and then remembering that it was still day I took several of the daytime drugs as well. After that my remaining contact with reality seems to have slid away from me. I don't know when it was that Vi visited me. I am not even quite sure if she did, or if I dreamed it. Certainly Sarah was a bad dream: Sarah walking all the way to the weir, turbulent and swollen with exceptionally heavy spring rains, Sarah walking into the weir until it was too deep to walk any more, Sarah lying face downwards on the water and being carried like some obscene Ophelia with her grey hair streaming, until the swirls and eddies pushing her limp body around ballooned her skirts over her head, and at last dumped her on the mud flats below my church. It was there we tried to bury her. I inscribed on her epitaph: 'Her name was writ in water.' I was worried because I knew that epitaph belonged to someone else; and I was annoyed because we couldn't dig a hole deep enough to make the headstone stand. No matter how much we scrabbled with our hands the muddy water oozed in, filling it up.

I have been told that it was not all nightmare, that Vi came to tell me of Sarah's suicide and found me in a comatose state. It was Vi who called Dr Marten, and he who arranged for my admission to hospital. So that's how I ended up here among all the other nuts being cracked.

It's Hannah's joke. Not a very good one, I know, but apt. The psychiatrists hope that by cracking open my mind I will reveal the core (but will it be the cure?) of my weakness. I don't see the need of it myself. I know what's wrong. I'm just a failed clergyman – failed man, in fact. Somebody – was it Sartre? – said Hell is other people; but he was wrong. Hell is myself.

I have written to the Bishop. He got wind of what was happening at Mudcott when it was all over, and has invited me to go and see him and have a talk. He's probably a kind man, possibly even an understanding one. I've written, giving this address, and asking to be relieved of my responsibilities, since I am no longer fit, and probably never was, for the priesthood. I went into the Church through fear rather than for the love of God. I wanted to escape from a harsh, dangerous world. I hoped it would prove in Gerard Manley Hopkins's words a 'Heaven-Haven.'

> I have desired to go
> Where springs not fail,
> To fields where flies no sharp and sided hail
> And a few lilies blow.

Hannah was one of the lilies; but it was she who brought down the hailstones on my head.

I was admitted for observation in April. It must be July now, for I can see below my window geraniums blooming in formal beds, with salvias all round, making a blot of bright unblinking red. I fear the gardener must be a long-term patient with an obsessional desire for blood.

Yesterday Vi came to see me again. Sarah I hear is not interred in mud but under the blackthorn hedge in the very spot I'd chosen for Emily. Vi tried to be kind. She tried to reduce my load of guilt by telling me things about Sarah's long-ago youth which I had never known before; but sadly this new knowledge has only made matters worse. It seems that when Sarah was fifteen, before the war, she worked for a poultry farmer in this district, by whom she became pregnant. He was already married, so there was no question of marriage for her. When she was six months gone her family hid her in a back room in their cottage, saying first that she was ill, then that she'd gone away to relatives in Devon for the sake of her health. When her time came and she gave birth her parents didn't help the babe to breathe

(Vi's words, not mine). They buried the little creature at night in the back garden under the rubbish tip, and then raked cinders over it. It never once took in a gasp of air, nor uttered a cry; it never had a name; it was a thing, not a person; neither its birth nor its death was ever registered. Nobody except her family knew of it. Poor Sarah carried her guilty secret all these years in silence. When Hannah and her happy baby broke into our quiet, uneventful existence at the vicarage Sarah was forced to live through all over again her griefs and fears by experiencing the resurrection of her buried shame. No wonder the balance of her mind became deranged. And I in my selfishness guessed nothing of her agony.

Hannah comes to see me often. She holds my hand and says I'm getting better. 'No more men for me!' she says. Her tone is derisive, but I fear she doth protest too much, and so on. . . . The female cousin with the strange hair is a great help to her, which only goes to show you can't judge by appearances. It seems they have both enrolled for a course of training in cookery. I only hope their fritters will one day be as good as Gran's.

'Marleen took me on the back of her motor bike to Grovesend to see my Auntie May,' Hannah told me. 'She's living in a place called Meadowsweet. A nursing home it is. And ever so nice.' I'm glad for both their sakes that Hannah has found another relative.

I have been thinking over a suggestion made to me about the library. Yes, I think I could catalogue the books and tidy up the index. I am interested, too, by some histories I have seen there of ancient physicians and the weird therapies they used, such as beating the Devil out of madmen and burning it out of crazy old witches. Even in the more enlightened Age of Reason and Science one illustrious fore-runner in psychiatry used a very drastic remedy: the whirling chair, in which the patient who had lost his wits was spun at high speed until he became so giddy that he vomited. I suppose the distinguished doctor argued that the centrifugal force generated would hurl the chaos in the lunatic head into an orderly circle inside the circumference of his skull. Electroconvulsions had not yet arrived.

And yes, I will borrow the tape of Beethoven's Ninth. I might even feel gloriously happy when I hear the chorus singing Schiller's Hymn to Joy. All men become brothers when possessed by great joy. Someone suggested it might be something to wrap around me. It is more than that. It is a life-jacket.

Tale End

Mary's new dog Chu-Chin had not the temperamental panache of Buzzby, her Irish setter of times past. She was a two-year-old bitch, a big Chow with a leonine face framed by a stiff ruff of sandy-coloured hair which she loved Mary to comb out, standing stock still during the grooming and as complacent as any monarch with a Divine Right to homage while receiving it. Although she looked fierce she was in fact hopelessly sentimental. She was a dog who appreciated her creature comforts, but she did also love rushing madly across fields for no particular reason other than to express a sheer joy in living; and this was in keeping with Mary's own mood. They were both delighted just to be alive.

There had been one or two burglaries in the district recently so Mary thought it unwise to leave the house empty during her absences. Tom and Marge had left for their new job in Northampton, taking their Welsh collie with them, and the cottage had been sold to newcomers whom Mary felt she didn't know well enough to ask favours of; but Beryl and her husband were willing to take charge of Gatt's Rise when she went away with Chu-Chin.

The land was now all let to the Trotters, father and son, the lease providing an income for Mary. She had kept about an acre of garden, including the apple orchard, the walled garden where she grew strawberries and raspberries and, with occasional help from old Mikey, vegetables, and she was making a flower garden with Fading's advice, laying out terraces which would in time be full of shrubs and bulbs. Mary walked round the back of the house to inspect her young horse-chestnut trees growing where once elms had flourished, and lower down the slope the straggle of native English cherries she had planted. They were only small saplings as yet, but in her mind's eye she could see them all as great trees, heavy with bursting bud. Some day when she was old and her cooling blood needed warming she would be delighted by the sight of their flowering glory.

She opened the car door and pushed Chu-Chin into the back seat where the bitch settled sulkily, blinking her eyes reproachfully at Mary, who knew very well that she preferred sitting in the front seat but for reasons obscure and annoying to Chu-Chin she forbade that pleasure.

The late August sun fell across the road in great yellow splashes as they drove, the roadside trees cast intermittent shade from the sun not yet at its noon height. This was to be the last time Mary would stay in David's house. She had grown quite fond of it, filled as it was with the aura of joyful days and nights spent there, but it was not after all Gatt's Rise. Fortunately David had agreed readily to moving in with her, since in any case he had to sell his house before taking up his new partnership with Preene, Parsons and Parsons. It was funny how things worked out, she thought, as she turned a corner rather too quickly and had to apologise to Chu-Chin for causing her to swerve on her seat. . . . Funny really to think that David was taking Gregory Barton's place in that old-established firm of solicitors, though not as clerk of court. When Barton retired that vacancy had been immediately filled by a temporary clerk who very soon became a permanent one.

David's mother had been living in some sort of seventh heaven of her own since the news of his appointment reached her, especially now that his divorce had come through and he could be married to Mary. And as if that wasn't enough joy they were to be married in St Colm's in Upper Coldacre where the vicar had agreed to overlook, this once, the misdemeanour of David's divorce, and marry them in church. And the bells would boom out so loudly at the wedding that her cottage in Colm's Walk would shudder at the sound. All this excitement had entirely routed from her concentration the details of a book she was writing on the local *History of Frenester and its Surrounding Villages*. The page devoted to the peasant rising and fate of Christoferus Twigge (to be illustrated with a black-and-white print of the illuminated text the martyr had been working on) would have to wait, and the chapter devoted to Luddite smashings of newfangled looms and her great-grandfather's part in the Chartist struggle to obtain manhood suffrage for working men, and for their wives to get cheaper bread through a repeal of the Corn Laws, would have to be written at a time of calm reflection quite impossible to achieve in the present state of affairs.

When Mary shut her car door, leaving a rebellious Chu-Chin inside, and walked up the steps into the many-odoured hall of Meadowsweet she heard singing in the lounge above. Flora was giving her singsong session. As she mounted the stairs Mary could hear above the tinkle of Flora's fingers on the piano a rather familiar voice singing solo, and as she approached the doorway a full young voice broke on her ears, making her heart bump inside her chest with the sudden shock of recognition:

'Hand me down ma walkin' cane,
Hand me down ma walkin' cane
Oh hand me down ma walkin' cane,
I'm gonna get on that midnight train,
For all my sins are taken away!'

And there beside the piano, beside Flora seated on the piano stool, stood Hannah with her mouth open on a triumphant note, Hannah with her mass of dark curls and her energetic young body buttoned up inside a blue uniform – not, Mary noted, royal blue like the trained nurses' dresses, but a paler, prettier turquoise colour.

Hannah stopped singing when she saw Mary. For a moment the two women, silenced by surprise, stared at each other. Then Hannah ran towards her and flung herself weeping into Mary's arms.

It took some time to extricate explanations of how this reunion had come about from all the cries of pleasure and astonishment at its happening. It all became clearer to Mary when she entered Matron's office to pay her mother's monthly account.

'Well, you see, her aunt is here with us,' said Matron. 'She has been here for some years now. And when I saw how good Hannah was with the elderly whenever she came to visit Auntie May – and when I heard she was a school-leaver in need of a job I took her on as Assistant Nurse in Training. She hasn't any O levels, I know, but she has had a few months' training in cookery. So she helps in the kitchen – helps all round, really. As a matter of fact she's invaluable. The patients all love her. Their little ray of sunshine is what they call her. And she actually seems to love the old – which is something that not everybody does. "It's because of Gran," she says. "She loved me when she was old, you know." I suppose that's a good enough reason. But whatever the reason a liking for the elderly is not too common – even in our profession.' She stopped speaking, and a look of regret passed over her features, perhaps because she was sorry so few people loved the old, or perhaps because she had indiscreetly admitted it.

'Is she living here?' Mary asked.

'Oh no. We haven't any rooms to spare. But there is a boarding-house round the corner where some of our staff have rooms. Hannah can't afford the rent on what she earns as a school-leaver in training, but her Aunt May is seeing to that.'

'Really?' Mary was surprised, till she remembered hearing a few months ago that the mill had been bought by a local heritage conservation society. 'Yes I do remember that the mill was sold.'

'There is a mill, then? Hannah talks rather charmingly about the mill on her Blissy Brook, but I always wondered how much of her talk was fairy tales.'

'No, no,' Mary assured her. 'The mill exists all right. And so does Blissy Brook, which is a run-off from our River Frene. But the building's been falling into rack and ruin for years, and the brook is a stagnant millpond now.'

Mary returned to the lounge to make the acquaintance of Auntie May, who was one of the human effigies she had overlooked before: a white-haired figure bent double in a chair, her hands and feet swollen and deformed by rheumatoid arthritis and her face puffy from taking steroids, as she explained, perfectly rationally, to Mary. She was happy to talk, grateful that someone seemed interested in her plight.

'I'm going to be married next week, Hannah,' Mary dropped her bombshell. 'But very quietly. No guests, only two witnesses.'

'Never!' cried Hannah. 'Are you really getting married?'

'Yes I am. And in St Colm's church in Upper Coldacre too. Not in a long white dress, of course – I'm too old for that – but in an ivory-coloured suit and a close-fitting hat made of pheasants' feathers. I wondered if you'd care to act as my maid of honour on the day?'

Hannah blushed scarlet, and her eyes filled with tears.

'It's nothing to cry about, Silly!' scolded her aunt. It's a happy occasion. And she wants you to be bridesmaid. So say yes!'

Flora sat on her piano stool listening, and no doubt feeling left out of things, so Mary crossed the room and kissed her cheek. 'I'll come in again tomorrow, Flora,' she said. 'And I'll bring in some designs for you to look at. You must help choose a dress for Hannah to wear. You know more about these things than I do.'

Flora's face brightened at once. 'Well, you haven't left me much time for all this,' she grumbled.

'I think it's just possible to fit it in,' said Mary. 'I've found this wonderful dressmaker in Grovesend, you see. She used to work for a London designer before she married. She made my wedding outfit. And I'm sure she'll manage to run up the right dress for Hannah in a few days. I've got to rush now, Flora, but we'll have a full dress rehearsal here for you in a few days' time.'

Mary gave Hannah a quick hug before she went downstairs. She was followed by singing, the tune surging and receding like the sound of keening from voices not quite human. Flora had resumed her singsong and Mary could just discern the words: 'Smoke gets in your eyes'.... She could imagine the scene: the old dears sitting in a semi-circle, Flora at the piano with her eyelids screwed up against the smoke from her fag (secreted in her pocket with its lighter till the nurse had left the room), and the ash growing, crumbling and falling on the keys. It was remarkable really that those claws of hers, in spite of her years of boozing, were still able to hit the notes with sharp rhythmic precision. Mary wondered in what deep layer of consciousness as yet undamaged her gift for accurate timing lay. It was strange, too, that Flora with her damaged liver, her chain-smoking and her patchy memory had against all the odds survived when Colly's sharp mind and seemingly so fit and active body had fallen beneath the inevitable axe. Every time she thought of it Mary still felt a small chill shudder through her soul, as if she were watching a Greek tragedy on the stage. Nemesis had overtaken Colly and he had fallen with the elms. Those great trees which stood like giant bearded sages across the length and breadth of Severnvale for centuries had harboured within the channels of their bark the cause of their own destruction: a fungus inexorably spreading, on which the invading beetles fed and thrived, stealing the nutriment from their ancient hosts, which slowly withered. Millions of elms died in that pandemic and disappeared entirely from the landscape. It was a disease as catastrophic in the plant world as the Black Death of the Middle Ages was to the human species. Like the elms Colly had seemed to stand, a sage respected, an honourable man. Since childhood she had accepted his position and values, till time and events revealed to her the flaws in his strength and he was swept away along with the black rookeries of raucous birds, which when their nesting sites had been destroyed returned no more.

So many familiar landmarks in her life were gone; but the house remained, squat and solid on her hill, the dormer windows in her roof still blinking down on the green fields below, her walls waiting to receive new occupants.

'I shall be sorry to leave this house, David,' said Mary. She opened the bedroom window and leaned out. It was a hot still summer night. The black outlines of trees at the end of the garden stood like silhouette cut-outs against a deep blue sky. It was very quiet. Nocturnal animals – rats, field mice, foxes, badgers – and moths and beetles of all sorts must be moving through shrubs in gardens and in the undergrowth of woods beyond the town, but they made no sound. And out there beyond where they moved so silently and secretly were the undulating spaces of Exmoor. 'I've been so happy here,' she said.

David stood beside her looking out. He said nothing. His own memories of his house were longer than hers and not all so happy. 'I've got the tickets,' he said. 'We fly from Heathrow. And I've got the tickets for the opera in Verona too.'

They sat down on the bed to examine the tempting pictures displayed in their holiday brochure. They were going to stay at a lakeside hotel in Riva del Garda, and their bedroom would have a balcony overlooking the water.

'There's a swimming pool in the hotel too,' said David.

'What's this?' asked Mary pointing to the word *Aliscafo* and a photograph of boats on the water.

'I think it must mean winged boat. It's some sort of hydrofoil.'

'We could take that and go across the lake to Limone,' said Mary. 'The Romans planted lemon groves there.' She smiled, thinking how much Colly would have enjoyed that. 'And we must take a bus into the Dolomites too, one day.'

'I'm looking forward to some of those regional specialities like Parma ham with Valpolicella. Did you know you're marrying a man with the double-barrelled name of Greedy-Guts? You've still time to back out if you have misgivings.'

Mary had no misgivings. 'What opera are we booked for?' she asked.

'*Aida*. Just imagine it in that great open-air arena!'

She imagined it: the roll of the hundred-throated chorus booming in the hollow stone space, the sound of the Italian tenor voice, full of the warm south, making the roots of hair at the base of her scalp tingle, and her skin flush as if she had really drunk a beaker from Keats's blushful Hippocrene. . . . 'It all seems too good to come true,' she said cautiously.

'We're going to make it come true,' declared David.

Chu-Chin, annoyed at being ignored, crept out from under the bed and pushed her nose against Mary's legs. She dropped a hand to tickle her dog behind the ears. 'I'm sorry you won't be coming with us, my pet,' she said. 'But I think you'd be bored by *Aida*. And Fading will look after you very well till we come home. I just hope you won't kill that little dachshund of hers with your jealousy.'

Colly would have been bored too. He would have been restless and ill at ease, unable to let himself be engulfed and carried away by the magic of Verdi's music, unable to lose his identity in the communal act of rapt listening. And edgy at being trapped there, almost as untamed as one of the lions in that amphitheatre in Roman times, his eyes would have roamed angrily over the crowd. He would of course have noted and rejoiced in the geometry of Roman architecture, in the correct placement of pillars and arches;

he would have expressed satisfaction that Roman work and orderly planning had lasted so many centuries. Mary was able to remember his idiosyncrasies now with tolerant amusement. David caught her smile, and being a little jealous of any of her thoughts from which he was excluded he turned her head towards him and kissed her lips.

'No misgivings then?' he murmured.

'Absolutely none,' was her reply.

NORA NAISH

The Butterfly Box

The butterfly box is a small art nouveau cigarette case which has been in Lucy Marshall's family for years. Together with a family portrait allegedly by Klimt, it has been passed down through four generations of mothers and daughters.

But the butterfly box hides a secret, which is revealed when the family come together at Lucy's home in the Cotswolds to celebrate her eighteenth birthday. Around her Lucy gathers her daughter Beena, granddaughter Joanna, who is bringing her new boyfriend to meet them for the first time, and, in spirit, her mother Louise. It is Louise's journals, left in Lucy's keeping and long unread, which reveal that the box lies at the centre of a family scandal far darker than anyone suspected.

'An engaging portrait of mothers and daughters who know each other and love each other'
Daily Mail

'Dr Naish knows how to tell a good story . . . this is the perfect holiday read'
Evening Standard

CAROL BIRCH

Songs of the West

'In Carol Birch's skilful novel, prosperous foreign incomers to furthest south-west Ireland buy large houses and establish "affirmation centres", make yoghurt and criticise commercialism. Meanwhile, the local country people get on with earning a living. Essie, middle-class and English, with seventeen rings in her ears and a stud in her tongue, makes earthenware knick-knacks. Rosanna is an anarchic alcoholic. Their friend Marie is a respectable wife and mother. One summer Marie falls for a writer from Dublin who passes through in his yellow caravan . . . Carol Birch writes beautifully about a place she must know and love, and has an acute ear for dialogue'
Sunday Telegraph

'Full of richly imagined characters, written with a fluent assurance'
Sunday Times

'*Songs of the West* is extremely hard to put aside . . . it is good to read the work of a writer who looks and listens so closely'
Times Literary Supplement

'Bustles with characters . . . a rich, often funny novel'
New Statesman

JANE BEESON

Scarhill

Kate Merlin has farmed Scarhill, on the remote Devon moors, for more than fifteen years.

Now, abandoned by her husband with two children to raise, she has no choice but to sell the farm. When an offer is made by a neighbouring farmer, Kate accepts, but later, taking her land agent's advice, she allows a rich London family to gazump.

But the arrival of the Deneuves has a devastating effect on the local community – not least because of the manipulative Alec Deneuve's plans to exploit the surrounding moor. And while his wayward son Jude, mysteriously sent down from Oxford, starts a disastrous relationship with Kate's daughter, Astra, and his glamorous wife Sophie flirts with the local vicar before embarking on an altogether more dangerous affair, Kate's backward and trusting son, Benjy, acts as the innocent observing eye . . .

'An acute, sensitive observer of human relationships'
The Times

A Selected List of Fiction Available from Mandarin

While every effort is made to keep prices low, it is sometimes necessary to increase prices at short notice. Mandarin Paperbacks reserves the right to show new retail prices on covers which may differ from those previously advertised in the text or elsewhere.

The prices shown below were correct at the time of going to press.

All these books are available at your bookshop or newsagent, or can be ordered direct from the address below. Just tick the titles you want and fill in the form below.

Cash Sales Department, PO Box 5, Rushden, Northants NN10 6YX.
Fax: 01933 414047 : Phone: 01933 414000.

Please send cheque, payable to 'Reed Book Services Ltd.', or postal order for purchase price quoted and allow the following for postage and packing:

£1.00 for the first book, 50p for the second; **FREE POSTAGE AND PACKING FOR THREE BOOKS OR MORE PER ORDER.**

NAME (Block letters) ....

ADDRESS ....

....

☐ I enclose my remittance for ....

☐ I wish to pay by Access/Visa Card Number ☐☐☐☐☐☐☐☐☐☐☐☐☐☐☐☐

Expiry Date ☐☐☐☐

Signature ....

Please quote our reference: MAND